Larry Niven was born in 1938 in California,
where he has spent most of his life. He
started college in California and graduated
with a degree in Mathematics from
Washburn University, Kansas.
Now working as a full-time writer, he lives
with his wife in Los Angeles.

Winner of both the Hugo and Nebula
awards, Larry Niven has written many
successful sf books, including *A Gift From
Earth*, *Neutron Star* and *Ringworld*.

Inconstant Moon

LARRY NIVEN

SPHERE BOOKS LIMITED
30/32 Gray's Inn Road, London WC1X 8JL

First published in Great Britain
by Victor Gollancz Ltd 1973
Copyright © Larry Niven 1973
Published by Sphere Books 1974

The original edition of this book contained twelve stories.
The Sphere edition contains eleven.

Set in Intertype Baskerville

Printed in Great Britain by
Hazell Watson & Viney Ltd
Aylesbury, Bucks

ISBN 0 7221 6383 5

CONTENTS

ACKNOWLEDGMENTS

INCONSTANT MOON

I

I was watching the news when the change came, like a flicker of motion at the corner of my eye. I turned towards the balcony window. Whatever it was, I was too late to catch it.

The moon was very bright tonight.

I saw that, and smiled, and turned back. Johnny Carson was just starting his monologue.

When the first commercials came on I got up to re-heat some coffee. Commercials came in strings of three and four, going on midnight. I'd have time.

The moonlight caught me coming back. If it had been bright before, it was brighter now. Hypnotic. I opened the sliding glass door and stepped out on to the balcony.

The balcony wasn't much more than a railed ledge, with standing room for a man and a woman and a portable barbecue set. These past months the view had been lovely, especially around sunset. The Power and Light Company had been putting up a glass-slab style office building. So far it was only a steel framework of open girders. Shadow-blackened against a red sunset sky, it tended to look stark and surrealistic and hellishly impressive.

Tonight . . .

I had never seen the moon so bright, not even in the desert. *Bright enough to read by,* I thought, and immediately, *but that's an illusion.* The moon was never bigger (I had read somewhere) than a quarter held nine feet away. It couldn't possibly be bright enough to read by.

It was only three-quarters full!

But, glowing high over the San Diego Freeway to the west, the moon seemed to dim even the streaming automobile headlights. I blinked against its light, and thought of men walking on the moon, leaving corrugated footprints. Once, for the sake of an article I was writing, I had been allowed to pick up a bone-dry moon rock and hold it in my hand. . . .

I heard the show starting again, and I stepped inside. But, glancing once behind me, I caught the moon glowing even brighter – as if it had come from behind a wisp of scudding cloud.

Now its light was brain-searing, lunatic.

The phone rang five times before she answered.

'Hi,' I said. 'Listen—'

'Hi,' Leslie said sleepily, complainingly. Damn. I'd hoped she was watching television, like me.

I said, 'Don't scream and shout, because I had a reason for calling. You're in bed, right? Get up and – can you get up?'

'What time is it?'

'Quarter of twelve.'

'Oh, Lord.'

'Go out on your balcony and look around.'

'Okay.'

The phone clunked. I waited. Leslie's balcony faced north, and west, like mine, but it was ten storeys higher, with a correspondingly better view.

Through my own window, the moon burned like a textured spotlight.

'Stan? You there?'

'Yah. What do you think of it?'

'It's gorgeous. I've never seen anything like it. What could make the moon light up like that?'

'I don't know, but isn't it gorgeous?'

'You're supposed to be the native.' Leslie had only moved out here a year ago.

'Listen, I've *never* seen it like this. But there's an old legend,' I said. 'Once every hundred years the Los Angeles smog rolls away for a single night, leaving the air as clear as interstellar space. That way the gods can see if Los Angeles is still there. If it is, they roll the smog back so they won't have to look at it.'

'I used to know all that stuff. Well, listen, I'm glad you woke me up to see it, but I've got to work tomorrow.'

'Poor baby.'

'That's life. 'Night.'

'Night.

Afterwards I sat in the dark, trying to think of someone else to call. Call a girl at midnight, invite her to step outside and look at the moonlight . . . and she may think it's romantic or she may be furious, but she won't assume you called six others.

So I thought of some names. But the girls who belonged to them had all dropped away over the past year or so, after I started spending all my time with Leslie. One could hardly blame them. And now Joan was in Texas and Hildy was getting married, and if I called Louise I'd probably get Gordie too. The English girl? But I couldn't remember her number. Or her last name.

Besides, everyone I knew punched a time clock of one kind or another. Me, I worked for a living, but as a free-lance writer I picked my hours. Anyone I woke up tonight, I'd be ruining her morning. Ah, well . . .

The Johnny Carson Show was a swirl of grey and a roar of static when I got back to the living-room. I turned the set off and went back out on to the balcony.

The flow was brighter than the flow of headlights on the freeway, brighter than Westwood Village off to the right. The Monica Mountains had a magical pearly glow. There were no stars near the moon. Stars could not survive that glare.

I wrote science and how-to articles for a living. I ought to be able to figure out what was making the moon do that. Could the moon be suddenly larger?

. . . Inflating like a balloon? No. Closer, maybe. The moon, falling?

Tides! Waves fifty feet high . . . and earthquakes! San Andreas Fault splitting apart like the Grand Canyon! Jump in my car, head for the hills . . . no, too late already . . .

Nonsense. The moon was brighter, not bigger. I could see that. And what could possibly drop the moon on our heads like that?

I blinked, and the moon left an after-image on my retinae. It was *that* bright.

A million people must be watching the moon right now, and wondering, like me. An article on the subject would sell big . . . if I wrote it before anyone else did . . .

There must be some simple, obvious explanation.

9

Well, how could the moon grow brighter? Moonlight was reflected sunlight. Could the sun have got brighter? It must have happened after sunset, then, or it would have been noticed. . . .

I didn't like that idea.

Besides, half the Earth was in direct sunlight. A thousand correspondents for *Life* and *Time* and *Newsweek* and *Associated Press* would be calling in from all over Europe, Asia, Africa . . . unless they were all hiding in cellars. Or dead. Or voiceless, because the sun was blanketing everything with static, radio and phone systems and television . . . television. Oh my God.

I was just barely beginning to be afraid.

All right, start over. The moon had become very much brighter. Moonlight, well, moonlight was reflected sunlight; any idiot knew that. Then . . . something had happened to the sun.

II

'Hello?'

'Hi. Me,' I said, and then my throat froze solid. Panic! What was I going to *tell* her?

'I've been watching the moon,' she said dreamily. 'It's wonderful. I even tried to use my telescope, but I couldn't see a thing; it was too bright. It lights up the whole city. The hills are all silver.'

That's right, she kept a telescope on her balcony. I'd forgotten.

'I haven't tried to go back to sleep,' she said. 'Too much light.'

I got my throat working again. 'Listen, Leslie love, I started thinking about how I woke you up and how you probably couldn't get back to sleep, what with all this light. So let's go out for a midnight snack.'

'Are you out of your mind?'

'No, I'm serious. I mean it. Tonight isn't a night for sleeping. We may never have a night like this again. To hell with your diet. Let's celebrate. Hot fudge sundaes, Irish coffee—'

'That's different. I'll get dressed.'

10

'I'll be right over.'

Leslie lived on the fourteenth floor of Building C of the Barrington Plaza. I rapped for admission, and waited.

And waiting, I wondered without any sense of urgency : Why Leslie?

There must be other ways to spend my last night on Earth, than with one particular girl. I could have picked a different particular girl, or even several not too particular girls, except that that didn't really apply to me, did it? Or I could have called my brother, or either set of parents—

Well, but brother Mike would have wanted a good reason for being hauled out of bed at midnight. 'But, Mike, the moon is so beautiful—' Hardly. Any of my parents would have reacted similarly. Well, I had a good reason, but would they believe me?

And if they did, what then? I would have arranged a kind of wake. Let 'em sleep through it. What I wanted was someone who would join my . . . farewell party without asking the wrong questions.

What I wanted was Leslie. I knocked again.

She opened the door just a crack for me. She was in her underwear. A stiff, misshapen girdle in one hand brushed my back as she came into my arms. 'I was about to put this on.'

'I came just in time, then.' I took the girdle away from her and dropped it. I stooped to get my arms under her ribs, straightened up with effort, and walked us to the bedroom with her feet dangling against my ankles.

Her skin was cold. She must have been outside.

'So !' she demanded. 'You think you can compete with a hot fudge sundae, do you?'

'Certainly. My pride demands it.' We were both somewhat out of breath. Once in our lives I had tried to lift her cradled in my arms, in more conventional movie style. I'd damn near broken my back. Leslie was a big girl, my height, and almost too heavy around the hips.

I dropped us on the bed, side by side. I reached around her from both sides to scratch her back, knowing it would leave her helpless to resist me, *ah* ha hahahaha. She made sounds of pleasure to tell me where to scratch. She pulled

11

my shirt up around my shoulders and began scratching my back.

We pulled pieces of clothing from ourselves and each other, at random, dropping them over the edges of the bed. Leslie's skin was warm now, almost hot . . .

All right, now *that's* why I couldn't have picked another girl. I'd have to teach her how to scratch. And there just wasn't time.

Some nights I had a nervous tendency to hurry our lovemaking. Tonight we were performing a ritual, a rite of passage. I tried to slow it down, to make it last. I tried to make Leslie like it more. It paid off incredibly. I forgot the moon and the future when Leslie put her heels against the backs of my knees and we moved into the ancient rhythm.

But the image that came to me at the climax was vivid and frightening. We were in a ring of blue-hot fire that closed like a noose. If I moaned in terror and ecstasy, then she must have thought it was ecstasy alone.

We lay side by side, drowsy, torpid, clinging together. I was minded to go back to sleep then, renege on my promise, sleep and let Leslie sleep . . . but instead I whispered into her ear: 'Hot fudge sundae.' She smiled and stirred and presently rolled off the bed.

I wouldn't let her wear the girdle. 'It's past midnight. Nobody's going to pick you up, because I'd thrash the blackguard, right? So why not be comfortable?' She laughed and gave in. We hugged each other once, hard, in the elevator. It felt much better without the girdle.

III

The grey-haired counter waitress was cheerful and excited. Her eyes glowed. She spoke as if confiding a secret. 'Have you noticed the moonlight?'

Ships's was fairly crowded, this time of night and this close to UCLA. Half the customers were university students. Tonight they talked in hushed voices, turning to look out through the glass walls of the twenty-four-hour restaurant. The moon was low in the west, low enough to compete with the street globes.

'We noticed,' I said. 'We're celebrating. Get us two hot fudge sundaes, will you?' When she turned her back I slid a ten dollar bill under the paper place mat. Not that she'd ever spend it, but at least she'd have the pleasure of finding it. I'd never spend it either.

I felt loose, casual. A lot of problems seemed suddenly to have solved themselves.

Who would have believed that peace could come to Vietnam and Cambodia in a single night?

This thing had started around eleven thirty, here in California. That would have put the noon sun just over the Arabian Sea, with all but a few fringes of Asia, Europe, Africa, and Australia in direct sunlight.

Already Germany was reunited, the Wall melted or smashed by shock waves. Israelis and Arabs had laid down their arms. Apartheid was dead in Africa.

And I was free. For me there were no more consequences. Tonight I could satisfy all my dark urges, rob, kill, cheat on my income tax, throw bricks at plate glass windows, burn my credit cards. I could forget the article on explosive metal forming, due Thursday. Tonight I could substitute cinnamon candy for Leslie's Pills. Tonight—

'Think I'll have a cigarette.'

Leslie looked at me oddly. 'I thought you'd given that up.'

'You remember. I told myself if I got any overpowering urges, I'd have a cigarette. I did that because I couldn't stand the thought of never smoking again.'

'But it's been months!' she laughed.

'But they keep putting cigarette ads in my magazines!'

'It's a plot. All right, go have a cigarette.'

I put coins in the machine, hesitated over the choice, finally picked a mild filter. It wasn't that I wanted a cigarette. But certain events call for champagne, and others for cigarettes. There is the traditional last cigarette before a firing squad . . .

I lit up. *Here's to lung cancer.*

It tasted just as good as I remembered; though there was a faint stale undertaste, like a mouthful of old cigarette butts. The third lungful hit me oddly. My eyes

13

unfocused and everything went very calm. My heart pulsed loudly in my throat.

'How does it taste?'

'Strange, I'm buzzed,' I said.

Buzzed! I hadn't even heard the word in fifteen years. In high school we'd smoked to get that buzz, that quasi-drunkenness produced by capillaries constricting in the brain. The buzz had stopped coming after the first few times, but we'd kept smoking, most of us . . .

I put it out. The waitress was picking up our sundaes.

Hot and cold, sweet and bitter: there is no taste quite like that of a hot fudge sundae. To die without tasting it again would have been a crying shame. But with Leslie it was a *thing,* a symbol of all rich living. Watching her eat was more fun than eating myself.

Besides . . . I'd killed the cigarette to taste the ice-cream. Now, instead of savouring the ice cream, I was anticipating Irish coffee.

Too little time.

Leslie's dish was empty. She stage-whispered, 'Aahh!' and patted herself over the navel.

A customer at one of the small tables began to go mad.

I'd noticed him coming in. A lean scholarly type wearing sideburns and steel-rimmed glasses, he had been continually twisting around to look out at the moon. Like others at other tables, he seemed high on a rare and lovely natural phenomenon.

Then he got it. I saw his face changing, showing suspicion, then disbelief, then horror, horror and helplessness.

'Let's go,' I told Leslie. I dropped quarters on the counter and stood up.

'Don't you want to finish yours?'

'Nope. We've got things to do. How about some Irish coffee?'

'And a Pink Lady for me? Oh, look!' She turned full around.

The scholar was climbing up on a table. He balanced, spread wide his arms and bellowed, 'Look out your windows!'

14

'You get down from there!' a waitress demanded, jerking emphatically at his pants leg.

'The world is coming to an end! Far away on the other side of the sea, death and hellfire—'

But we were out of the door, laughing as we ran. Leslie panted, 'We may have – escaped a religious – riot in there!'

I thought of the ten I'd left under my plate. Now it would please nobody. Inside, a prophet was shouting his message of doom to all who would hear. The grey-haired woman with the glowing eyes would find the money and think : They knew it too.

Buildings blocked the moon from the Red Barn's parking lot. The street lights and the indirect moonglare were pretty much the same colour. The night only seemed a bit brighter than usual.

I didn't understand why Leslie stopped suddenly in the driveway. But I followed her gaze straight up to where a star burned very brightly just south of the zenith.

'Pretty,' I said.

She gave me a very odd look.

There were no windows in the Red Barn. Dim artificial lighting, far dimmer than the queer cold light outside, showed on dark wood and quietly cheerful customers. Nobody seemed aware that tonight was different from other nights.

The sparse Tuesday night crowd was gathered mostly around the piano bar. A customer had the mike. He was singing some half-familiar song in a wavering weak voice, while the black pianist grinned and played a schmaltzy background.

I ordered two Irish coffees and a Pink Lady. At Leslie's questioning look I only smiled mysteriously.

How ordinary the Red Barn felt. How relaxed; how happy. We held hands across the table, and I smiled and was afraid to speak. If I broke the spell, if I said the wrong thing . . .

The drinks arrived. I raised an Irish coffee glass by the stem. Sugar, Irish whiskey, and strong black coffee, with thick whipped cream floating on top. It coursed

15

through me like a magical potion of strength, dark and hot and powerful.

The waitress waved back my money. 'See that man in the turtleneck, there at the end of the piano bar? He's buying,' she said with relish. 'He came in two hours ago and handed the bartender a hundred dollar bill.'

So that was where all the happiness was coming from. Free drinks! I looked over, wondering what the guy was celebrating.

A thick-necked, wide-shouldered man in a turtleneck and sports coat, he sat hunched over into himself, with a wide bar glass clutched tight in one hand. The pianist offered him the mike, and he waved it by, the gesture giving me a good look at his face. A square, strong face, now drunk and miserable and scared. He was ready to cry from fear.

So I knew what he was celebrating.

Leslie made a face. 'They didn't make the Pink Lady right.'

There's one bar in the world that makes a Pink Lady the way Leslie likes it, and it isn't in Los Angeles. I passed her the other Irish coffee, grinning an I-told-you-so grin. Forcing it. The other man's fear was contagious. She smiled back, lifted her glass and said, 'To the blue moonlight.'

I lifted my glass to her, and drank. But it wasn't the toast I would have chosen.

The man in the turtleneck slid down from his stool. He moved carefully towards the door, his course slow and straight as an ocean liner cruising into dock. He pulled the door wide, and turned around, holding it open, so that the weird blue-white light streamed past his broad black silhouette.

Bastard. He was waiting for someone to figure it out, to shout out the truth to the rest. *Fire of doom—*

'Shut the door!' someone bellowed.

'Time to go!' I said softly.

'What's the hurry?'

The hurry? He might *speak!* But I couldn't say that

. . .

Leslie put her hand over mine. 'I know. I *know.* But we can't run away from it, can we?'

A fist closed hard on my heart. She'd known, and I hadn't noticed?

The door closed, leaving the Red Barn in reddish dusk. The man who had been buying drinks was gone.

'Oh, God. When did you figure it out?'

'Before you came over,' she said. 'But when I tried to check it out, it didn't work.'

'Check it out?'

'I went out on the balcony and turned the telescope on Jupiter. Mars is below the horizon these nights. If the sun's gone nova, all the planets ought to be lit up like the moon, right?'

'Right. Damn.' I should have thought of that myself. But Leslie was the stargazer. I knew some astrophysics, but I couldn't have found Jupiter to save my life.

'But Jupiter wasn't any brighter than usual. So then I didn't know *what* to think.'

'But then—' I felt hope dawning fiery hot. Then I remembered. 'That star, just overhead. The one you stared at.'

'Jupiter.'

'All lit up like a fucking neon sign. Well, that tears it.'

'Keep your voice down.'

I *had* been keeping my voice down. But for a wild moment I wanted to stand up on a table and scream! *Fire and doom*— What right had they to be ignorant?

Leslie's hand closed tight on mine. The urge passed. It left me shuddering. 'Let's get out of here. Let 'em think there's going to be a dawn.'

'There is.' Leslie laughed a bitter, barking laugh like nothing I'd ever heard from her. She walked out while I was reaching for my wallet – and remembering that there was no need.

Poor Leslie. Finding Jupiter its normal self must have looked like a reprieve – until the white spark flared to shining glory an hour and a half late. An hour and a half, for sunlight to reach Earth by way of Jupiter.

When I reached the door Leslie was half-running down Westwood towards Santa Monica. I cursed and ran to catch up, wondering if she'd suddenly gone crazy.

Then I noticed the shadows ahead of us. All along the

17

other side of Santa Monica Boulevard: moon shadows, in horizontal patterns of dark and blue-white bands.

I caught her at the corner.

The moon was setting.

A setting moon always looks tremendous. Tonight it glared at us through the gap of sky beneath the freeway, terribly bright, casting an incredible complexity of lines and shadows. Even the unlighted crescent glowed pearly bright with earthshine.

Which told me all I wanted to know about what was happening on the lighted side of Earth.

And on the moon? The men of Apollo Nineteen must have died in the first few minutes of nova sunlight. Trapped out on a lunar plain, hiding perhaps behind a melting boulder . . . Or were they on the night side? I couldn't remember. Hell, they could outlive us all. I felt a stab of envy and hatred.

And pride. We'd put them there. We reached the moon before the nova came. A little longer, we'd have reached the stars.

The disc changed oddly as it set. A dome, a flying saucer, a lens, a line . . .

Gone.

Gone. Well, that was that. Now we could forget it; now we could walk around outside without being constantly reminded that something was *wrong*. Moonset had taken all the queer shadows out of the city.

But the clouds had an odd glow to them. As clouds glow after sunset, tonight the clouds shone livid white at their western edges. And they streamed too quickly across the sky. As if they tried to run . . .

When I turned to Leslie, there were big tears rolling down her cheeks.

'Oh, damn.' I took her arm. 'Now stop it. Stop it.'

'I can't. You know I can't stop crying once I get started.'

'This wasn't what I had in mind. I thought we'd do things we've been putting off, things we like. It's our last chance. Is this the way you want to die, crying on a street corner?'

'I don't want to die at all!'

'Tough shit!'

'Thanks a lot.' Her face was all red and twisted. Leslie was crying as a baby cries, without regard for dignity or appearance. I felt awful. I felt guilty, and I *knew* the nova wasn't my fault, and it made me angry.

'I don't want to die either!' I snarled at her. 'You show me a way out and I'll take it. Where would we go? The South Pole? It'd just take longer. The moon must be molten all across its day side. Mars? When this is over Mars will be part of the sun, like the Earth. Alpha Centauri? The acceleration we'd need, we'd be spread across a wall like peanut butter and jelly—'

'Oh, shut up.'

'Right.'

'Hawaii. Stan, we could get to the airport in twenty minutes. We'd get two hours extra, going west! Two hours more before sunrise!'

She had something there. Two hours was worth any price! But I'd worked this out before, staring at the moon from my balcony. 'No. We'd die sooner. Listen, love, we saw the moon go bright about midnight. That means California was at the back of the Earth when the sun went nova.'

'Yes, that's right.'

'Then we must be furthest from the shock wave.'

She blinked. 'I don't understand.'

'Look at it this way. First the sun explodes. That heats the air and the oceans, all in a flash, all across the day side. The steam and superheated air expand *fast*. A flaming shock wave comes roaring over into the night side. It's closing on us right now. Like a noose. But it'll reach Hawaii first. Hawaii is two hours closer to the sunset line.'

'Then we won't see the dawn. We won't live even that long.'

'No.'

'You explain things so well,' she said bitterly. 'A flaming shock wave. So graphic.'

'Sorry. I've been thinking about it too much. Wondering what it will be like.'

'Well, stop it.' She came to me and put her face in my shoulder. She cried quietly. I held her with one arm and used the other to rub her neck, and I watched the streaming clouds, and I didn't think about what it would be like.

Didn't think about the ring of fire closing on us.

It was the wrong picture anyway.

I thought of how the oceans had boiled on the day side, so that the shock wave had been mostly steam to start with. I thought of the millions of square miles of ocean it had to cross. It would be cooler and wetter when it reached us. And the Earth's rotation would spin it like the whirlpool in a bathtub.

Two counter-rotating hurricanes of live steam, one north, one south. That was how it would come. We were lucky. California would be near the eye of the northern one.

A hurricane wind of live steam. It would pick a man up and cook him in the air, strip the steamed flesh from him and cast him aside. It was going to hurt like hell.

We would never see the sunrise. In a way that was a pity. It would be spectacular.

Thick parallel streamers of clouds were drifting across the stars, too fast, their bellies white by city light. Jupiter dimmed, then went out. Could it be starting already? Heat lightning jumped—

'Aurora,' I said.

'What?'

'There's a shock wave from the sun, too. There should be an aurora like nothing anybody's ever seen before.'

Leslie laughed suddenly, jarringly. 'It seems so strange, standing on a street corner talking like this! Stan, are we dreaming it?'

'We could pretend—'

'No. Most of the human race must be dead already.'

'Yah.'

'And there's nowhere to go.'

'Damn it, you figured that out long ago, all by yourself. Why bring it up now?'

'You could have let me sleep,' she said bitterly. 'I was dropping off to sleep when you whispered in my ear.'

I didn't answer. It was true.

' "Hot fudge sundae",' she quoted. Then, 'It wasn't a bad idea, actually. Breaking my diet.'

I started to giggle.

'Stop that.'

'We could go back to your place now. Or my place. To sleep.'

'I suppose. But we couldn't sleep, could we? No, don't say it. We take sleeping pills, and five hours from now we wake up screaming. I'd rather stay awake. At least we'll know what's happening.'

But if we took all the pills . . . but I didn't say it. I said, 'Then how about a picnic?'

'Where?'

'The beach, maybe. Who cares? We can decide later.'

IV

All the markets were closed. But the liquor store next to the Red Barn was one I'd been using for years. They sold us foie gras, crackers, a couple of bottles of chilled champagne, six kinds of cheese and a hell of a lot of nuts – I took one of everything – more crackers, a bag of ice, frozen rumaki hors d'oeuvres, a fifth of an ancient brandy that cost twenty-five bucks, a matching fifth of Cherry Heering for Leslie, six-packs of beer and Bitter Orange . . .

By the time we had piled all that into a dinky store cart, it was raining. Big fat drops spattered in flurries across the acre of plate glass that fronted the store. Wind howled around the corners.

The salesman was in a fey mood, bursting with energy. He'd been watching the moon all night. 'And now this!' he exclaimed as he packed our loot into bags. He was a small, muscular old man with thick arms and shoulders. 'It *never* rains like this in California. It comes down straight and heavy when it comes at all. Takes days to build up.'

'I know.' I wrote him a cheque, feeling guilty about it. He'd known me long enough to trust me. But the cheque was good. There were funds to cover it. Before opening hours the cheque would be ash, and all the banks in the world would be bubbling in the heat of the sun. But that was hardly my fault.

He piled our bags in the cart, set himself at the door.

'Now when the rain lets up, we'll run these out. Ready?' I got ready to open the door. The rain came like someone had thrown a bucket of water at the window. In a moment it had stopped, though water still streamed down the glass. 'Now!' cried the salesman, and I threw the door open and we were off. We reached the car laughing like maniacs. The wind howled around us, sweeping up spray and hurling it at us.

'We picked a good break. You know what this weather reminds me of? Kansas,' said the salesman. 'During a tornado.'

Then suddenly the sky was full of gravel! We yelped and ducked, and the car rang to a million tiny concussions, and I got the car door unlocked and pulled Leslie and the salesman in after me. We rubbed our bruised heads and looked out at white gravel bouncing everywhere.

The salesman picked a small white pebble out of his collar. He put it in Leslie's hand, and she gave a startled squeak and handed it to me, and it was cold.

'Hail,' said the salesman. 'Now I really don't get it.'

Neither did I. I could only think that it had something to do with the nova. But what? How?

'I've got to get back,' said the salesman. The hail had expended itself in one brief flurry. He braced himself, then went out of the car like a marine taking a hill. We never saw him again.

The clouds were churning up there, forming and disappearing, sliding past each other faster than I'd ever seen clouds move; their bellies glowing by city light.

'It must be the nova,' Leslie said shivering.

'But how? If the shock wave were here already, we'd be *dead* – or at least deaf. Hail?'

'Who cares? Stan, we don't have *time*!'

I shook myself. 'All right. What would you like to do most, right now?'

'Watch a baseball game.'

'It's two in the morning,' I pointed out.

'That lets out a lot of things, doesn't it?'

'Right. We've hopped our last bar. We've seen our last play, and our last clean movie. What's left?'

'Looking in jewellery store windows.'

22

'Seriously? Your last night on Earth?'

She considered, then answered. 'Yes.'

By damn, she meant it. I couldn't think of anything duller. 'Westwood or Beverly Hills?'

'Both.'

'Now, *look—*'

'Beverly Hills, then.'

We drove through another spatter of rain and hail – a capsule tempest. We parked half a block from the Tiffany salesroom.

The sidewalk was one continuous puddle. Second-hand rain dripped on us from various levels of the buildings overhead. Leslie said, 'This is great. There must be half a dozen jewellery stores in walking distance.'

'I was thinking of driving.'

'No no no, you don't have the proper attitude. One must window shop on foot. It's in the rules.'

'But the rain!'

'You won't die of pneumonia. You won't have time,' she said, too grimly.

Tiffany's had a small branch office in Beverly Hills, but they didn't put expensive things in the windows at night. There were a few fascinating toys, that was all.

We turned up Rodeo Drive – and struck it rich. Tibor showed an infinite selection of rings, ornate and modern, large and small, in all kinds of precious and semi-precious stones. Across the street, Van Cleef and Arpel showed brooches, men's wristwatches of elegant design, bracelets with tiny watches in them, and one window that was all diamonds.

'Oh, lovely,' Leslie breathed, caught by the flashing diamonds. 'What they must look like in daylight! . . . Wups—'

'No, that's a good thought. Imagine them at dawn, flaming with nova light, while the windows shatter to let the raw daylight in. Want one? The necklace?'

'Oh, *May* I? Hey, hey, I was kidding! Put that down, you idiot, there must be alarms in the glass.'

'Look, nobody's going to be wearing any of that stuff between now and morning. Why shouldn't we get some good out of it?'

'We'd be caught!'

'Well, you *said* you wanted to window shop . . .'

'I don't want to spend my last hour in a cell. If you'd brought the car we'd have *some* chance—'

'– Of getting away. Right. I *wanted* to bring the car —' But at that point we both cracked up entirely, and had to stagger away holding on to each other for balance.

There were a good half-dozen jewellery stores on Rodeo. But there was more. Toys, books, shirts and ties in odd and advanced styling. In Francis Orr, a huge plastic cube full of new pennies. A couple of damn strange clocks further on. There was an extra kick in window shopping, knowing that we could break a window and take anything we wanted badly enough.

We walked hand in hand, swinging our arms. The sidewalks were ours alone; all others had fled the mad weather. The clouds still churned overhead.

'I wish I'd known it was coming,' Leslie said suddenly. 'I spent the whole day fixing a mistake in a programme. Now we'll never run it.'

'What would you have done with the time? A baseball game?'

'Maybe. No. The standings don't matter now.' She frowned at dresses in a store window. 'What would you have done?'

'Gone to the Blue Sphere for cocktails,' I said promptly. 'It's a topless place. I used to go there all the time, I hear they've gone full nude now.'

'I've never been to one of those. How late are they open?'

'Forget it. It's almost two-thirty.'

Leslie mused, looking at giant stuffed animals in a toy store window. 'Isn't there someone you would have murdered, if you'd had the time?'

'Now, you *know* my agent lives in New York.'

'Why him?'

'My child, why would any writer want to murder his agent? For the manuscripts he loses under other manuscripts. For his ill-gotten ten per cent, and the remaining ninety per cent that he sends me grudgingly and late. For—'

Suddenly the wind roared and rose up against us. Leslie

24

pointed, and we ran for a deep doorway that turned out to be Gucchi's. We huddled against the glass.

The wind was suddenly choked with hail the size of marbles. Glass broke somewhere, and alarms lifted thin, frail voices into the wind. There was more than hail in the wind! There were rocks!

I caught the smell and taste of seawater.

We clung together in the expensively wasted space in front of Gucchi's. I coined a short-lived phrase and screamed, 'Nova weather! How the blazes did it—' But I couldn't hear myself, and Leslie didn't even know I was shouting.

Nova weather. How did it get here so fast? Coming over the pole, the nova shock wave would have to travel about four thousand miles – at least a five-hour trip.

No. The shock wave would travel in the stratosphere, where the speed of sound was higher, then propagate down. Three hours was plenty of time. Still, I thought, it should not have come as a rising wind. On the other side of the world, the exploding sun was tearing our atmosphere away and hurling it at the stars. The shock should have come as a single vast thunderclap.

For an instant the wind gentled, and I ran down the sidewalk pulling Leslie after me. We found another doorway as the wind picked up again. I thought I heard a siren coming to answer the alarm.

At the next break we splashed across Wilshire and reached the car. We sat there panting, waiting for the heater to warm up. My shoes felt squishy. The wet clothes stuck to my skin.

Leslie shouted, 'How much longer?'

'I don't know! We ought to have *some* time.'

'We'll have to spend our picnic indoors!'

'Your place or mine? Yours,' I decided, and pulled away from the kerb.

v

Wilshire Boulevard was flooded to the hub caps in spots. The spurt of hail and sleet had become a steady, pounding rain. Fog lay flat and waist deep ahead of us, broke swirling over our hood, churned in a wake behind us. Weird weather.

Nova weather. The shock wave of scalding super-heated steam hadn't happened. Instead, a mere hot wind roaring through the stratosphere, the turbulence eddying down to form strange storms at ground level.

We parked illegally on the upper parking level. My one glimpse of the lower level showed it to be flooded. I opened the trunk and lifted two heavy paper bags.

'We must have been crazy,' Leslie said, shaking her head. 'We'll never use all this.'

'Let's take it up anyway.'

She laughed at me. 'But why?'

'Just a whim. Will you help me carry it?'

We took double armfuls up to the fourteenth floor. That still left a couple of bags in the trunk. 'Never mind them,' Leslie said. 'We've got the rumaki and the bottles and the nuts. What more do we need?'

'The cheeses. The crackers. The foie gras.'

'Forget 'em.'

'No.'

'You're out of your mind,' she explained to me, slowly so that I would understand. 'You could be steamed dead on the way down! We might not have more than a few minutes left, and you want food for a week! *Why?*'

'I'd rather not say.'

'Go then!' She slammed the door with terrible force.

The elevator was an ordeal. I kept wondering if Leslie was right. The shrilling of the wind was muffled, here at the core of the building. Perhaps it was about to rip electrical cables somewhere, leave me stranded in a darkened box. But I made it down. The upper level was knee deep in water.

My second surprise was that it was lukewarm, like old bath-water, unpleasant to wade through. Steam curdled on the surface, then blew away on a wind that howled through the concrete echo chamber like the screaming of the damned.

Going up was another ordeal. If what I was thinking was wish fulfilment, if a roaring wind of live steam caught me now . . . I'd feel like such an idiot. . . . But the doors opened, and the lights hadn't even flickered.

26

Leslie wouldn't let me in.

'Go away!' She shouted through the locked door. 'Go eat your cheese and crackers somewhere else!'

'You got another date?'

That was a mistake. I got no answer at all.

I could almost see her viewpoint. The extra trip for the extra bags was no big thing to fight about; but why did it have to be? How long was our love affair going to last, anyway? An hour, with luck. Why back down on a perfectly good argument, to preserve so ephemeral a thing?

'I wasn't going to bring this up,' I shouted, hoping she could hear me through the door. The wind must be three times as loud on the other side. 'We may need food for a week! And a place to hide!'

Silence. I began to wonder if I could kick the door down. Would I be better off waiting in the hall? Eventually she'd have to—

The door opened. Leslie was pale. 'That was cruel,' she said quietly.

'I can't promise anything. I wanted to wait, but you forced it. I've been wondering if the sun really has exploded.'

'That's cruel. I was just getting used to the idea.' She turned her face to the door jamb. Tired, she was tired. I'd kept her up too late. . . .

'Listen to me. It was all wrong,' I said. 'There should have been an aurora borealis to light up the night sky from pole to pole. A shock wave of particles exploding out of the sun, travelling at an inch short of the speed of light, would rip into the atmosphere like – why, we'd have seen blue fire over every building!

'Then, the storm came too slow,' I screamed, to be heard above the thunder. 'A nova would rip away the sky over half the planet. The shock wave would move around the night side with a sound to break all the glass in the world, all at once! And crack concrete and marble – and, Leslie love, it just hasn't happened. So I started wondering.'

She said it in a mumble. 'Then what is it?'

'A flare. The worst—'

She shouted it at me like an accusation. 'A flare! A

27

solar flare! You think the sun could light up like that—'

'Easy, now—'

'— could turn the moon and planets into so many torches, then fade out as if nothing had happened! Oh, you idiot—'

'May I come in?'

She looked surprised. She stepped aside, and I bent and picked up the bags and walked in.

The glass doors rattled as if giants were trying to beat their way in. Rain had squeezed through the cracks to make dark puddles on the rug.

I set the bags on the kitchen counter. I found bread in the refrigerator, dropped two slices in the toaster. While they were toasting I opened the foie gras.

'My telescope's gone,' she said. Sure enough, it was. The tripod was all by itself on the balcony, on its side.

I untwisted the wire on a champagne bottle. The toast popped up, and Leslie found a knife and spread both slices with foie gras. I held the bottle near her ear, figuring to trip conditioned reflexes.

She did smile fleetingly as the cork popped. She said, 'We should set up our picnic grounds here. Behind the counter. Sooner or later the wind is going to break those doors and shower glass all over everything.'

That was a good thought. I slid around the partition, swept all the pillows off the floor and the couch and came back with them. We set up a nest for ourselves.

It was kind of cosy. The kitchen counter was three and a half feet high, just over our heads, and the kitchen alcove itself was just wide enough to swing our elbows comfortably. Now the floor was all pillows. Leslie poured the champagne into brandy snifters, all the way to the lip.

I searched for a toast, but there were just too many possibilities, all depressing. We drank without toasting. And then carefully set the snifters down and slid forward into each other's arms. We could sit that way, face to face, leaning sideways against each other.

'We're going to die,' she said.

'Maybe not.'

'Get used to the idea, I have,' she said. 'Look at you, you're all nervous now. Afraid of dying. Hasn't it been a lovely night?'

'Unique. I wish I'd known in time to take you to dinner.'

Thunder came in a string of six explosions. Like bombs in an air raid. 'Me too,' she said when we could hear again.

'I wish I'd known this afternoon.'

'Pecan pralines!'

'Farmer's Market. Double-roasted peanuts. Who would *you* have murdered, if you'd had the time?'

'There was a girl in my sorority—'

– and she was guilty of sibling rivalry, so Leslie claimed. I named an editor who kept changing his mind. Leslie named one of my old girl friends, I named her only old boy friend that I knew about, and it got to be kind of fun before we ran out. My brother Mike had forgotten my birthday once. The fiend.

The lights flickered, then came on again.

Too casually, Leslie asked, 'Do you really think the sun might go back to normal?'

'It better *be* back to normal. Otherwise we're dead anyway. I wish we could see Jupiter.'

'Dammit, answer me! Do you think it was a flare?'

'Yes.'

'Why?'

'Yellow dwarf stars don't go nova.'

'What if ours did?'

'The astronomers know a lot about novas,' I said. 'More than you'd guess. They can see them coming months ahead. Sol is a gee-nought yellow dwarf. They don't go nova at all. They have to wander off the main sequence first, and that takes millions of years.'

She pounded a fist softly on my back. We were cheek to cheek; I couldn't see her face. 'I don't want to believe it. I don't dare. Stan, nothing like this has ever happened before. How can you know?'

'Something did.'

'What? I don't believe it. We'd remember.'

'Do you remember the first moon landing? Aldrin and Armstrong?'

'Of course. We watched it at Earl's Lunar Landing Party.'

'They landed on the biggest, flattest place they could find on the moon. They sent back several hours of jumpy

29

home movies, took a lot of very clear pictures, left corrugated footprints all over the place. And they came home with a bunch of rocks.

'Remember? People said it was a long way to go for rocks. But the first thing anyone noticed about those rocks was that they were half melted.

'Something in the past, oh, say the past hundred thousand years; there's no way of marking it closer than that – the sun flared up. It didn't stay hot enough long enough to leave any marks on the Earth. But the moon doesn't have an atmosphere to protect it. All the rocks melted on one side.'

The air was warm and damp. I took off my coat, which was heavy with rainwater. I fished the cigarettes and matches out, lit a cigarette and exhaled past Leslie's ear.

'We'd remember. It *couldn't* have been this bad.'

'I'm not so sure. Suppose it happened over the Pacific? It wouldn't do *that* much damage. Or over the American continents. It would have sterilized some plants and animals and burned down a lot of forests, and who'd know? The sun went back to normal, that time. It might again. The sun is a four per cent variable star. Maybe it gets a touch more variable than that, every so often.'

Something shattered in the bedroom. A window? A wet wind touched us, and the shriek of the storm was louder.

'Then we could live through this,' Leslie said hesitantly.

'I believe you've put you're finger on the crux of the matter. Skol!' I found my champagne and drank deep. It was past three in the morning, with a hurricane beating at our doors.

'Then shouldn't we be doing something about it?'

'We are.'

'Something like trying to get up into the hills! Stan, there's going to be floods!'

'You bet your ass there are, but they won't rise this high. Fourteen storeys. Listen, I've thought this through. We're in a building that was designed to be earthquake proof. You told me so yourself. It'd take more than a hurricane to knock it over.

'As for heading for the hills, what hills? We won't get far tonight, not with the streets flooded already. Suppose we could get up into the Santa Monica Mountains; then what? Mudslides, that's what. That area won't stand up to what's coming. The flare must have boiled away enough water to make another ocean. It's going to rain for forty days and forty nights! Love, this is the safest place we could have reached tonight.'

'Suppose the polar caps melt?'

'Yeah . . . well, we're pretty high, even for that. Hey, maybe that last flare was what started Noah's Flood. Maybe it's happening again. Sure as hell, there's not a place on Earth that isn't the middle of a hurricane. Those two great counter-rotating hurricanes, by now they must have broken up into hundreds of little storms—'

The glass doors exploded inward. We ducked, and the wind howled about us and dropped rain and glass on us.

'At least we've got food!' I shouted. 'If the floods maroon us here, we can last it out!'

'But if the power goes, we can't cook it! And the refrigerator—'

'We'll cook everything we can. Hardboil all the eggs—'

The wind rose about us. I stopped trying to talk.

Warm rain sprayed us horizontally and left us soaked. Try to cook in a hurricane? I'd been stupid; I'd waited too long. The wind would tip boiling water on us if we tried it. Or hot grease—

Leslie screamed, 'We'll have to use the oven!'

Of course. The oven couldn't possibly fall on us.

We set it for 400° and put the eggs in, in a pot of water. We took all the meat out of the meat drawer and shoved it in on a broiling pan. Two artichokes in another pot. The other vegetables we could eat raw.

What else? I tried to think.

Water. If the electricity went, probably the water and telephone lines would too. I turned on the faucet over the sink and started filling things: pots with lids, Leslie's thirty-cup percolator that she used for parties, her wash bucket. She clearly thought I was crazy, but I didn't trust the rain as a water source; I couldn't control it.

The sound. Already we'd stopped trying to shout through it. Forty days and nights of this and we'd be stone deaf. Cotton? Too late to reach the bathroom. Paper towels! I tore and wadded and made four plugs for our ears.

31

Sanitary facilities? Another reason for picking Leslie's place over mine. When the plumbing stopped, there was always the balcony.

And if the flood rose higher than the fourteenth floor, there was the roof. Twenty storeys up. If it went higher than that, there would be damn few people left when it was over.

And if it was a nova?

I held Leslie a bit more closely, and lit another cigarette one-handed. All the wasted planning, if it was a nova. But I'd have been doing it anyway. You don't stop planning just because there's no hope.

And when the hurricane turned to live steam, there was always the balcony. At a dead run, and over the railing, in preference to being boiled alive.

But now was not the time to mention it.

Anyway, she'd probably thought of it herself.

The lights went out about four. I turned off the oven, in case the power should come back. Give it an hour to cool down, then I'd put all the food in Baggies.

Leslie was asleep, sitting up in my arms. How could she sleep, not knowing? I piled pillows behind her and let her back easy.

For some time I lay on my back, smoking, watching the lightning make shadows on the ceiling. We had eaten all the foie gras and drunk one bottle of champagne. I thought of opening the brandy, but decided against it, with regret.

A long time passed. I'm not sure what I thought about. I didn't sleep, but certainly my mind was in idle. It only gradually came to me that the ceiling, between lightning flashes, had turned grey.

I rolled over, gingerly, soggily. Everything was wet.

My watch said it was nine-thirty.

I crawled around the partition into the living-room. I'd been ignoring the storm sounds for so long that it took a faceful of warm whipping rain to remind me. There was a hurricane going on. But charcoal-grey light was filtering through the black clouds.

So. I was right to have saved the brandy. Floods, storms, intense radiation, fires lit by the flare – if the toll of destruction was as high as I expected, then money was about to become worthless. We would need trade goods.

I was hungry. I ate two eggs and some bacon – still warm – and started putting the rest of the food away. We had food for a week, maybe . . . but hardly a balanced diet. Maybe we could trade with other apartments. This was a big building. There must be empty apartments, too, that we could raid for canned soup and the like. And refugees from the lower floors to be taken care of, if the water rose high enough . . .

Damn! I missed the nova. Life had been simplicity itself last night. Now . . . Did we have medicines? Were there doctors in the building? There would be dysentery and other plagues. And hunger. There was a supermarket near here; could we find a scuba rig in the building?

But I'd get some sleep first. Later we could start exploring the building. The day had become a lighter charcoal grey. Things could be worse, far worse. I thought of the radiation that must have sleeted over the far side of the world, and wondered if our children would colonize Europe, or Asia, or Africa.

BORDERED IN BLACK

ONLY ONE FIGURE stood in the airlock, though it was a cargo lock, easily big enough to hold both men. Lean and sandy-haired, the tiny figure was obviously Carver Rappaport. A bushy beard now covered half its face. It waited patiently while the ramp was run up, and then it started down.

Turnbull, waiting at the bottom, suppressed growing uneasiness. Something was wrong. He'd known it the moment he heard that the *Overcee* was landing. The ship must have been in the solar system for hours. Why hadn't she called in?

And where was Wall Kameon?

Returning spacers usually sprinted down the ramp, eager to touch honest concrete again. Rappaport came down with slow, methodical speed. Seen close, his beard was ragged, unkempt. He reached bottom, and Turnbull saw that the square features were set like cement.

Rappaport brushed past him and kept walking.

Turnbull ran after him and fell into step, looking and feeling foolish. Rappaport was a good head taller, and where he was walking, Turnbull was almost running. He shouted above the background noise of the spaceport, 'Rappaport, where's Kameon?'

Like Turnbull, Rappaport had to raise his voice. 'Dead.'

'Dead? Was it the ship? Rappaport, did the *ship* kill him?'

'No.'

'Then what? Is his body aboard?'

'Turnbull, I don't want to talk about it. No, his body isn't aboard. His —' Rappaport ground the heels of his hands into his eyes, like a man with a blinding headache. 'His grave,' he said, emphasizing the word, 'has a nice black border around it. Let's leave it at that.'

But they couldn't, of course.

Two security officers caught up with them near the edge of the field. 'Stop him,' said Turnbull, and they each took an arm. Rappaport stopped walking and turned.

'Have you forgotten that I'm carrying a destruct capsule?'

'What about it?' For the moment Turnbull really didn't understand what he meant.

'Any more interference and I'll use it. Understand this, Turnbull. I don't care any more. Project Overcee is over. I don't know where I go from here. The best thing we can do is blow up that ship and stay in our own solar system.'

'Man, have you gone crazy? What *happened* out there? You – meet aliens?'

'No comment— No, I'll answer that one. We didn't meet aliens. Now tell your comedian friends to let go.'

Turnbull let himself realize that the man wasn't bluffing. Rappaport was prepared to commit suicide. Turnbull, the instinctive politician, weighed chances and gambled.

'If you haven't decided to talk in twenty-four hours we'll let you go. I promise that. We'll keep you here 'til then, by force if necessary. Just to give you an opportunity to change your mind.'

Rappaport thought it over. The security men still held his arms, but cautiously, now, standing as far back as they could, in case his personal bomb went off.

'Seems fair,' he said at last, 'if you're honest. Sure, I'll wait twenty-four hours.'

'Good.' Turnbull turned to lead the way back to his office. Instead, he merely stared.

The *Overcee* was red hot at the nose, glaring white at the tail. Mechs and techs were running in all directions. As Turnbull watched, the solar system's first faster-than-light spacecraft slumped and ran in a spreading, glowing pool.

. . . It had started a century ago, when the first ramrobot left the solar system. The interstellar ramscoop robots could make most of their journey at near lightspeed, using a conical electro-magnetic field two hundred miles across to scoop hydrogen fuel from interstellar space. But no man had ever ridden a ramrobot. None ever would. The ramscoop magnetic field did horrible things to chordate organisms.

Each ramrobot had been programmed to report back only if it found a habitable world near the star to which

35

it had been assigned. Twenty-six had been sent out. Three had reported back – so far.

. . . It had started twelve years ago, when a well-known mathematician worked out a theoretical hyperspace over Einsteinian fourspace. He did it in his spare time. He considered the hyperspace a toy, an example of pure mathematics. And when has pure mathematics been anything but good clean fun?

. . . It had started ten years ago, when Ergstrom's brother Carl demonstrated the experimental reality of Ergstrom's toy universe. Within a month the UN had financed Project Overcee, put Winston Turnbull in charge, and set up a school for faster-than-light astronauts. The vast number of applicants was winnowed to ten 'hypernauts'. Two were Belters; all were experienced spacers. The training began in earnest. It lasted eight years, while Project Overcee built the ship.

. . . It had started a year and a month ago, when two men climbed into the almost luxurious lifesystem of the *Overcee,* ran the ship out to Neptune's orbit under escort, and vanished.

One was back.

Now his face was no stonier than Rappaport's. Turnbull had just watched his work of the last ten years melt and run like quicksilver. He was mad clean through; but his mind worked furiously. Part of him, the smaller part, was wondering how he would explain the loss of ten billion dollars' worth of ship. The rest was reviewing everything it could remember about Carver Geoffrey Rappaport and William (Wall) Kameon.

Turnbull entered his office and went straight to the bookshelf, sure that Rappaport was following. He pulled out a leather-bound volume, did something to the binding and poured two paper cups full of amber fluid. The fluid was bourbon, and it was more than ice cold.

Rappaport had seen this bookcase before, yet he wore a faintly puzzled frown as he took a cup. He said, 'I didn't think I'd ever anticipate anything again.'

'The bourbon?'

Rappaport didn't answer. His first swallow was a gulp. 'Did you destroy your ship?'

36

'Yes. I set the controls so it would only melt. I didn't want anyone hurt.'

'Commendable. And the *Overcee* motor? You left it in orbit?'

'I hard-landed it on the Moon. It's gone.'

'That's great. Just great. Carver, that ship cost ten billion dollars to build. We can duplicate it for four, I think, because we won't be making any false starts, but you—'

'Hell you wouldn't.' Rappaport swirled the bourbon in his cup, looking down into the miniature whirlpool. He was twenty to thirty pounds lighter than he had been a year ago. 'You build another *Overcee* and you'll be making one enormous false start. We were wrong, Turnbull. It's not our universe. There's nothing out there for us.'

'It *is* our universe.' Turnbull let the quiet certainty show in his politician's voice. He needed to start an argument – he needed to get this man to talking. But the certainty was real, and always had been. It was humanity's universe, ready for the taking.

Over the rim of his cup Rappaport looked at him in exasperated pity. 'Turnbull, can't you take my word for it? It's not our universe, and it's not worth having anyway. What's out there is—' He clamped his mouth shut and turned away in the visitor's chair.

Turnbull waited ten seconds to point up the silence. Then he asked, 'Did you kill Kameon?'

'Kill Wall? You're out of your mind!'

'Could you have saved him?'

Rappaport froze in the act of turning around. 'No,' he said. And again, 'No. I tried to get him moving, but he wouldn't – stop it! Stop needling me. I can walk out anytime, and you couldn't stop me.'

'It's too late. You've aroused my curiosity. What about Kameon's black-bordered grave?'

No answer.

'Rappaport, you seem to think that the UN will just take your word and dismantle Project Overcee. There's not a prayer of that. Probability zero. In the past century we've spent tens of billions of dollars on the ramrobots and the *Overcee,* and now we can rebuild her for four.

37

The only way to stop that is to tell the UN exactly why they shouldn't.'

Rappaport didn't answer, and Turnbull didn't speak again. He watched Rappaport's cigarette burning unheeded in the ashtray, leaving a strip of charred wet paper. It was uncharacteristic of the former Carver Rappaport to forget burning cigarettes, or to wear an untrimmed beard and sloppily cut hair. That man had been always clean shaven; that man had lined up his shoes at night, every night, even when staggering drunk.

Could he have killed Kameon for being sloppy – and then turned messy himself as he lost his self-respect. Stranger things had happened in the days when it took eight months to reach Mars— No, Rappaport had not done murder; Turnbull would have bet high on that. And Kameon would have won any fair fight. Newspapermen had nicknamed him The Wall when he was playing guard for the Berlin Nazis.

'You're right. Where do I start?'

Turnbull was jerked out of his abstraction. 'Start at the beginning. When you went into hyperspace.'

'We had no trouble there. Except with the windows. You shouldn't have put windows on the *Overcee*.'

'Why not? What did you see?'

'Nothing.'

'Well then?'

'You ever try to find your blind spot? You put two dots on a piece of paper, maybe an inch apart, and you close one eye, focus on one dot and slowly bring the paper up to your face. At some point the other dot disappears. Looking at the window in *Overcee* is like your blind spot expanding to a two-foot square with rounded corners.'

'I assume you covered them up.'

'Sure. Would you believe it, we had trouble finding those windows? When you wanted them they were invisible. We got them covered with blankets. Then every so often we'd catch each other looking under the blankets. It bothered Wall worse than me. We could have made the trip in five months instead of six, but we had to keep coming for a look around.'

'Just to be sure the universe was still there.'

'Right.'
'But you did reach Sirius.'
'Yes. We reached Sirius . . .'

Ramrobot No. 6 had reported from Sirius B, half a century ago. The Sirius stars are an unlikely place to look for habitable worlds, since both stars are blue-white giants. Still, the ramrobots had been programmed to test for excessive ultraviolet. Sirius B was worth a look.

The ship came out where Sirius was two bright stars. It turned its sharp nose towards the dimmer star and remained motionless for twenty minutes, a silver torpedo shape in a great, ungainly cradle studded with heavy electromagnetic motors. Then it was gone again.

Now Sirius B was a searing ball of light. The ship began to swing about, like a hound sniffing the breeze, but slowly, ponderously.

'We found four planets,' said Rappaport. 'Maybe there were more, but we didn't look. Number Four was the one we wanted. It was a cloudly ball about twice the size of Mars, with no moon. We waited until we'd found it before we started celebrating.'

'Champagne?'

'Hah! Cigars and drunk pills. And Wall shaved off his grubby beard. My God, we were glad to be out in space again! Near the end it seemed like those blind spots were growing around the edges of the blankets. We smoked our cigars and sucked our drunk pills and yakked about the broads we'd known. Not that we hadn't done *that* before. Then we slept it off and went back to work . . .'

The cloud cover was nearly unbroken. Rappaport moved the telescope a bit at a time, trying to find a break. He found several, but none big enough to show him anything. 'I'll try infra-red,' he said.

'Just get us down,' Wall said irritably. He was always irritable lately. 'I want to get to work.'

'And I want to be sure we've got a place to land.'

Carv's job was the ship. He was pilot, astrogator, repairman, and everything but the cook. Wall was the cook. Wall was also the geologist, astrophysicist, biologist, and chemist – the expert on habitable planets, in theory Each man had been trained nine years for his job, and each had some training as backup man for the other; and in each case the training had been based largely on guesswork.

The picture on the scope screen changed from a featureless disc to a patterned ball as Carv switched to infra-red. 'Now which is water?' he wondered.

'The water's brighter on the night side and darker on the day side. See?' Wall was looking over his shoulder. 'Looks like about forty per cent land. Carv, those clouds might cut out enough of the ultra-violet to let people live in what gets through.'

'Who'd want to? You couldn't see the stars.' Carv turned a knob to raise the magnification.

'Hold it right there, Carv. Look at that. There's a white line around the edge of that continent.'

'Dried salt?'

'No. It's warmer than what's around it. And it's just as bright on the night side as on the day.'

'I'll get us a closer look.'

The *Overcee* was in orbit, three hundred miles up. By now the continent with the 'hot' border was almost entirely in shadow. Of the three supercontinents, only one showed a white shoreline under infra-red.

Wall hung at the window, looking down. To Rappaport he looked like a great ape. 'Can we do a re-entry glide?'

'In this ship? The *Overcee* would come apart like a cheap meteor. We'll have to brake to a full stop above the atmosphere. Want to strap down?'

Kameon did, and Carv watched him do it before he went ahead and dropped the *Overcee* motor. *I'll be glad to be out of here,* he thought. *It's getting so Wall and I hate the sight of each other.* The casual, uncaring way Kameon fastened his straps jarred his teeth. He knew that Kameon thought he was finicky to the point of psychasthenia.

The fusion drive started and built up to one gee. Carv swung the ship around. Only the night side showed below, with the faint blue light of Sirius A shining softly off the cloud cover. Then the edge of dawn came up in

40

torn blue-white cloud. Carv saw an enormous rift in the cloud bank and turned ship to shift their path over it.

Mountains and valleys, and a wide river . . . Patches of wispy cloud shot by, obscuring the view, but they could see down. Suddenly there was a black line, a twisting ribbon of India ink, and beyond that the ocean.

Only for a moment the ocean showed, and then the rift jogged east and was gone. But the ocean was an emerald green.

Wall's voice was soft with awe. 'Carv, there's life in that water.'

'You sure?'

'No. It could be copper salts or something. Carv, we've got to get *down* there!'

'Oh, wait your turn. Did you notice that your hot border is black in visible light?'

'Yah. But I can't explain it. Would it be worth our while to turn back after you get the ship slowed?'

Carv fingered his neatly trimmed Vandyke. 'It'd be night over the whole continent before we got back there. Let's spend a few hours looking at the green ocean.'

The *Overcee* went down on her tail, slowly, like a cautious crab. Layer after layer of cloud swallowed her without trace, and darkness fell as she dropped. The key to this world was the word 'moonless'. Sirius B-IV had had no oversized moon to strip away most of her atmosphere. Her air pressure would be comfortable at sea level, but only because the planet was too small to hold more air. That same low gravity produced a more gentle pressure gradient, so that the atmosphere reached three times as high as on Earth. There were cloud layers from ground to 130 kilometres up.

The *Overcee* touched down on a wide beach on the western shore of the smallest continent. Wall came out first, then Carv lowered a metal oblong as large as himself and followed it down. They wore lightly pressurized vac suits. Carv did nothing for twenty minutes while Wall opened the box out flat and set the carefully packed instruments into their grooves and notches. Finally Wall signalled, in an emphatic manner. By taking off his helmet.

Carv waited a few seconds, then followed suit.

Wall asked, 'Were you waiting to see if I dropped dead?'

'Better you than me.' Carv sniffed the breeze. The air was cool and humid, but thin. 'Smells good enough. No. No, it doesn't. It smells like something rotting.'

'Then I'm right. There's life here. Let's get down to the beach.'

The sky looked like a raging thunderstorm, with occasional vivid blue flashes that might have been lightning. They were flashes of sunlight penetrating tier upon tier of cloud. In that varying light Carv and Wall stripped off their suits and went down to look at the ocean, walking with shuffling steps in the light gravity.

The ocean was thick with algae. Algae were a bubbly green blanket on the water, a blanket that rose and fell like breathing as the insignificant waves ran beneath. The smell of rotting vegetation was no stronger here than it had been a quarter of a mile back. Perhaps the smell pervaded the whole planet. The shore was a mixture of sand and green scum so rich that you could have planted crops in it.

'Time I got to work,' said Wall. 'You want to fetch and carry for me?'

'Later maybe. Right now I've a better idea. Let's get to hell out of each other's sight for an hour.'

'That *is* brilliant. But take a weapon.'

'To fight off maddened algae?'

'Take a weapon.'

Carv was back at the end of an hour. The scenery had been deadly monotonous. There was water below a green blanket of scum six inches deep; there was loamy sand, and beyond that dry sand: and behind the beach were white cliffs, smoothed as if by countless rainfalls. He had found no target for his laser cutter.

Wall looked up from a binocular microscope, and grinned when he saw his pilot. He tossed a depleted pack of cigarettes. 'And don't worry about the air plant!' he called cheerfully.

Carv came up beside him, 'What news?'

'It's algae. I can't name the breed, but there's not much

42

difference between this and any terrestial algae, except that this sample is all one species.'

'That's unusual?' Carv was looking around him in wonder. He was seeing a new side to Wall. Aboard ship Wall was sloppy almost to the point of being dangerous, at least in the eyes of a Belter like Carv. But now he was at work. His small tools were set in neat rows on portable tables. Bulkier instruments with legs were on flat rock, the legs carefully adjusted to leave their platforms exactly horizontal. Wall handled the binocular microscope as if it might dissolve at a touch.

'It is,' said Wall. 'No little animalcules moving among the strands. No variations in structure. I took samples from depths up to six feet. All I could find was the one alga. But otherwise – I even tested for proteins and sugars. You could eat it. We came all this way to find pond scum.'

They came down on an island five hundred miles south. This time Carv helped with the collecting. They got through faster that way, but they kept getting in each other's way. Six months spent in two small rooms had roused tempers too often. It would take more than a few hours on ground before they could bump elbows without a fight.

Again Carv watched Wall go through his routines. He stood just within voice range, about fifty yards away, because it felt so good to have so much room. The care Wall exercised with his equipment still amazed him. How could he reconcile it with Wall's ragged fingernails and his thirty hour's growth of beard?

Well, Wall was a flatlander. All his life he'd had a whole planet to mess up, and not a crowded pressure dome or the cabin of a ship. No flat ever learned real neatness.

'Same breed,' Wall called.

'Did you test for radiation?'

'No. Why?'

'This thick air must screen out a lot of gamma rays. That means your algae can't mutate without local radiation from the ground.'

'Carv, it had to mutate to get to its present form. How could all its cousins just have died out?'

'That's your field.'

A little later Wall said, 'I can't get a respectable background reading anywhere. You were right, but it doesn't explain anything.'

'Shall we go somewhere else?'

'Yah.'

They set down in deep ocean, and when the ship stopped bobbing Carv went out of the airlock with a glass bucket. 'It's a foot thick out there,' he reported. 'No place for a Disneyland. I don't think I'd want to settle here.'

Wall sighed his agreement. The green scum lapped thickly at the *Overcee*'s gleaming metal hull, two yards below the sill of the airlock.

'A lot of planets must be like this,' said Carv. 'Habitable, but who needs it?'

'And I wanted to be the first man to found an interstellar colony.'

'And get your name in the newstapes, the history books—'

'—And my unforgettable face on every trivis in the solar system. Tell me, shipmate, if you hate publicity so much, why have you been trimming that Vandyke so prettily?'

'Guilty. I like being famous. Just not as much as you do.'

'Cheer up then. We may yet get all the hero worship we can stand. This may be something bigger than a new colony.'

'What could be bigger than that?'

'Set us down on land and I'll tell you.'

On a chunk of rock just big enough to be called an island, Wall set up his equipment for the last time. He was testing for food content again, using samples from Carv's bucket of deep ocean algae.

Carv stood by, a comfortable distance away, watching the weird variations in the clouds. The very highest were moving across the sky at enormous speeds, swirling and changing shape by the minutes and seconds. The noonday light was subdued and pearly. No doubt about it, Sirius B-IV had a magnificent sky.

'Okay, I'm ready.' Wall stood up and stretched. 'This stuff isn't just edible. I'd guess it would taste as good as the food supplements they were using on Earth before the fertility laws cut the population down to something reasonable. I'm going to taste it now.'

The last sentence hit Carv like an electric shock. He was running before it was quite finished, but long before he could get there his crazy partner had put a dollup of green scum in his mouth, chewed and swallowed. 'Good,' he said.

'You – utter – damned – fool.'

'Not so. I knew it was safe. The stuff has an almost cheesy flavour. You could get tired of it fast, I think, but that's true of anything.'

'Just *what* are you trying to *prove*?'

'That this alga was tailored as a food plant by biological engineers. Carv, I think we've landed on somebody's private farm.'

Carv sat down heavily on a rainwashed white rock. 'Better spell that out,' he said, and heard that his voice was hoarse.

'I was going to. Suppose there was a civilization that had cheap, fast interstellar travel. Most of the habitable planets they found would be sterile, wouldn't they? I mean, life is an unlikely sort of accident.'

'We don't have the vaguest idea how likely it is.'

'All right, pass that. Say somebody finds this planet, Sirius B-IV, and decides it would make a nice farm planet. It isn't good for much else, mainly because of the variance in lighting, but if you dropped a specially bred food alga in the ocean, you'd have a dandy little farm. In ten years there'd be oceans of algae, free for the carting. Later, if they *did* decide to colonize, they could haul the stuff inland and use it for fertilizer. Best of all, it wouldn't mutate. Not here.'

Carv shook his head to clear it. 'You've been in space too long.'

'Carv, the planet looks *bred* – like a pink grapefruit. And where did all its cousins go? Now I can tell you.'

45

They got poured out of the breeding vat because they weren't good enough.'

Low waves rolled in from the sea, low and broad beneath their blanket of cheesy green scum. 'All right,' said Carv. 'How can we disprove it?'

Wall looked startled. '*Disprove* it? Why would we want to do that?'

'Forget the glory for a minute. If you're right, we're trespassing on somebody's property without knowing anything about the owner – except that he's got dirt-cheap interstellar travel, which would make him a tough enemy. We're also introducing our body bacteria into his pure edible algae culture. And how would we explain, if he suddenly showed up?'

'I hadn't thought of it that way.'

'We ought to cut and run right now. It's not as if the planet were worth anything.'

'No. No, we can't do that.'

'Why not?'

The answer gleamed in Wall's eyes.

Turnbull, listening behind his desk with his chin resting in one hand, interrupted for the first time in minutes. 'A good question. I'd have got out right then.'

'Not if you'd just spent six months in a two-room cell with the end of everything creeping around the blankets.'

'I see.' Turnbull's hand moved almost imperceptibly, writing, *NO WINDOW IN OVERCEE No. 2! Oversized viewscreen?*

'It hadn't hit me that hard. I think I'd have taken off if I'd been sure Wall was right, and if I could have talked him into it. But I couldn't, of course. Just the thought of going home then was enough to set Wall shaking. I thought I might have to knock him on the head when it came time to leave. We had some hibernation drugs aboard, just in case.'

He stopped. As usual, Turnbull waited him out.

'But then I'd have been all alone.' Rappaport finished his drink, his second, and got up to pour a third. The bourbon didn't seem to affect him. 'So we stood there on that rocky beach, both of us afraid to leave and both afraid to stay . . .'

Abruptly Wall got up and started putting his tools away. 'We can't disprove it, but we can prove it easily enough. The owners must have left artifacts around. If we find one, we run. I promise.'

'There's a big area to search. If we had any sense we'd run now.'

'Will you drop that? All we've got to do is find the ramrobot probe. If there's anyone watching this place they must have seen it come down. We'll find footprints all over it.'

'And if there aren't any footprints? Does that make the whole planet clean?'

Wall closed his case with a snap. Then he stood, motionless, looking very surprised. 'I just thought of something,' he said.

'Oh, not again.'

'No, this is for real, Carv. The owners must have left a long time ago.'

'Why?'

'It must be thousands of years since there were enough algae here to use as a food supply. We should have seen ships taking off and landing as we came in. They'd have started their colony too, if they were going to. Now it's gone beyond that. The planet isn't fit for anything to live on, with the soupy oceans and the smell of things rotting.'

'No.'

'Dammit, it makes sense!'

'It's thin. It sounds thin even to me, and I *want* to believe it. Also, it's too pat. It's just too close to the best possible solution we could dream up. You want to bet our lives on it?'

Wall hoisted his case and moved towards the ship. He looked like a human tank, moving in a stormy darkness lit by shifting, glaring beams of blue light. Abruptly he said, 'There's one more point. That black border. It has to be contaminated algae. Maybe a land-living mutant; that's why it hasn't spread across the oceans. It would have been cleaned away if the owners were still interested.'

'All *right*. Hoist that thing up and let's get inside.'

'Hmph?'

47

'You've finally said something we can check. The eastern shore must be in daylight by now. Let's get aboard.'

At the border of space they hovered, and the Sun burned small and blinding white at the horizon. To the side Sirius A was a tiny dot of intense brilliance. Below, where gaps in the cloud cover penetrated all the way to the surface, a hair-thin black line ran along the twisting beach of Sirius B-IV's largest continent. The silver thread of a major river exploded into a forking delta, and the delta was a black triangle shot with lines of silvery green.

'Going to use the scope?'

Carv shook his head. 'We'll see it close in a few minutes.'

'You're in quite a hurry, Carv.'

'You bet. According to you, if that black stuff is some form of life, then this farm's been deserted for thousands of years at least. If it isn't, then what is it? It's too regular to be a natural formation. Maybe it's a conveyor belt.'

'That's right. Calm me down. Reassure me.'

'If it is, we go up fast and run all the way home.' Carv pulled a lever and the ship dropped from under them. They fell fast. Speaking with only half his attention, Carv went on. 'We've met just one other sentient race, and they had nothing like hands and no mechanical culture. I'm not complaining, mind you. A world wouldn't be fit to live in without dolphins for company. But why should we get lucky twice? I don't want to meet the farmer, Wall.'

The clouds closed over the ship. She dropped more slowly with every kilometre. Ten kilometres up she was almost hovering. Now the coast was spread below them. The black border was graded: black as night on Pluto along the sea, shading off to the colour of the white sand and rocks along the landward side.

Wall said, 'Maybe the tides carry the dead algae inland. They'd decay there. No, that won't work. No moon. Nothing but solar tides.'

They were a kilometre up. And lower, And lower.

The black was moving, flowing like tar, away from the drive's fusion flame.

Rappaport had been talking down into his cup, his words coming harsh and forced, his eyes refusing to meet Turnbull's. Now he raised them. There was something challenging in that gaze.

Turnbull understood. 'You want me to guess? I won't. What was the black stuff?'

'I don't know if I want to prepare you or not. Wall and I, we weren't ready. Why should you be?'

'All right, Carver, go ahead and shock me.'

'It was people.'

Turnbull merely stared.

'We were almost down when they started to scatter from the downblast. Until then it was just a dark field, but when they started to scatter we could see moving specks, like ants. We sheered off and landed on the water offshore. We could see them from there.'

'Carver, when you say people, do you mean – people? Human?'

'Yes. Human. Of course they didn't act much like it . . .'

A hundred yards offshore, the *Overcee* floated nose up. Even seen from the airlock the natives were obviously human. The telescope screen brought more detail.

They were no terrestrial race. Nine feet tall, men and women both, with wavy black hair growing from the eyebrows back to half-way down the spine, hanging almost to the knees. Their skins were dark, as dark as the darkest Negro, but they had chisel noses and long heads and small, thin-lipped mouths.

They paid no attention to the ship. They stood or sat or lay where they were, men and women and children jammed literally shoulder to shoulder. Most of the seaside population was grouped in large rings with men on the outside and women and children protected inside.

'All around the continent,' said Wall.

Carv could no more have answered than he could have taken his eyes off the scope screen.

Every few minutes there was a seething in the mass as some group that was too far back pulled forward to reach the shore, the food supply. The mass pushed back. On the fringes of the circles there were bloody fights, slow fights in which there were apparently no rules at all.

'How?' said Carv. 'How?'

Wall said, 'Maybe a ship crashed. Maybe there was a caretaker's family here, and nobody ever came to pick them up. They must be the farmer's children, Carv.'

'How long have they been here?'

'Thousands of years at least. Maybe tens or hundreds of thousands.' Wall turned his empty eyes away from the screen. He swivelled his couch so he was looking at the back wall of the cabin. His dreary words flowed out into the cabin.

'Picture it, Carv. Nothing in the world but an ocean of algae and a few people. Then a few hundred people, then hundreds of thousands. They'd never have been allowed near here unless they'd had the bacteria cleaned out of them to keep the algae from being contaminated. Nothing to make tools out of, nothing but rock and bone. No way of smelting ores, because they wouldn't even have fire. There's nothing to *burn*. They had no diseases, no contraceptives, and no recreation but breeding. The population would have exploded like a bomb. Because nobody would starve to death, Carv. For thousands of years nobody would starve on Sirius B-IV.'

'They're starving now.'

'Some of them. The ones that can't reach the shore.' Wall turned back to the scope screen. 'One continual war,' he said after a while. 'I'll bet their height comes from natural selection.'

Carv hadn't moved for a long time. He had noticed that there were always a few men inside each protective circle, and that there were always men outside going inside and men inside going outside. Breeding more people to guard each circle. More people for Sirius B-IV.

The shore was a seething blackness. In infra-red light it would have shown brightly, at a temperature of 98.6° Fahrenheit.

'Let's go home,' said Wall.

'Okay.'

'And did you?'

'No.'

'In God's name, why not?'

'We *couldn't*. We had to see it all, Turnbull. I don't

understand it, but we did, both of us. So I took the ship up and dropped it a kilometre inshore, and we got out and started walking towards the sea.

'Right away, we started finding skeletons. Some were clean. A lot of them looked like Egyptian mummies, skeletons with black dried skin stretched tight over the bones. Always there was a continuous low rustle of – well, I guess it was conversation. From the beach. I don't know what they could have had to talk about.

'The skeletons got thicker as we went along. Some of them had daggers of splintered bone. One had a chipped stone fist axe. You see, Turnbull, they were intelligent. They could make tools, if they could find anything to make tools out of.

'After we'd been walking awhile we saw that some of the skeletons were alive. Dying and drying under that overcast blue sky. I'd thought that sky was pretty once. Now it was – horrible. You could see a shifting blue beam spear down on the sand and sweep across it like a spotlight until it picked out a mummy. Sometimes the mummy would turn over and cover its eyes.

'Wall's face was livid, like a dead man's. I knew it wasn't just the light. We'd been walking about five minutes, and the dead and living skeletons were all around us. The live ones all stared at us, apathetically, but still staring, as if we were the only things in the world worth looking at. If they had anything to wonder with, they must have been wondering what it was that could move and still not be human. We couldn't have looked human to them. We had shoes and coveralls on, and we were too small.

'Wall said, 'I've been wondering about the clean skeletons. There shouldn't be any decay bacteria here.'

'I didn't answer. I was thinking how much this looked like a combination of Hell and Belsen. The only thing that might have made it tolerable was the surrealistic blue lighting. We couldn't really believe what we were seeing.

'There weren't enough fats in the algae,' said Wall. 'There was enough of everything else, but no fats.'

'We were closer to the beach now. And some of the mummies were beginning to stir. I watched a pair behind a dune who looked like they were trying to kill each other, and then suddenly I realized what Wall had said.

51

'I took his arm and turned to go back. Some of the long skeletons were trying to get up. I knew what they were thinking. *There may be meat in those limp coverings. Wet meat, with water in it. There just may.* I pulled at Wall and started to run.

'He wouldn't run. He tried to pull loose. I had to leave him. They couldn't catch me, they were too starved, and I was jumping like a grasshopper. But they got Wall, all right. I heard this destruct capsule go off. Just a muffled pop.'

'So you came home.'

'Uh huh.' Rappaport looked up like a man waking from a nightmare. 'It took seven months. All alone.'

'Any idea why Wall killed himself?'

'You crazy? He didn't want to get *eaten.*'

'Then why wouldn't he run?'

'It wasn't that he wanted to kill himself, Turnbull. He just decided it wasn't worthwhile saving himself. Another six months in the *Overcee,* with the blind spots pulling at his eyes and that nightmare of a world constantly on his mind – it wasn't worth it.'

'I'll bet the *Overcee* was a pigpen before you blew it up.'

Rappaport flushed. 'What's that to you?'

'You didn't think it was worthwhile either. When a Belter stops being neat it's because he wants to die. A dirty ship is deadly. The air plant gets fouled. Things float around loose, ready to knock your brains out when the drive goes on. You forget where you put the meteor patches—'

'All right. I made it, didn't I?'

'And now you think we should give up space.'

Rappaport's voice went squeaky with emotion. 'Turnbull, aren't you convinced *yet*? We've got a paradise here, and you want to leave it for – that. Why? Why?

'To build other paradises, maybe. Ours didn't happen by accident. Our ancestors did it all, starting with not much more than what was on Sirius B-IV.'

'They had a *hell*uva lot more.' A faint slurring told that the bourbon was finally getting to Rappaport.

'Maybe they did at that. But now there's a better reason. These people you left on the beach. They need our help.

52

And with a new *Overcee*, we can give it to them. What do they need most, Carver? Trees or meat animals?'

'Animals.' Rappaport shuddered and drank.

'Well, that could be argued. But pass it. First we'll have to make soil.' Turnbull leaned back in his chair, face upturned, talking half to himself. 'Algae mixed with crushed rock. Bacteria to break the rock down. Earthworms. Then grass . . .'

'Got it all planned out, do you? And you'll take the UN into it, too. Turnbull, you're good. But you've missed something.'

'Better tell me now then.'

Rappaport got carefully to his feet. He came over to the desk, just a little unsteadily, and leaned on it so that he stared down into Turnbull's eyes from a foot away. 'You've been assuming that those people on the beach really were the farmer's race. That Sirius B-IV has been deserted for a long, long time. But what if some kind of carnivore seeded that planet? Then what? The algae wouldn't be for them. They'd let the algae grow, plant food animals, then go away until the animals were jammed shoulder to shoulder along the coast. Food animals! You understand, Turnbull?'

'Yes. I hadn't thought of that. And they'd breed them for *size* . . .'

The room was deadly quiet.

'*Well*?'

'Well, we'll simply have to take that chance, won't we?'

HOW THE HEROES DIE

ONLY SHEER RUTHLESSNESS could have taken him out of town alive. The mob behind Carter hadn't tried to guard the Mars buggies, since Carter would have needed too much time to take a buggy through the vehicular airlock. They could have caught him there, and they knew it. Some were guarding the personnel lock, hoping he'd try for that. He might have; for if he could have closed the one door in their faces and opened the next, the safeties would have protected him while he went through the third and fourth and outside. On the Marsbuggy he was trapped in his bubble.

There was room to drive around in. Less than half the prefab houses had been erected so far. The rest of the bubbletown's floor was flat and fused sand, empty but for scattered piles of foam-plastic walls and ceilings and floors. But they'd get him eventually. Already they were starting up another buggy.

They never expected him to run his vehicle through the bubble wall.

The Marsbuggy tilted, then righted itself. A blast of breathing-air roared out around him, picked up a cloud of fine sand, and hurled it explosively away into the thin, poisoned atmosphere. Carter grinned as he looked behind him. They would die now, all of them. He was the only one wearing a pressure suit. In an hour he could come back and repair the rip in the bubble. He'd have to dream up a fancy story to tell when the next ship came . . .

Carter frowned. What were they—

At least ten wind-harried men were wrestling with the wall of a prefab house. As Carter watched, they picked the wall up off the fused sand, balanced it almost upright, and let go. The foam-plastic wall rose into the wind and slapped hard against the bubble, over the ten-foot rip.

Carter stopped his buggy to see what would happen.

Nobody was dead. The air was not shrieking away but leaking away. Slowly, methodically, a line of men climbed into their suits and filed through the personnel lock to repair the bubble.

A buggy entered the vehicular lock. The third and last was starting to life. Carter turned his buggy and was off.

Top speed for a Marsbuggy is about twenty-five miles per hour. The buggy rides on three wide balloon-tyred wheels, each mounted at the end of a five-foot arm. What those wheels can't go over, the buggy can generally hop over on the compressed-air jet mounted underneath. The motor and the compressor are both powered by a Litton battery holding a tenth as much energy as the original Hiroshima bomb.

Carter had been careful, as careful as he had had time for. He was carrying a full load of oxygen, twelve four-hour tanks in the air bin behind him, and an extra tank rested against his knees. His batteries were nearly full; he would be out of air long before his power ran low. When the other buggies gave up he could circle round and return to the bubble in the time his extra tank would give him.

His own buggy and the two behind him were the only such vehicles on Mars. At twenty-five miles per hour he fled, and at twenty-five miles per hour they followed. The closest was half a mile behind.

Carter turned on his radio.

He found the middle of a conversation. '– Can't afford it. One of you will have to come back. We could lose two of the buggies, but not all three.'

That was Shute, the bubbletown's research director and sole military man. The next voice, deep and sarcastic, belonged to Rufus Doolittle, the biochemist. 'What'll we do, flip a coin?'

'Let me go,' the third voice said tightly. 'I've got a stake in this.'

Carter felt apprehension touch the nape of his neck.

'Okay, Alf. Good luck,' said Rufus. 'Good hunting,' he added maliciously, as if he knew Carter were listening.

'You concentrate on getting the bubble fixed. I'll see that Carter doesn't come back.'

Behind Carter, the rearmost buggy swung in a wide loop towards town. The other came on. And it was driven by the linguist, Alf Harness.

55

Most of the bubble's dozen men were busy repairing the ten-foot rip with heaters and plastic sheeting. It would be a long job but an easy one, for by Shute's orders the bubble had been deflated. The transparent plastic had fallen in folds across the prefab houses, forming a series of interconnected tents. One could move about underneath with little difficulty.

Lieutenant-Major Michael Shute watched the men at work and decided they had things under control. He walked away like a soldier on parade, stooping as little as possible as he moved beneath the dropping folds.

He stopped and watched Gondot operating the airmaker. Gondot noticed him and spoke without looking up.

'Mayor, why'd you let Alf chase Carter alone?'

Shute accepted his nickname. 'We couldn't lose both tractors.'

'Why not just post them on guard duty for two days?'

'And what if Carter got through the guard? He must be determined to wreck the dome. He'd catch us with our pants down. Even if some of us got into suits, could we stand another rip in the bubble?'

Gondot reached to scratch his short beard. His fingertips rapped helmet plastic and he looked annoyed. 'Maybe not. I can fill the bubble anytime you're ready, but then the airmaker'll be empty. We'll be almost out of tanked air by the time they finish mending that rip. Another'd finish us.'

Shute nodded and turned away. All the air anyone could use – tons of nitrogen and oxygen – was right outside; but it was in the form of nitrogen dioxide gas. The airmaker could convert it three times as fast as men could use it. But if Carter tore the dome again, that would be too slow.

But Carter wouldn't. Alf would see to that. The emergency was over – this time.

And so Lieutenant-Major Shute could go back to worrying about the emergency's underlying causes.

His report on those causes had been finished a month ago. He had reread it several times since, and always it had seemed complete and to the point. Yet he had the feeling it could be written better. He ought to make it as effective as possible. What he had to say could only be said

56

once, and then his career would be over and his voice silenced.

Cousins had sold some fiction once, writing as a hobby. Perhaps he would help. But Shute was reluctant to involve anyone else in what amounted to his own rebellion.

Yet – he'd have to rewrite that report now, or at least add to it. Lew Harness was dead, murdered. John Carter would be dead within two days. All Shute's responsibility. All pertinent.

The decision wasn't urgent. It would be a month before Earth was in reach of the bubbletown's sending station.

Most of the asteroids spend most of their time between Mars and Jupiter, and it often happens that one of them crosses a planet where theretofore it had crossed only an orbit. There are asteroid craters all over Mars. Old eroded ones, sharp new ones, big ones, little ones, ragged and smooth ones. The bubbletown was at the centre of a large, fairly recent crater four miles across : an enormous, poorly cast ashtray discarded on the reddish sand.

The buggies ran over cracked glass, avoiding the occasional tilted blocks, running uphill towards the broken rim. A sky the colour of blood surrounded a tiny, brilliant sunset precisely at the zenith.

Inevitably Alf was getting closer. When they crossed the rim and started downhill they would pull apart. It was going to be a long chase.

Now was the time for regrets, if there ever was such a time. But Carter wasn't the type, and he had nothing to be ashamed of anyway. Lew Harness had needed to die; had as much as *asked* to die. Carter was only puzzled that his death should have provoked so violent a reaction. Could they *all* be – the way Lew had been? Unlikely. If he'd stayed and explained—

They'd have torn him apart. Those vulpine faces, with the distended nostrils and the bared teeth !

And now he was being chased by one man. But that man was Lew's brother.

Here was the rim, and Alf was still well behind. Carter slowed as he went over, knowing that the way down would be rougher. He was just going over the edge when a rock ten yards away exploded in white fire.

57

Alf had a flare pistol.

Carter just stopped himself from scrambling out of the buggy to hide in the rocks. The buggy lurched downward and, like it or not, Carter had to forget his terror to keep the vehicle upright.

The rubble around the crater's rim slowed him still further. Carter angled the buggy for the nearest rise of sloping sand. As he reached it, Alf came over the rim, a quarter-mile behind. His silhouette hesitated there against the bloody sky, and another flare exploded, blinding bright and terrifyingly close.

Then Carter was on the straightaway, rolling down sloping sand to a perfectly flat horizon.

The radio said, 'Gonna be a long one, Jack.'

Carter pushed to transmit. 'Right. How many flares do you have left?'

'Don't worry about it.'

'I won't. Not the way you're throwing them away.'

Alf didn't answer. Carter left the radio band open, knowing that ultimately Alf must talk to the man he needed to kill.

The crater which was home dropped behind and was gone. Endless flat desert rose before the buggies, flowed under the oversized wheels and dropped behind. Gentle crescent dunes patterned the sand, but they were no barrier to a buggy. Once there was a martian well. It stood all alone on the sand, a weathered cylindrical wall seven feet high and ten in circumference, made of cut diamond blocks. The wells, and the slanting script written deep into their 'dedication blocks', were responsible for the town's presence on Mars. Since the only martian ever found – a mummy centuries dead, at least – had exploded at the first contact with water, it was generally assumed that the wells were crematoriums. But it wasn't certain. Nothing was certain about Mars.

The radio maintained an eerie silence. Hours rolled past; the sun slid towards the deep red horizon, and still Alf did not speak. It was as if Alf had said everything there was to say to Jack Carter. And that was wrong! Alf should have needed to justify himself!

It was Carter who sighed and gave up. 'You can't catch me, Alf.'

'No, but I can stay behind you as long as I need to.'

'You can stay behind me just twenty-four hours. You've got forty-eight hours of air. I don't believe you'll kill yourself just to kill me.'

'Don't count on it. But I won't need to. Noon tomorrow, you'll be chasing me. You need to breathe, just like I do.'

'Watch this,' said Carter. The O-tank resting against his knee was empty. He tipped it over the side and watched it roll away.

'I had an extra tank,' he said. He smiled in relief at his release from that damning weight. 'I can live four hours longer than you can. Want to turn back, Alf?'

'No.'

'He's not worth it, Alf. He was nothing but a queer.'

'Does that mean he's got to die?'

'It does if the son of a bitch propositions me. Maybe you're a little that way yourself?'

'No. And Lew wasn't queer 'til he came here. They should have sent half men, half women.'

'Amen.'

'You know, lots of people get a little sick to their stomachs about homosexuals. I do myself, and it hurt to see it happening to Lew. But there's only one type who goes looking for 'em so he can beat up on 'em.'

Carter frowned.

'Latents. Guys who think they might turn queer themselves if you gave 'em the opportunity. They can't stand queers around because queers are temptation.'

'You're just returning the compliment.'

'Maybe.'

'Anyway, the town has enough problems without – things like that going on. This whole project could have been wrecked by someone like your brother.'

'How bad do we need killers?'

'Pretty badly, this time.' Suddenly Carter knew that he was now his own defence attorney. If he could convince Alf that he shouldn't be executed, he could convince the rest of them. If he couldn't – then he must destroy the bubble, or die. He went on talking as persuasively as he knew how.

'You see, Alf, the town has two purposes. One is to find

out if we can live in an environment as hostile as this one. The other is to contact the martians. Now there are just fifteen of us in town—'

'Twelve. Thirteen when I get back.'

'Fourteen if we both do. Okay. Each of us is more or less necessary to the functioning of the town. But I'm needed in both fields. I'm the ecologist, Alf. I not only have to keep the town from dying from some sort of imbalance, I also have to figure out how the martians live, what they live on, how martian life forms depend on each other. You see?'

'Sure. How 'bout Lew? Was he necessary?'

'We can get along without him. He was the radio man. At least a couple of us have training enough to take over communications.'

'You make me so happy. Doesn't the same go for you?'

Carter thought hard and fast. Yes, Gondot in particular could keep the town's life support system going with a little help. But – 'Not with the martian ecology. There isn't—'

'There isn't any martian ecology. Jack, has anyone ever found *any* life on Mars besides that man-shaped mummy? You can't be an ecologist without something to make deductions from. You've got nothing to investigate. So what good are you?'

Carter kept talking. He was still arguing as the sun dropped into the sea of sand and darkness closed down with a snap. But he knew now it was no use. Alf's mind was closed.

By sunset the bubble was taut, and the tortured scream of incoming breathing-air had dropped to a tired sigh. Lieutenant-Major Shute unfastened the clamps at his shoulders and lifted his helmet, ready to jam it down fast if the air were too thin. It wasn't. He set the helmet down and signalled thumbs-up to the men watching him.

Ritual. Those dozen men had known the air would be safe. But rituals had grown fast where men worked in space, and the most rigid was that the man in charge fastened his helmet last and unfastened it first. Now suits were being removed. Men moved about their duties. Some moved towards the kitchen to clean up the vacuum-induced havoc so Hurley could get dinner.

Shute stopped Lee Cousins as he went by. 'Lee, could I see you a minute?'

'Sure, Mayor.' Shute was 'the Mayor' to all bubbletown.

'I want your help as a writer,' said Shute. 'I'm going to send in a quite controversial report when we get within range of Earth, and I'd like you to help me make it convincing.'

'Fine. Let's see it.'

The ten streetlamps came on, dispelling the darkness which had fallen so suddenly. Shute led the way to his prefab bungalow, unlocked the safe, and handed Cousins the manuscript. Cousins hefted it. 'Big,' he said. 'Might pay to cut it.'

'By all means, if you find anything unnecessary.'

'I'll bet I can,' Cousins grinned. He dropped on the bed and began to read.

Ten minutes later he asked, 'Just what *is* the incidence of homosexuality in the Navy?'

'I haven't the faintest idea.'

'Then it's not powerful evidence. You might quote a limerick to show that the problem's proverbial. I know a few.'

'Good.'

A little later Cousins said, 'A lot of schools in England *are* coeducational. More every year.'

'I know. But the present problem is among men who graduated from boys' schools when they were much younger.'

'Make that clearer. Incidentally, was your high-school coeducational?'

'No.'

'Any queers?'

'A few. At least one in every class. The senior used to use paddles on the ones they suspected.'

'Did it help?'

'No. Of course not.'

'Okay. You've got two sets of circumstances under which a high rate of homosexuality occurs. In both cases you've got three conditions: a reasonable amount of leisure, no women, and a disciplinary pecking order. You need a third example.'

'I couldn't think of one.'

'The Nazi organization.'

'Oh?'

'I'll give you details.' Cousins went on reading. He finished the report and put it aside. 'This'll cause merry hell,' he said.

'I know.'

'The worst thing about it is your threat to give the whole thing to the newspapers. If I were you I'd leave that out.'

'If you were me you wouldn't,' said Shute. 'Everyone who had anything to do with WARGOD knew they were risking everything that's happened. The preferred to let us take that risk rather than risk public opinion themselves. There are hundreds of Decency Leagues in the United States. Maybe thousands, I don't know. But they'd all come down on the government like harpies if anyone tried to send a mixed crew to Mars or anywhere else in space. The only way I can make the government act is to give them a greater threat.'

'You win. This is a greater threat.'

'Did you find anything else to cut out?'

'Oh, hell yes. I'll go through this again with a red pencil. You talk too much, you use too many words that are too long, and you generalize. You'll have to give details or you'll lose impact.'

'Can't be helped. We've got to have women on Mars, and right now. Rufe and Timmy are building up to a real spitting fight. Rufe thinks he caused Lew's death by leaving him. Timmy keeps taunting him with it.'

'All right,' said Shute. He stood up. He had been sitting erect throughout the discussion, as if sitting at attention. 'Are the buggies still in radio range?'

'They can't hear us, but we can hear them. Timmy's working the radio.'

'Good. I'll keep him on it until they go out of range. Shall we get dinner?'

Phobos rose where the sun had set, a scattering of moving dots of light, like a crescent of dim stars. It grew brighter as it rose: a new moon becoming a half-moon in hours. Then it was too high to look at. Carter had to keep his eyes on the triangle of desert lit by his headlights. The headlight beams were the colour of earthly sunlight, but to Carter's Mars-adapted eyes they turned everything blue.

He had chosen his course well. The desert ahead was flat for more than seven hundred miles. There would be no low hills rising suddenly before him to trap him into jet-jumping in faint moonlight or waiting for Alf to come down on him. Alf's turnover point would come at high noon tomorrow, and then Carter would have won.

For Alf would turn back towards the bubble, and Carter would go on into the desert. When Alf was safely over the horizon, Carter would turn left or right, go on for an hour, and then follow a course parallel to Alf's. He would be in sight of the bubble an hour later than Alf, with three hours in which to plan.

Then would come the hardest part. Certainly there would be someone on guard. Carter would have to charge past the guard – who might be armed with a flare pistol – tear the bubble open, and somehow confiscate the supply of O-tanks. Ripping the bubble open would probably kill everyone inside, but there would be men in suits outside. He would have to load some of the O-tanks on his buggy and open the stopcocks of the rest, all before anyone reached him.

What bothered him was the idea of charging a flare pistol . . . But perhaps he could just aim the buggy and jump out. He would have to see.

His eyelids were getting heavy, and his hands were cramped. But he dared not slow down, and he dared not sleep.

Several times he had thought of smashing the come-hither in his suit radio. With that thing constantly beeping, Alf could find him anytime he pleased. But Alf could find him anyway. His headlights were always behind, never catching up, never dropping away. If he ever got out of Alf's sight, that come-hither would have to go. But there was no point in letting Alf know that. Not yet.

Stars dropped into the black western horizon. Phobos rose again, brighter this time, and again became too high to watch. Deimos now showed above the steady shine of Alf's headlights.

Suddenly it was day, and there were thin black shadows pointing to a yellow horizon. Stars still glowed in a red-black sky. There was a crater ahead, a glass dish set in the desert, not too big to circle around. Carter angled left. The buggy behind him also angled. If he kept turning like this, Alf couldn't help but gain on him. Carter sucked water and nutrient solution from the nipples of his helmet, and concentrated on steering. His eyes felt gritty, and his mouth belonged to a martian mummy.

'Morning,' said Alf.

'Morning. Get plenty of sleep?'

'Not enough. I only slept about six hours, in snatches. I kept worrying you'd turn off and lose me.'

For a moment Carter went hot and cold. Then he knew that Alf was needling him. He'd no more slept than Carter had.

'Look to your right,' said Alf.

To their right was the crater wall. And – Carter looked again to be sure – there was a silhouette on the rim, a man-shaped shadow against the red sky. With one hand it balanced something tall and thin.

'A martian,' Carter said softly. Without thinking he turned his buggy to climb the wall. Two flares exploded in front of him, a second apart, and he frantically jammed the tiller bar hard left.

'God damn it, Alf! That was a *martian*! We've got to go *after* it!'

The silhouette was gone. No doubt the martian had run for its life when it saw the flares.

Alf said nothing. Nothing at all. And Carter rode on, past the crater, with a murderous fury building in him.

It was eleven o'clock. The tips of a range of hills were pushing above the western horizon.

'I'm just curious,' Alf said, 'but what would you have said to that martian?'

Carter's voice was tight and bitter. 'Does it matter?'

'Yah. The best you could have done was scare him. When we get in touch with the martians, we'll do it just the way we planned.'

Carter ground his teeth. Even without the accident of Lew Harness' death. there was no telling how long the translation plan would take. It involved three steps; sending pictures of the writings on the crematory wells and other artifacts to Earth, so that computers could translate the language; writing messages in that language to leave near the wells where martians would find them; and then waiting for the martians to make a move. But there was no reason to believe that the script on the wells wasn't from more than one language, or from the same language as it had changed over thousands of years. There was no reason to assume the martians would be interested in strange beings living in a glorified balloon, regardless of whether the invaders knew how to write. And could the martians read their own ancestors' script?

An idea ... 'You're a linguist,' said Carter.

No answer.

'Alf, we've talked about whether the town needed Lew, and we've talked about whether the town needs me. How about you? Without you we'd *never* get the well-script translated.'

'I doubt that. The Cal Tech computers are doing most of the work, and anyhow I left notes. But so what?'

'If you keep chasing me you'll force me to kill you. Can the town afford to lose you?'

'You can't do it. But I'll make you a deal if you want. It's eleven now. Give me two of your O-tanks, and we'll go back to town. We'll stop two hours from town, leave your buggy, and you'll ride the rest of the way tied up in the air bin. Then you can stand trial.'

'You think they'll let me off?'

'Not after the way you ripped the bubble open on your way out. That was a blunder, Jack.'

'Why don't you just take one tank?' If Alf did that, Carter would get back with two hours to spare. He knew, now, that he would have to wreck the bubble. He had no alternative. But Alf would be right behind him with the flare gun ...

'No deal. I wouldn't feel safe if I didn't know you'd run out of air two hours before we got back. You want me to feel safe, don't you?'

It was better the other way. Let Alf turn back in an hour. Let Alf be in the bubble when Carter returned to tear it open.

'Carter turned him down,' said Timmy. He haunched

65

over the radio, holding his earphones with both hands, listening with every nerve for voices which had almost died into the distance.

'He's planning something,' Gondot said uneasily.

'Naturally,' said Shute. 'He wants to lose Alf, return to the bubble, and wreck it. What other hope has he?'

'But he'd die too,' said Timmy.

'Not necessarily. If he killed us all, he could mend the new rip while he lived on the O-tanks we've got left. I think he could keep the bubble in good enough repair to keep one man alive.'

'My *Lord*! What can we do?'

'Relax, Timmy. It's simple math.' It was easy for Lieutenant-Major Shute to keep his voice light, and he didn't want Timmy to start a panic. 'If Alf turns back at noon, Carter can't get here before noon tomorrow. At four he'll be out of air. We'll just keep everyone in suits for four hours.' Privately he wondered if twelve men could repair even a small rip before they used up the bottled air. It would be one tank every twenty minutes . . . but perhaps they wouldn't be tested.

'Five minutes of twelve,' said Carter. 'Turn back, Alf. You'll only get home with ten minutes to spare.'

The linguist chuckled. A quarter-mile behind, the blue dot of his buggy didn't move.

'You can't fight mathematics, Alf. Turn back.'

'Too late.'

'In five minutes it will be.'

'I started this trip short of an O-tank. I should have turned two hours ago.'

Carter had to wet his lips from the water nipple before he answered. 'You're lying. Will you stop bugging me? Stop it!'

Alf laughed. 'Watch me turn back.'

His buggy came on.

It was noon, and the case would not end. At twenty-five miles per, two Marsbuggies a quarter of a mile apart moved serenely through an orange desert. Chemical stains of green rose ahead and fell behind. Crescent dunes drifted by, as regular as waves on an ocean. The ghostly path of a meteorite touched the northern horizon in a momentary white flash. The hills were higher now, humps of smooth rock-like animals sleeping beyond the horizon. The sun burned small and bright in a sky reddened by nitrogen dioxide and, near the horizon, blackened by its thinness to the colour of bloody India ink.

Had the chase really started at noon? Exactly noon? But it was twelve-thirty now, and he was *sure* that was too late.

Alf had doomed himself – to doom Carter.

But he *wouldn't*.

'Great minds think alike,' he told the radio.

'Really?' Alf's tone said he couldn't have cared less.

'You took an extra tank. Just like me.'

'No I didn't, Jack.'

'You must have. If there's one thing I'm sure of in life, it's that *you* are *not* the type to kill yourself. All right, Alf, I quit. Let's go back.'

'Let's not.'

'We'd have three hours to chase that martian.'

A flare exploded behind his buggy. Carter sighed raggedly. At two o'clock both buggies would turn back to bubbletown, where Carter would probably be executed.

But suppose I turn back now?

That's easy. Alf will shoot me with the flare gun.

He might miss. If I let him choose my course, I'll die for certain.

Carter sweated and cursed himself, but he couldn't do it. He couldn't deliberately turn into Alf's gun.

At two o'clock the base of the range came over the horizon. The hills were incredibly clear, almost as clear as they would have been on the Moon. But they were horribly weathered, and the sea of sand lapped around them as if eager to finish them off, to drag them down.

Carter rode with his eyes turned behind. His watch hands moved on, minute to minute, and Carter watched in disbelief as Alf's vehicle continued to follow. As the time approached and reached two-thirty, Carter's disbelief faded. It didn't matter, now, how much oxygen Alf had. They had passed Carter's turnover point.

'You've killed me,' he said.

No answer.

'I killed Lew in a fistfight. What you've done to me is

67

much worse. You're killing me by slow torture. You're a demon, Alf.'

'Fistfight my aunt's purple asterisk. You hit Lew in the throat and watched him drown in his own blood. Don't tell *me* you didn't know what you were doing. Everybody in town knows you know karate.'

'He died in minutes. I'll need a whole day !'

'You don't like that? Turn around and rush my gun. It's right here waiting.'

'We could get back to the crater in time to search for that martian. That's why I came to Mars. To learn what's here. So did you, Alf. Come on, let's turn back.'

'You first.'

But he couldn't. He *couldn't*. Karate can defeat any hand-to-hand weapon but a quarterstaff, and Carter had quarterstaff training too. But he couldn't charge a flare gun ! Not even if Alf meant to turn back. And Alf didn't.

A faint whine vibrated through the bubble. The sand-storm was at the height of its fury, which made it about as dangerous an an enraged caterpillar. At worst it was an annoyance. The shrill, barely audible whine could get on one's nerves, and the darkness made streetlamps necessary. Tomorrow the bubble would be covered a tenth of an inch deep in fine, Moon-dry silt. Inside the bubble it would be darker than night until someone blew the silt away with an O-tank.

To Shute the storm was depressing. Here on Mars was Lieutenant-Major Shute, Boy Hero, facing terrifying dangers on the frontiers of human exploration ! A sand-storm that wouldn't have harmed an infant. Nobody here faced a single danger that he had not brought with him.

Would it be like this forever? Men travelling enormous distances to face themselves?

There had been little work done since noon today. Shute had given up on that. On a stack of walls sat Timmy, practically surrounding the buggy-pickup radio, sur-rounded in turn by the bubble's population.

Timmy stood up as Shute approached the group. They're gone,' he announced, sounding very tired. He turned off the radio. The men looked at each other, and some got to their feet.

68

'Tim! How'd you lose them?'

Timmy noticed him. 'They're too far away, Mayor.'

'They never turned around?'

'They never did. They just kept going out into the desert. Alf must have gone insane. Carter's not worth dying for.'

Shute thought, *But he was once.* Carter had been one of the best: tough, fearless, bright, enthusiastic. Shute had watched him deteriorate under the boredom and the close quarters aboard ship. He had seemed to recover when they reached Mars, when all of them suddenly had work to do. Then, yesterday morning – murder.

Alf. It was hard to lose Alf. Lew had been little loss, but Alf—

Cousins dropped into step beside him. 'I've got that red-pencil work done.'

'Thanks, Lee. I'll have to do it all over now.'

'Don't do it over. Write an addendum. Show how and why three men died. Then you can say, "I told you so." '

'You think so?'

'My professional judgment. When's the funeral?'

'Day after tomorrow. That's Sunday. I thought it would be appropriate.'

'You can say all three services at once. Good timing.'

To all bubbletown, Jack Carter and Alf Harness were dead. But they still breathed—

The mountains came towards them: the only fixed points in an ocean of sand. Alf was closer now, something less than four hundred yards behind. At five o'clock Carter reached the base of the mountains.

They were too high to go over on the air jet. He could see spots where he might have landed the buggy while the pump filled the jet tank for another hop. But for what?

Better to wait for Alf.

Suddenly Carter knew that that was the one thing in the world Alf wanted. To roll up alongside in his buggy. To watch Carter's face until he was sure Carter knew exactly what was to come. And then to blast Carter down in flames from ten feet away, and watch while a

69

bright magnesium-oxidizer flare burned through his suit and skin and vitals.

The hills were low and shallow. Even from yards away he might have been looking at the smooth flank of a sleeping beast – except that this beast was not breathing. Carter took a deep breath, noticing how stale the air had become despite the purifier unit, and turned on the compressed-air jet.

The air on Mars is terribly thin, but it can be compressed; and a rocket will work anywhere, even a compressed-air rocket. Carter went up, leaning as far back in the cabin as he could to compensate for the loss of weight in the O-tanks behind him, to put as little work as possible on gyroscopes meant to spin only in emergencies. He rose fast, and he tilted the buggy to send it skating along the thirty-degree slope of the hill. There were flat places along the slope, but not many. He should reach the first one easily ...

A flare exploded in his eyes. Carter clenched his teeth and fought the urge to look behind. He tilted the buggy backward to slow him down. The jet pressure was dropping.

He came down like a feather two hundred feet above the desert. When he turned off the jet he could hear the gyros whining. He turned the stabilizer off and let them run down. Now there was only the chugging of the compressor, vibrating through his suit.

Alf was out of his buggy, standing at the base of the mountains, looking up.

'Come on,' said Carter. 'What are you waiting for?'

'Go on over if you want to.'

'What's the matter? Are your gyros fouled?'

'Your brain is fouled, Carter. Go on over.' Alf raised one arm stiffly out. The hand showed flame, and Carter ducked instinctively.

The compressor had almost stopped, which meant the tank was nearly full. But Carter would be a fool to take off before it was completely full. You got the greatest acceleration from an air jet during the first seconds of flight. The rest of the flight you get just enough pressure to keep you going.

But – Alf was getting into his buggy. Now the buggy was rising.

Carter turned on his jet and went up.

He came down hard, three hundred feet high, and only then dared to look down. He heard Alf's nasty laugh, and he saw that Alf was still at the foot of the mountains. It had been a bluff!

But *why* wasn't Alf coming after him?

The third hop took him to the top. The first downhill hop was the first he'd ever made, and it almost killed him. He had to do his decelerating on the last remnants of pressure in the jet tank! He waited till his hands stopped shaking, then continued the rest of the way on the wheels. There was no sign of Alf as he reached the foot of the range and started out into the desert.

Already the sun was about to go. Faint bluish stars in a red-black sky outlined the yellow hills behind him.

Still no sign of Alf.

Alf spoke in his ear, gently, almost kindly. 'You'll just have to come back, Jack.'

'Don't hold your breath.'

'I'd rather not have to. That's why I'm telling you this. Look at your watch.'

It was about six-thirty.

'Did you look? Now count it up. I started with forty-four hours of air. You started with fifty-two. That gave us ninety-six breathing hours between us. Together we've used up sixty-one hours. That leaves thirty-five between us.

'Now, I stopped moving an hour ago. From where I am it's almost thirty hours back to base. Sometime in the next two and a half hours, you've got to get my air and stop me from breathing. Or I've got to do the same for you.'

It made sense. Finally, everything made sense. 'Alf, are you listening? Listen,' said Carter, and he opened his radio panel and, moving by touch, found a wire he'd located long ago. He jerked it loose. His radio crackled deafeningly, then stopped.

'Did you hear that, Alf? I just jerked my come-hither loose. Now you couldn't find me even if you wanted to.'

'I wouldn't have it any other way.'

Then Carter realized what he'd done. There was now no possibility of Alf finding him. After all the miles and hours of the chase, now it was Carter chasing Alf. All Alf had to do was wait.

The dark fell on the west like a heavy curtain.

Carter went south, and he went immediately. It would take him an hour or more to cross the range. He would have to leapfrog to the top with only his headlights to guide him. His motor would not take him uphill over such a slope. He could use the wheels going down, with luck, but he would have to do so in total darkness. Deimos would not have risen; Phobos was not bright enough to help.

It had gone exactly as Alf had planned. Chase Carter to the range. If he attacks there, take his tanks and go home. If he chooses to cross, he may be killed. Take his tanks. If he makes it, show him why he has to come back. Time it so he has to come back in darkness. If by some miracle he makes it this time – well, there's always the flare gun.

Carter could give him only one surprise. He would cross six miles south of where he was expected, and approach Alf's buggy from the *southeast*.

Or was Alf expecting that too?

It didn't matter. Carter was beyond free will.

The first jump was like jumping blindfolded from a ship's airlock. He'd pointed the headlights straight down, and as he went up he watched the circle of light expand and dim. He angled east. First he wasn't moving at all. Then the slope slid towards him, far too fast. He back-angled. Nothing seemed to happen. The pressure under him died slowly, but it was dying, and the slope was a wavering blur surrounded by dark.

It came up, clarifying fast.

The landing jarred him from coccyx to cranium. He held himself rigid, waiting for the buggy to tumble end-for-end down the hill. But though the buggy was tilted at a horrifying angle, it stayed.

Carter sagged and buried his helmet in his arms. Two enormous hanging tears, swollen to pinballs in the low gravity, dropped on to his faceplate and spread. For the first time he regretted all of it. Killing Lew, when a kick in the kneecap would have put him out of action and taught him a permanent, memorable lesson. Snatching the buggy instead of surrendering himself for trial. Driving through the bubble – and making every man on Mars his mortal enemy. Hanging around to watch what would happen – when, perhaps, he could have run beyond the horizon before Alf came out the vehicular airlock. He clenched his fists and pressed them against his faceplate, remembering his attitude of mild interest as he sat watching Alf's buggy roll into the lock.

Time to go. Carter readied himself for another jump. This one would be horrible. He'd be taking off with the buggy canted thirty degrees backward . . .

Wait a minute.

There was something wrong with that picture of Alf's buggy as it rolled towards the lock surrounded by trotting men. Definitely something wrong there. But what?

It would come to him. He gripped the jet throttle and readied his other hand to flip on the gyros the moment he was airborne.

–Alf had planned so carefully. How had he come away with one O-tank too few?

And – if he really had everything planned, *how did Alf expect to get Carter's tanks if Carter crashed*?

Suppose Carter crashed his buggy against a hill, right now, on his second jump. How would Alf know? He wouldn't, not until nine o'clock came and Carter hadn't shown up. Then he'd know Carter had crashed somewhere. But it would be too late!

Unless Alf had lied.

That was it, that was what was wrong with his picture of Alf in the vehicular airlock. Put one O-tank in the air bin and it would stand out like a sore thumb. Fill the air bin and then remove one tank, and the hole in the hexagonal array would show like Sammy Davis III on the Berlin Nazis football team! There had been no such hole.

Let Carter crash now, and Alf would know it with four hours in which to search for his buggy.

Carter swung his headlights up to normal position, then moved the buggy backward in a dead-slow half-circle. The buggy swayed but didn't topple. Now he could move down behind his headlights . . .

Nine o'clock. If Carter was wrong then he was dead now. Even now Alf might be unfastening his helmet, his eyes blank with the ultimate despair, still wondering where Carter had got to. But if he was right . . .

Then Alf was nodding to himself, not smiling, merely confirming a guess. Now he was deciding whether to wait another five minutes on the chance that Carter was late, or to start searching now. Carter sat in his dark cabin at the foot of the black mountains, his left hand clutching a wrench, his eyes riveted to the luminous needle of the direction finder.

The wrench had been the heaviest in his toolbox. He'd found nothing sharper than a screwdriver, and that wouldn't have penetrated suit fabric.

The needle pointed straight towards Alf.

And it wasn't moving.

Alf had decided to wait.

How long would he wait?

Carter caught himself whispering, not loudly, *Move, idiot. You've got to search both sides of the range. Both sides and the top. Move. Move!*

Ye gods! Had he shut off his radio? Yes, the switch was down.

Move.

The needle moved. It jerked once, infinitesimally, and was quiet.

It was quiet a long time – seven or eight minutes. Then it jerked in the opposite direction. Alf was searching the wrong side of the hills !

And then Carter saw the flaw in his own plan. Alf must now assume he was dead. And if he, Carter, was dead, then he wasn't using air. Alf had two hours extra, but he thought he had four !

The needle twitched and moved – a good distance. Carter sighed and closed his eyes. Alf was coming over. He had sensibly decided to search this side first; for if Carter was on this side, dead, then Alf would have to cross the range again to reach home.

Twitch.

Twitch. He must be at the top.

74

Then the long, slow, steady movement down.

Headlights. Very faint, to the north. Would Alf turn north?

He turned south. Perfect. The headlights grew brighter . . . and Carter waited, with his buggy buried to the windshield in the sand at the base of the range.

Alf still had the flare gun. Despite all his certainty that Carter was dead, he was probably riding with the gun in his hand. But he was using his headlights, and he was going slowly, perhaps fifteen miles per hour.

He would pass . . . twenty yards west . . .

Carter gripped the wrench. *Here he comes.*

There was light in his eyes. *Don't see me.* And then there wasn't. Carter swarmed out of the buggy and down the sloping sand. The headlights moved away, and Carter was after them, leaping as a moonie leaps, both feet pushing at once into the sand, a second spent in flying, legs straddled and feet reaching forward for the landing and another leap.

One last enormous kangaroo jump – and he was on the O-tanks, falling on knees and forearms with feet lifted high so the metal wouldn't clang. One arm landed on nothing at all where empty O-tanks were missing. His body tried to roll off on to the sand. He wouldn't let it.

The transparent bubble of Alf's helmet was before him. The head inside swept back and forth, sweeping the triangle created by the headlights.

Carter crept forward. He poised himself over Alf's head, raised the wrench high, and brought it down with all his strength.

Cracks starred out in the plastic. Alf looked up with his eyes and mouth all wide open, his amazement unalloyed by rage or terror. Carter brought the weight down again.

There were more cracks, longer cracks. Alf winced and – finally – brought up the flare gun. Carter's muscles froze for an instant as he looked into its hellish mouth. Then he struck for what he knew must be the last time.

The wrench smashed through transparent plastic and scalp and skull. Carter knelt on the O-tank for a moment, looking at the unpleasant thing he'd done. Then he lifted the body out by the shoulders, tumbled it over the side, and climbed into the cabin to stop the buggy.

It took him a few minutes to find his own buggy where he'd buried it in the sand. It took longer to uncover it. That was all right. He had plenty of time. If he crossed the range by 12:30 he would reach bubbletown on the last of his air.

There would be little room for finesse. On the other hand, he would be arriving an hour before dawn. They'd never see him. They would have stopped expecting him, or Alf, at noon tomorrow – even assuming they didn't know Alf had refused to turn back.

The bubble would be empty of air before anyone could get into a suit.

Later he could repair and fill the bubble. In a month Earth would hear of the disaster: how a meteorite had touched down at a corner of the dome, how John Carter had been outside at the time, the only man in a suit. They'd take him home and he could spend the rest of his life trying to forget.

He knew which tanks were his empties. Like every man in town, he had his own method of arranging them in the air bin. He dumped six and stopped. It was a shame to throw away empties. The tanks were too hard to replace.

He didn't know Alf's arrangement scheme. He'd have to test Alf's empties individually.

Already Alf had thrown some away. (To leave space for Carter's tanks?) One by one, Carter turned the valve of each tank. If it hissed, he put it in his own air bin. If it didn't, he dropped it.

One of them hissed. Just one.

Five O-tanks. He couldn't possibly make a thirty-hour trip on five O-tanks.

Somewhere, Alf had left three O-tanks where he could find them again. Just on the off chance: just in case something went terribly wrong for Alf, and Carter captured his buggy, Carter still wouldn't go home alive.

Alf must have left the tanks where he could find them easily. He must have left them near here; for he had never been out of Carter's sight until Carter crossed the range, and furthermore he'd kept just one tank to reach them. The tanks were nearby, and Carter had just two hours to find them.

In fact, he realized, they must be on the other side of the range. Alf hadn't stopped anywhere on this side.

But he could have left them on the hillside during his jumps to the top . . .

In a sudden frenzy of hurry, Carter jumped into his buggy and took it up. The headlights showed his progress to the top and over.

The first red rays of sunlight found Lee Cousins and Rufe Doolittle already outside the bubble. They were digging a grave. Cousins dug in stoic silence. In a mixture of pity and disgust he endured Rufe's constant compulsive flow of words.

'. . . first man to be buried on another planet. Do you think Lew would have liked that? No, he'd hate it. He'd say it wasn't worth dying for. He wanted to go home. He would have, too, on the next ship . . .'

The sand came up in loose, dry shovelsful. Practice was needed to keep it on the shovel. It tried to flow like a viscous liquid.

'I tried to tell the Mayor he'd have liked a well burial. The Mayor wouldn't listen. He said the martians might not – hey!'

Cousins' eyes jerked up, and the movement caught them – a steadily moving fleck on the crater wall. Martian! was his first thought. What else could be moving out there? And then he saw that it was a buggy.

To Lee Cousins it was like a corpse rising from its grave. The buggy moved like a blind thing down the tilted blocks of old glass, touched the drifted sand in the crater floor, all while he stood immobile. At the corner of his eye he saw Doolittle's shovel flying wide as Doolittle ran for the bubble.

The buggy only grazed the sand, then began reclimbing the crater. Cousins' paralysis left him and he ran for the town's remaining buggy.

The ghost was moving at half speed. He caught it a mile beyond the crater rim. Carter was in the cockpit. His helmet was in his lap clutched in a rigid death-grip.

Cousins reported, 'He must have aimed the buggy

along his direction finder when he felt his air going. Give him credit,' he added, and lifted a shovelful from the second grave. 'He did that much. He sent back the buggy.'

Just after dawn a small biped form came around a hill to the east. It walked directly to the sprawled body of Alf Harness, picked up a foot in both delicate-looking hands, and began to tug the corpse across the sand, looking rather like an ant tugging a heavy bread crumb. In the twenty minutes it needed to reach Alf's buggy the figure never stopped to rest.

Dropping its prize, the martian climbed the pile of empty O-tanks and peered into the air bin, then down at the body. But there was no way such a small, weak being could lift such a mass.

The martian seemed to remember something. It scrambled down the O-tanks and crawled under the buggy's belly.

Minutes later it came out, dragging a length of nylon line. It tied each end of the line to one of Alf's ankles, then dropped the loop over the buggy's trailer-attachment knob.

For a time the figure stood motionless above Alf's broken helmet, contemplating its work. Alf's head might take a beating, riding that way; but as a specimen Alf's head was useless. Wherever nitrogen dioxide gas had touched moisture, red fuming nitric acid had formed. By now the rest of the body was dry and hard, fairly well preserved.

The figure climbed into the buggy. A little fumbling, surprisingly little, and the buggy was rolling. Twenty yards away it stopped with a jerk. The martian climbed out and walked back. It knelt beside the three O-tanks which had been tied beneath the buggy with the borrowed nylon line, and it opened the stopcocks of each in turn. It leapt back in horrid haste when the noxious gas began hissing out.

Minutes later the buggy was moving south. The O-tanks hissed for a time, then were quiet.

78

AT THE BOTTOM OF A HOLE

TWELVE STOREYS BELOW the roof gardens were citrus groves, grazing pastures, and truck farms. They curved out from the base of the hotel in neat little squares, curved out and up, and up, and up and over. Five miles overhead was the fusion sunlight tube, running down the radius of the slightly bulging cylinder that was Farmer's Asteroid. Five miles above the sunlight tube, the sky was a patchwork of small squares, split by a central wedding ring of lake and by tributary rivers, a sky alive with the tiny red glints of self-guided tractors.

Lucas Garner was half-daydreaming, letting his eyes rove the solid sky. At the Belt government's invitation he had entered a bubbleworld for the first time, combining a vacation from United Nations business with a chance at a brand new experience – a rare thing for a man seventeen decades old. He found it pleasantly kooky to look up into a curved sky of fused rock and imported topsoil.

'There's nothing immoral about smuggling,' said Lit Shaeffer.

The surface overhead was dotted with hotels, as if the bubbleworld were turning to city. Garner knew it wasn't. Those hotels, and the scattered hotels in the other bubbleworld, served every Belter's occasional need for an earth-like environment. Belters don't need houses. A Belter's home is the inside of his pressure suit.

Garner returned his attention to his host. 'You mean smuggling's like picking pockets on Earth?'

'That's just what I don't mean,' Shaeffer said. The Belter reached into his coverall pocket, pulled out something flat and black, and laid it on the table. 'I'll want to play that in a minute. Garner, picking pockets is legal on Earth. Has to be, the way you crowd together. You couldn't enforce a law against picking pockets. In the Belt smuggling is against the law, but it isn't immoral. It's like a flatlander forgetting to feed the parking meter.

79

There's no loss of self-respect. If you get caught you pay the fine and forget it.'

'Oh.'

'If a man wants to send his earnings through Ceres, that's up to him. It costs him a straight thirty per cent. If he thinks he can get past the goldskins, that too is his choice. But if we catch him we'll confiscate his cargo, and everybody will be laughing at him. Nobody pities an inept smuggler.'

'Is that what Muller tried to do?'

'Yah. He had a valuable cargo, twenty kilos of pure north magnetic poles. The temptation was too much for him. He tried to get past us, and we picked him up on radar. Then he did something stupid. He tried to whip around a hole.

'He must have been on course for Luna when we found him. Ceres was behind him with the radar. Our ships were ahead of him, matching course at two gee. His mining ship wouldn't throw more than point five gee, so eventually they'd pull alongside him no matter what he did. Then he noticed Mars was just ahead of him.'

'The hole.' Garner knew enough Belters to have learned a little of their slang.

'The very one. His first instinct must have been to change course. Belters learn to avoid gravity wells. A man can get killed half a dozen ways coming too close to a hole. A good autopilot will get him safely around it, or programme an in-and-out spin, or even land him at the bottom, God forbid. But miners don't carry good autopilots. They carry cheap autopilots, and they stay clear of holes.'

'You're leading up to something,' Garner said regretfully. 'Business?'

'You're too old to fool.'

Sometimes Garner believed that himself. Sometime between the first world war and the blowing of the second bubbleworld, Garner had learned to read faces as accurately as men read print. Often it saved time – and in Garner's view his time was worth saving.

'Go on,' he said.

'Muller's second thought was to use the hole. An in-and-out spin would change his course more than he could hope to do with the motor. He could time it so Mars would hide him from Ceres when he curved out. He could damn near touch the surface, too. Mars' atmosphere is as thin as a flatlander's dreams.'

'Thanks a lot. Lit, isn't Mars UN property?'

'Only because we never wanted it.'

Then Muller had been trespassing. 'Go on. What happened to Muller?'

'I'll let him tell it. This is his log.' Lit Shaeffer did something to the flat box, and a man's voice spoke.

April 20, 2112
The sky is flat, the land is flat, and they meet in a circle at infinity. No star shows but the big one, a little bigger than it shows through most of the Belt, but dimmed to red, like the sky.

It's the bottom of a hole, and I must have been crazy to risk it. But I'm *here*. I got down alive. I didn't expect to, not there at the end.

It was one crazy landing.

Imagine a universe half of which has been replaced by an ochre abstraction, too distant and far too big to show meaningful detail, moving past you at a hell of a clip. A strange, singing sound comes through the walls, like nothing you've ever heard before, like the sound of the wings of the angel of death. The walls are getting warm. You can hear the thermo-system whining even above the shriek of air whipping around the hull. Then, because you don't have enough problems, the ship shakes itself like a mortally wounded dinosaur.

That was my fuel tanks tearing loose. All at once and nothing first, the four of them sheered their mooring bars and went spinning down ahead of me, cherry red.

That faced me with two bad choices. I had to decide fast. If I finished the hyperbola I'd be heading into space on an unknown course with what fuel was left in my inboard cooling tank. My lifesystem wouldn't keep me alive more than two weeks. There wasn't much chance I could get anywhere in that time, with so little fuel, and I'd seen to it the goldskins couldn't come to *me*.

But the fuel in the cooling tank would get me down. Even the ships of Earth use only a little of their fuel getting in and out of their pet gravity well. Most of it gets burned getting them from place to place fast. And Mars is lighter than Earth.

But what then? I'd still have two weeks to live.

I remembered the old Lacis Solis base, deserted seventy years ago. Surely I could get the old lifesystems working well enough to support one man. I might even find enough water to turn some into hydrogen by electrolysis. It was a better risk than heading out into nowhere.

Right or wrong, I went down.

The stars are gone, and the land around me makes no sense. Now I know why they call planet dwellers 'flat-landers'. I feel like a gnat on a table.

I'm sitting here shaking, afraid to step outside.

Beneath a red-black sky is a sea of dust punctuated by scattered, badly cast glass ashtrays. The smallest, just outside the port, are a few inches in diameter. The largest are miles across. As I came down the deep-radar showed me fragments of much larger craters deep under the dust. The dust is soft and fine, almost like quicksand. I came down like a feather, but the ship is buried to half-way up the lifesystem.

I set down just beyond the lip of one of the largest craters, the one which houses the ancient flatlander base. From above the base looked like a huge transparent raincoat discarded on the cracked bottom.

It's a weird place. But I'll have to go out sometime; how else can I use the base lifesystem?

My Uncle Bat used to tell me stupidity carries the death penalty.

I'll go outside tomorrow.

April 21, 2112

My clock says it's morning. The Sun's around on the other side of the planet, leaving the sky no longer bloody. It looks almost like space if you remember to look away from gravity, though the stars are dim, as if seen through fogged plastic. A big star has come over the horizon, brightening and dimming like a spinning rock. Must be Phobos, since it came from the sunset region.

I'm going out.

Later:

A sort of concave glass shell surrounds the ship where the fusion flame splashed down. The ship's lifesystem, the half that shows above the dust, rests in the centre like a frog on a lilypad in Confinement Asteroid. The splashdown shell is all a spiderweb of cracks, but it's firm enough to walk on.

Not so the dust.

The dust is like thick oil. The moment I stepped on to it I started to sink. I had to swim to where the crater rim slopes out like the shore of an island. It was hard work. Fortunately the splashdown shell reaches to the crater rock at one point, so I won't have to do *that* again.

It's queer, this dust. I doubt you could find its like anywhere in the system. It's meteor debris, condensed from vaporized rock. On Earth dust this fine would be washed down to the sea by rain and turned to sedimentary rock, natural cement. On the Moon there would be vacuum cementing, the bugaboo of the Belt's microminiaturization industries. But here, there's just enough 'air' to be absorbed by the dust surface . . . to prevent vacuum cementing . . . and not nearly enough to stop a meteorite. Result: it won't cement, nohow. So it behaves like a viscous fluid. Probably the only rigid surfaces are the meteor craters and mountain ranges.

Going up the crater lip was rough. It's all cracked, tilted blocks of volcanic glass. The edges are almost sharp. This crater must be geologically recent. At the bottom, half submerged in a shallow lake of dust, is bubbletown. I can walk okay in this gravity; it's something less than my ship's gee max. But I almost broke my ankles a couple of times getting down over those tilted, slippery, dust-covered blocks. As a whole the crater is a smashed ashtray pieced loosely together like an impromptu puzzle.

The bubble covers the base like a deflated tent, with the airmaking machinery just outside. The airmaker is in a great cube of black metal, blackened by seventy years of martian atmosphere. It's huge. It must have been a bitch to lift. How they moved that mass from Earth to Mars with only chemical and ion rockets, I'll never know. Also *why*? What was on Mars that they wanted?

If ever there were a useless world, this is it. It's not close to Earth, like the Moon. The gravity's inconveniently high. There are no natural resources. Lose your suit pressure and it'd be a race against time, whether you died of blowout or of red fuming nitrogen dioxide eating your lungs.

The wells?

Somewhere on Mars there are wells. The first expedition found one in the 1990s. A mummified *something* was nearby. It exploded when it touched water, so nobody ever knew more about it, including just how old it was.

Did they expect to find live martians? If so, so what?

Outside the bubble are two two-seater Marsbuggies. They have an enormous wheelbase and wide, broad wheels, probably wide enough to keep the buggy above the dust while it's moving. You'd have to be careful where you stopped. I won't be using them anyway.

The airmaker will work, I think, if I can connect it to the ship's power system. Its batteries are drained, and its fusion plant must be mainly lead by now. Thousands of tons of breathing-air are all about me, tied up in nitrogen dioxide, NO_2. The airmaker will release oxygen and nitrogen, and will also pick up what little water vapour there is. I'll pull hydrogen out of the water for fuel. But can I get the power? There may be cables in the base.

It's for sure I can't call for help. My antennas burned off coming down.

I looked through the bubble and saw a body, a few feet away. He'd died of blowout. Odds are I'll find a rip in the bubble when I get around to looking.

Wonder what happened here?

April 22, 2112

I went to sleep at first sunlight. Mars' rotation is just a fraction longer than a ship's day, which is convenient. I can work when the stars show and the dust doesn't, and that'll keep me sane. But I've had breakfast and done clean-ship chores, and still it'll be two hours before sundown. Am I a coward? I *can't* go out there in the light.

Near the sun the sky is like fresh blood, tinged by nitrogen dioxide. On the other side it's almost black. Not a sign of a star. The desert is flat, broken only by craters and by a regular pattern of crescent dunes so shallow that they can be seen only near the horizon. Something like a straight lunar mountain range angles away into the desert; but it's terribly eroded, like something that died a long time ago. Could it be the tilted lip of an ancient asteroid crater? The Gods must have hated Mars, to put it right in the middle of the Belt. This shattered, pulverized land is like a symbol of age and corruption. Erosion seems to live only at the bottom of holes.

Almost dawn. I can see red washing out the stars.

After sundown I entered the base through the airlock, which still stands. Ten bodies are sprawled in what must have been the village square. Another was half-way into a suit in the administration building, and the twelfth was a few feet from the bubble wall, where I saw him yesterday. A dozen bodies, and they all died of blowout: explosive decompression if you want to be technical.

The circular area under the bubble is only half-full of buildings. The rest is a carefully fused sand floor. Other buildings lie in stacks of walls, ceiling, floors, ready to be put up. I suppose the base personnel expected others from Earth.

One of the buildings held electrical wiring. I've hooked a cable to the airmaker battery, and was able to adapt the other end to the contact on my fusion plant. There's a lot of sparking, but the airmaker works. I'm letting it fill the stack of empty O-tanks I found against a pile of walls. The nitrogen dioxide is draining into the bubble.

I know now what happened to the flatlander base.

Bubbletown died by murder. No question of it. When nitrogen dioxide started pouring into the bubble I saw dust blowing out from the edge of town. There was a rip. It was sharp-edged, as if cut by a knife. I can mend it if I can find a bubble repair kit. There must be one somewhere.

Meanwhile I'm getting oxygen and water. The oxygen tanks I can empty into the lifesystem as they fill. The ship takes it back out of the air and stores it. If I can find a way to get the water here I can just pour it into the john. Can I carry it here in the O-tanks?

April 23, 2112
Dawn.
The administration building is also a tape library. They

kept a record of the base doings, very complete and so far very boring. It reads like a ship's log sounds, but more gossipy and more detailed. Later I'll read it all the way through.

I found some bubble plastic and contact cement and used them to patch the rip. The bubble still wouldn't inflate. So I went out and found two more rips just like the first. I patched them and looked for more. Found three. When I got them fixed it was nearly sunup.

The O-tanks hold water, but I have to heat them to boil the water to get it out. That's hard work. Question : is it easier to do that or to repair the dome and do my electrolysis inside? How many rips are there?

I've found six. So how many killers were there? No more than three. I've accounted for twelve inside, and according to the log there were fifteen in the second expedition.

No sign of the goldskins. If they'd guessed I was here they'd have come by now. With several months' worth of air in my lifesystem, I'll be home free once I get out of this hole.

April 24, 2112

Two more rips in the bubble, a total of eight. They're about twenty feet apart, evenly spaced around the transparent plastic fabric. It looks like at least one man ran around the dome slashing at the fabric until it wasn't taut enough to cut. I mended the rips. When I left the bubble it was swelling with air.

I'm half-way through the town log, and nobody's seen a martian yet. I was right, that's what they came for. Thus far they've found three more wells. Like the first, these are made of cut diamond building blocks, fairly large, very well worn, probably tens or hundreds of thousands of years old. Two of the four have dirty nitrogen dioxide at the bottoms. The others are dry. Each of the four has a 'dedication block' covered with queer, partially eroded writing. From a partial analysis of the script, it seems that the wells were actually crematoriums : a deceased martian would explode when he touched water in the nitrogen dioxide at the bottom. It figures. Martians wouldn't have fire.

I still wonder why they came, the men of the base. What

86

could martians do for them? If they wanted someone to talk to, someone not human, there were dolphins and killer whales right in their own oceans. The trouble they took! And the risks! Just to get from one hole to another!

April 24, 2112

Strange. For the first time since the landing, I did not return to the ship when the sky turned light. When I did start back the sun was up. It showed as I went over the rim. I stood there between a pair of sharp obsidian teeth, staring down at my ship.

It looked like the entrance to Confinement Asteroid.

Confinement is where they take women when they get pregnant: a bubble of rock ten miles long and five miles across, spinning on its axis to produce one gee of outward pull. The children have to stay there for the first year, and the law says they have to spend a month out of each year there until they're fifteen. I've a wife named Letty waiting there now, waiting for the year to pass so she can leave with our daughter Janice. Most miners, they pay the fatherhood fee in one lump sum if they've got the money; it's about sixty thousand commercials, so some have to pay in instalments, and sometimes it's the woman who pays; but when they pay they forget about it and leave the women to raise the kids. But I've been thinking about Letty. And Janice. The monopoles in my hold would buy gifts for Letty, and raise Janice with enough left over so she could do some travelling, and *still* I'd have enough commercials left for more children. I'd have them with Letty, if she'd agree. I think she would.

How'd I get on to that? As I was saying before I was so rudely interrupted, my ship looks like the entrance to Confinement – or to Farmer's Asteroid, or any underground city. With the fuel tanks gone there's nothing left but the drive and the lifesystem and a small magnetically insulated cargo hold. Only the top half of the lifesystem shows above the sea of dust, a blunt steel bubble with a thick door, not streamlined like a ship of Earth. The heavy drive tube hangs from the bottom, far beneath the dust. I wonder how deep the dust is.

The splashdown shell will leave a rim of congealed glass

around my lifesystem. I wonder if it'll affect my takeoff?

Anyway, I'm losing my fear of daylight.

Yesterday I thought the bubble was inflating. It wasn't. More rips were hidden under the pool of dust, and when the pressure built up the dust blew away and down went the bubble. I repaired four rips today before sunlight caught me.

One man couldn't have made all those slashes.

That fabric's *tough*. Would a knife go through it? Or would you need something else, like an electric carving knife or a laser?

April 25, 2112

I spent most of today reading the bubbletown log.

There *was* a murder. Tensions among fifteen men with no women around can grow pretty fierce. On day a man named Carter killed a man named Harness, then ran for his life in one of the Marsbuggies, chased by the victim's brother. Neither came back. They must have run out of air.

Three dead out of fifteen leaves twelve.

Since I counted twelve bodies, who's left to slash the dome?

Martians?

In the entire log I find no mention of a martian being seen. Bubbletown never ran across any martian artifact, except the wells. If there are martians, where are they? Where are their cities? Mars was subjected to all kinds of orbital reconnaissance in the early days. Even a city as small as bubbletown would have been seen.

Maybe there are no cities. But where do the diamond blocks come from? Diamonds as big as the well material don't form naturally. It takes a respectable technology to make them that big. Which implies cities – I think.

That mummy. Could it have been hundreds of thousands of years old? A man couldn't last that long on Mars, because the water in his body would react with the nitrogen dioxide around him. On the moon, he could last millions of years. The mummified martian's body chemistry was and is a complete mystery, barring the napalmlike explosion when water touched it. Perhaps it *was* that durable, and perhaps one of the pair who left to die returned to cut the dome instead, and perhaps I'm seeing goblins. This is the place for it. If I ever get out of here, you *try* and catch me near another hole.

April 26, 2112

The sun shows clear and bright above a sharp-edged horizon. I stand at the port looking out. Nothing seems strange anymore. I've lived here all my life. The gravity is settling in my bones; I no longer stumble as I go over the crater lip.

The oxygen in my tanks will take me anywhere. Give me hydrogen and you'll find me on Luna, selling my monopoles without benefit of a middleman. But it comes slowly. I can get hydrogen only by carrying water here in the base O-tanks and then electrolysing it into the fuel-cooling tank, where it liquefies.

The desert is empty except for a strange rosy cloud that covers one arm of horizon. Dust? Probably. I heard the wind singing faintly through my helmet as I returned to the ship. Naturally the sound can't get through the hull.

The desert is empty.

I can't repair the bubble. Today I found four more rips before giving up. They must circle the bubble all the way 'round. One man couldn't have done it. Two men couldn't.

It looks like martians. But where are they?

They could walk on the sand, if their feet were flat and broad and webbed . . . and there'd be no footprints. The dust hides everything. If there were cities here the dust must have covered them ages ago. The mummy wouldn't have shown webbing; it would have been worn away.

Now it's starlessly black outside. The thin wind must have little trouble lifting the dust. I doubt it will bury me. Anyway the ship would rise to the surface.

Gotta sleep.

April 27, 2112.

It's oh four hundred by the clock, and I haven't slept at all. The sun is directly overhead, blinding bright in a clear red sky. No more dust storm.

The martians exist. I'm sure of it. Nobody else was left to murder the base.

But why don't they show themselves?

I'm going to the base, and I'm taking the log with me.

I'm in the village square. Oddly enough, it was easier making the trip in sunlight. You can see what you're stepping on, even in shadow, because the sky diffuses the light a little, like indirect lighting in a dome city.

The crater lip looks down on me from all sides, splintered shards of volcanic glass. It's a wonder I haven't cut my suit open yet, making that trip twice a day.

Why did I come here? I don't know. My eyes feel rusty, and there's too much light. Mummies surround me, with faces twisted by anguish and despair, and with fluids dried on their mouths. Blowout is an ugly death. Ten mummies here, and one by the edge of town, and one in the admin building.

I can see all of the crater lip from here. The buildings are low bungalows, and the square is big. True, the deflated bubble distorts things a little, but not much.

So. The martians came over the lip in a yelling swarm or a silent one, brandishing sharp things. Nobody would have heard them if they yelled.

But ten men were in a position to see them.

Eleven men. There's a guy at the edge . . . no, they might have come from the other direction. But still, ten men. And they just waited here? I don't believe it.

The twelfth man. He's half into a suit. What did he see that they didn't?

I'm going to go look at him.

By God. I was right. He's got two fingers on a zipper, and he's pulling down. He's not half into a suit, he's half out of it!

No more goblins.

But who cut the dome?

The hell with it. I'm sleepy.

April 28, 2112

A day and a half of log to catch up on.

My cooling tank is full, or nearly. I'm ready to try the might of the goldskins again. There's air enough to let me take my time, and less chance of a radar spotting me if I move slowly. Good-bye, Mars, lovely paradise for the manic-depressive.

That's not funny. Consider the men in the base.

Item: it took a lot of knives to make those slits.

Item: everyone was inside.

Item: no martians. They would have been seen.

Therefore the slits were made from inside. If someone was running around making holes in the bubble, why didn't someone stop him?

It looks like mass suicide. Facts are facts. They must have spread evenly out around the dome, slashed, and then walked to the town square against a driving wind of breathing-air roaring out behind them. Why? Ask 'em. The two who aren't in the square may have been dissenters; if so, it didn't help them.

Being stuck at the bottom of a hole is not good for a man. Look at the insanity records on Earth.

I am now going back to a minute-to-minute log.

1120

Ready to prime drive. The dust won't hurt the fusion tube, nothing could do that, but backblast might damage the rest of the ship. Have to risk it.

1124

The first shot of plutonium didn't explode. Priming again.

1130

The drive's dead. I can't understand it. My instruments swear the fusion shield is drawing power, and when I push the right button the hot uranium gas sprays in there. What's wrong?

Maybe a break in the primer line. How am I going to find out? The primer line's way down there under the dust.

1245

I've sprayed enough uranium into the fusion tube to make a pinch bomb. By now the dust must be hotter than Washington.

How am I going to repair that primer line? Lift the ship in my strong, capable hands? Swim down through the dust and do it by touch? I haven't anything that'll do a welding job under ten feet of fine dust.

I think I've had it.

Maybe there's a way to signal the goldskins. A big, black

91

SOS spread on the dust . . . if I could find something black to spread around. Have to search the base again.
1900

Nothing in the town. Signalling devices in plenty, for suits and Marsbuggies and orbital ships, but only the laser was meant to reach into space. I can't fix a seventy-year-old comm laser with spit and wire and good intentions.

I'm going off minute-to-minute. There'll be no takeoff.

April 29, 2112

I've been stupid.

Those ten suicides. What did they do with their knives after they were through cutting? Where did they get them in the first place? Kitchen knives won't cut bubble plastic. A laser might, but there can't be more than a couple of portable lasers in the base. I haven't found any.

And the airmaker's batteries were stone dead.

Maybe the martians kill to steal power. They wouldn't have fire. Then they took my uranium for the same reason, slicing my primer line under the sand and running it into their own container.

But how would they get down there? Dive under the dust?

Oh.

I'm getting out of here.

I made it to the crater. God knows why they didn't stop me. Don't they care? They've *got* my primer fuel.

They're under the dust. They live there, safe from meteors and violent temperature changes, and they build their cities there too. Maybe they're heavier than the dust, so they can walk around on the bottom.

Why, there must be a whole ecology down there! Maybe one-celled plants on top, to get energy from the sun, to be driven down by currents in the dust and by dust storms, to feed intermediate stages of life. Why didn't anybody *look*? Oh, I wish I could *tell* someone!

I haven't time for this. The town O-tanks won't fit my suit valves, and I can't go back to the ship. Within the next twenty-four hours I've got to repair and inflate the bubble, or die of runout.

Later :

Done. I've got my suit off, and I'm scratching like a madman. There were just three slits left to patch, none at all along the edge of the bubble where I found the lone mummy. I patched those three and the bubble swelled up like instant city.

When enough water flows in I'll take a bath. But I'll take it in the square, where I can see the whole rim.

I wonder how long it would take a martian to get over the rim and down here to the bubble?

Wondering won't help? I could still be seeing goblins.

April 30, 2112

The water feels wonderful. At least these early tourists took some luxuries with them.

I can see perfectly in all directions. Time has filmed the bubble a little, merely enough to be annoying. The sky is jet black, cut raggedly in half by the crater rim. I've turned on all the base lights. They light the interior of the crater, dimly, but well enough so I'd see anything creeping down on me. Unfortunately they also dim out the stars.

The goblins can't get me while I'm awake.

But I'm getting sleepy.

Is that a ship? No, just a meteor. The sky's lousy with meteors. Ive got nothing to do but talk to myself until something happens.

Later:

I strolled up to the rim to see if my ship was still there. The martians might have dragged it into the dust. They hadn't, and there's no sign of tampering.

Am I seeing goblins? I could find out. All I'd have to do is peep into the base fusion plant. Either there's a pile there, mostly lead by now . . . or the pile was stolen seventy years ago. Either way the residual radiation would punish my curiosity.

I'm watching the sun rise through the bubble wall. It has a strange beauty, unlike anything I've seen in space. I've seen Saturn from an infinity of angles when I pulled monopoles in the rings, but it can't compare to this.

Now I know I'm crazy. It's a hole! I'm at the bottom of a lousy hole!

The sun writes a jagged white line along the crater rim. I can see the whole rim from here, no fear of that. No matter how fast they move, I can get into my suit before they get down to me.

It would be good to see my enemy.

Why did they come here, the fifteen men who lived and died here? I know why I'm here : for love of money. Them too? A hundred years ago the biggest diamonds men could make looked like coarse sand. They may have come after the diamond wells. But travel was fiendishly expensive then. Could they have made a profit?

Or did they think they could develop Mars the way they developed the asteroids? Ridiculous! But they didn't have my hindsight. Any holes *can* be useful . . . like the raw lead deposits along Mercury's dawnside crescent. Pure lead, condensed from dayside vapour, free for the hauling. We'd be doing the same with martian diamonds if it weren't so cheap to make them.

Here's the sun. An anticlimax : I can't look into it, though it's dimmer than the rock miner's sun. No more postcard scenery 'til.

Wups.

I'd never reach my suit. One move and the bubble will be a sieve. Just now they're as motionless as I am, staring at me without eyes. I wonder how they sense me? Their spears are poised and ready. Can they really puncture bubble fabric? But the martians must know their own strength, and they've done this before.

All this time I've been waiting for them to swarm over the rim. They came out of the dust pool in the bottom of the crater. I should have realized the obsidian would be as badly cracked down there as elsewhere.

They *do* look like goblins.

For moments the silence was broken only by the twin humming of a nearby bumblebee and a distant tractor. Then Lit reached to turn off the log. He said, 'We'd have saved him if he could have held out.'

'You knew he was there?'

'Yah. The Deimos scope watched him land. We sent in a routine request for permission to land on UN property. Unfortunately flatlanders can't move as fast as a drugged snail, and we knew of no reason to hurry them up. A telescope would have tracked Muller if he'd tried to leave.'

'Was he nuts?'

'Oh, the martians were real enough. But we didn't know that until way too late. We saw the bubble inflate and stay that way for awhile, and we saw it deflate all of a sudden. It looked like Muller'd had an accident. We broke the law and sent a ship down to get him if he was still alive. And that's why I'm telling you all this, Garner. As First Speaker for the Belt Political Section, I hereby confess that two Belt ships have trespassed on United Nations property.'

'You had good reasons. Go on.'

'You'd have been proud of him, Garner. He didn't run for his suit; he knew perfectly well it was too far away. Instead, he ran towards an O-tank full of water. The martians must have slashed the moment he turned, but he reached the tank, stepped through one of the holes and turned the O-tank on the martians. In the low pressure it was like using a fire hose. He got six before he fell.'

'They burned?'

'They did. But not completely. There are some remains. We took three bodies, along with their spears, and left the others in situ. You want the corpses?'

'Damn right.'

'Why?'

'What do you mean, Lit?'

'Why do you want them? We took three mummies and three spears as souvenirs. To you they're not souvenirs. It was a Belter who died down there.'

'I'm sorry, Lit, but those bodies are important. We can find out what a martian's made of before we go down. It could make all the difference.'

'Go down.' Lit made a rude noise. 'Luke, why do you want to go down there? What could you possibly *want* from Mars? Revenge? A million tons of dust?'

'Abstract knowledge.'

'For what?'

'Lit, you amaze me. Why did Earth go to space in the first place, if not for abstract knowledge?'

Words crowded over each other to reach Lit's mouth. They jammed in his throat, and he was speechless. He spread his hands, made frantic gestures, gulped twice, and said, 'It's *obvious*!'

'Tell me slow. I'm a little dense.'

'There's *everything* in space. Monopoles. Metal. Vacuum for the vacuum industries. A place to build cheap without all kinds of bracing girders. Free fall for people with weak hearts. Room to test things that might blow up. A place to learn physics where you can watch it happen. Controlled environments—'

'Was it all that obvious before we got here?'

'Of course it was!' Lit glared at his visitor. The glare took in Garner's withered legs, his drooping, mottled, hairless skin, the decades that showed in his eyes – and Lit remembered his visitor's age '. . . Wasn't it?'

ONE FACE

AN ALARM RANG : a rising, falling crescendo, a mechanical shriek of panic. The baritone voice of the ship's Brain blared, 'Strac Astrophysics is not in his cabin! Strac Astrophysics, report to your cabin immediately! The *Hogan's Goat* will Jump in sixty seconds.'

Verd sat bold upright, then forced himself to lie down again. The *Hogan's Goat* had not lost a passenger through carelessness in all the nearly two centuries of Verd's captaincy. Passengers were *supposed* to be careless. If Strac didn't reach his room verd would have to postpone Jump to save his life : a serious breach of custom.

Above the green coffin which was his Jump couch the Brain said, 'Strac Astrophysics is in his cabin and protected.'

Verd relaxed.

'Five,' said the Brain. 'Four. Three . . .'

In various parts of the ship, twenty-eight bodies jerked like springs released. 'Oof,' came a complaint from the Jump couch next to Verd's. 'That felt strange. Dam' strange.'

'Um,' said Verd.

Lourdi Coursefinder tumbled out of her Jump couch. She was a blend of many subdivisions of man, bearing the delicate, willowy beauty born of low-gravity worlds. She was Verd's wife, and an experienced traveller. Now she looked puzzled and disturbed.

'Jump never felt like that. What do you suppose—?'

Verd grunted as he climbed out. He was a few pounds overweight. His face was beefy, smooth and unlined, fashionably hairless. So was his scalp, except for a narrow strip of black brush which ran straight up from between his brow ridges and continued across his scalp and downward until it faded out near the small of his back. Most of the hair had been surgically implanted. Neither wrinkled skin nor width of hair strip could number a man's years, and superficially Verd might have been anywhere from twenty to four hundred years old. It was in his economy of movement that his age showed. He hid things the easy way, the fast way. He never needed more than seconds to find it, and he always took that time. The centuries had taught him well.

'I don't know,' he said. 'Let's find out what it was. Brain!' he snapped at a wall speaker.

The silence stretched like a nerve.

'Brain?'

One wall arced over to become the ceiling, another jogged inwards to leave room for a piece of the total conversion drive, a third was all controls and indicators for the ship's Brain. This was the crew common room. It was big and comfortable, a good place to relax, and no crewman minded its odd shape. Flat ceilings were for passengers.

Verd Spacercaptain, Lourdi Coursefinder, and Parliss Lifesystems sat along one wall, watching the fourth member of the crew.

Chanda Metalminds was a tall, plain woman whose major beauty was her wavy black hair. A strip three inches wide down the centre of her scalp had been allowed to grow until it hung to the region of her coccyx. Satin black and satin smooth, it gleamed and rippled as she moved. She stood before the biggest of the Brain screens, which now showed a diagram of the *Hogan's Goat*, and she used her finger as a pointer.

'The rock hit here.' Chanda's finger rested almost half-way back along the spinal maze of lines and little black squares and lighted power sources which represented the Jumper section. The *Hogan's Goat* was a sculptured torpedo, and the Jumper machinery was its rounded nose and its thick spine and its trailing wasplike sting. You could see it in the diagram : the rest of the *Goat* had been desgned to fit the Jumper. And the Jumper was cut by a slanting line, bright red, next to Chanda's finger-tip.

'It was a chunk of dirty ice, a typical piece of comet head,' said Chanda. 'The meteor gun never had a chance at it. It was too close for that when we came out of overspace. Impact turned the intruder to plasma in the Jumper. The plasma cone knocked some secondary bits of metal loose, and they penetrated *here*. That rained droplets of high-speed molten metal all through the ship's Brain.'

Parliss whistled. He was tall, ash blond, and very young. 'That'll soften her up,' he murmured irreverently. He winced under Chanda's glare and added, 'Sorry.'

Chanda held the glare a moment before she continued. 'There's no chance or repairing the Brain ourselves. There are too many points of injury, and most of them too small to find. Fortunately the Brain can still solve problems and obey orders. Our worst problem seems to be this motor aphasia. The Brain can't speak, not in any language. I've circumvented that by instructing the Brain to use Winsel code. Since I don't know the extent of the damage precisely, I recommend we land the passengers by tug instead of trying to land the *Goat*.'

Verd cringed at the thought of what the tug captains would say. 'Is that necessary?'

'Yes, Verd. I don't even know how long the Brain will answer to Winsel code. It was one of the first things I tried. I didn't really expect it to work, and I doubt it would on a human patient.'

'Thanks Chanda.' Verd stood up and the Brain surgeon sat down. 'All I have to say, group, is that we're going to take a bad loss this trip. The Brain is sure to need expensive repairs, and the Jumper will have to be almost completely torn out. It gave one awful discharge when the meteor hit, and a lot of parts are fused – Lourdi, what's wrong? We can afford it.'

Lourdi's face was bloodless. Her delicate surgeon's fingers strangled the arms of her chair.

'Come on,' Verd said gently. What could have driven her into such a panic? 'We land on Earth and take a vacation while the orbital repair companies do the worrying. What's wrong with that?'

Lourdi gave her head a spastic shake. 'We can't do that. Oh, Eye of Kdapt, I didn't dare believe it. Verd, we've got to fix the Jumper out here.'

'Not a chance. But—'

'Then we've got trouble.' Lourdi had calmed a little, but it was the calm of defeat. 'I couldn't ask the Brain to do it, so I used the telescope myself. That's not Sol.'

The others looked at her.

'It's not the Sun. It's a greenish-white dwarf, a dead star. I couldn't find the Sun.'

Once it had its orders, the Brain was much faster with the telescope than Lourdi. It confirmed her description of the star which was where Sol should have been, and added that it was no star in the Brain's catalogue. Furthermore the Brain could not recognize the volume of space around it. It was still scanning stars, hoping to find its bearings.

'But the rock hit *after* we came out of overspace. *After*!' Verd said between his teeth. 'How could we have gone anywhere else?' Nobody was listening.

They sat in the crew common-room drinking droobleberry juice and vodka.

'We'll have to tell the passengers something,' said Chanda. Nobody answered, though she was dead right. Interstellar law gave any citizen free access to a computer. In space the appropriate computer was a ship's Brain. By now the passengers must have discovered that the Brain was incommunicado.

Lourdi stopped using her glass to make rings on the tabletop. 'Chanda, will you translate for me?'

Chanda looked up. 'Of course.'

'Ask the Brain to find the planet in this system which most resembles Saturn.'

'Saturn?' Chanda's homely face lost its hopeful expression. Nonetheless she began tapping on the rim of a Brain speaker with the end of a stylus, tapping in the rhythms of Winsel code.

Almost immediately a line of short and long white dashes began moving left and right across the top of the Brain screen. The screen itself went white, cleared, showed what looked like a picture of Saturn. But the ring showed too many gaps, too well defined. Chanda said, 'Fifth major planet from primary. Six moons. Period: 29.46 years. Distance from Sun: 9.45 A.U. Diameter: 72,018 miles. Type: gas giant. So?'

Lourdi nodded. Verd and Parliss were watching her intently. 'Ask it to show us the second and third planets.'

The second planet was in its quarter phase. The Brain

screen showed it looked like a large moon, but less badly pocked, and with a major difference : the intensely bright area across the middle. Chanda translated the marching dots : 'Distance : 1.18 A.U. Period : 401.4. Diameter : 7918 miles. No moons. No air.'

The third planet – 'That's Mars,' said Lourdi.

It was.

And the second planet was Earth.

'I believe I know what has happened.' Verd was almost shouting. Twenty-seven faces looked back at him across the dining-room. He was addressing crew and passengers, and he had to face them in person, for the Brain could no longer repeat his words over the stateroom speakers.

'You know that a Jumper creates an overspace in which the speed of light becomes infinite in the neighbourhood of the ship. When—'

'Almost infinite,' said a passenger.

'That's a popular misconception,' Verd snapped. He found that he did not like public speaking, not under these conditions. With an effort he resumed his speaking voice. 'The speed of light goes all the way to infinity. Our speed is kept finite by the braking spine, which projects out of the effective neighbourhood. Otherwise we'd go simultaneous : we'd be everywhere at once along a great circle of the universe. The breaking spine is that thing like a long stinger that points out behind the ship.

'Well, there was a piece of ice in our way, inside the range of our meteor gun, when we came out of overspace. It went through the Jumper and into the Brain.

'The damage to the Brain is secondary. Something happened to the Jumper while the meteor was in there. Maybe some metal vaporized and caused a short circuit. Anyway the *Goat* jumped back into the counterpart of overspace.' Verd stopped. Was he talking over their heads? 'You understand that when we say we travel in an overspace of Einsteinian space, we really mean a *subspace* of that overspace?'

A score of blank faces looked back at him. Doggedly Verd went on. 'We went into the counterpart of that subspace. The speed of light went to zero.'

A murmur of whispering rose and fell. Nobody laughed.

'The braking spine stuck out, or we'd have been in there until the bitter end of time. Well, then. In a region around the ship, the speed of light was zero. Our mass was infinite, our clocks and hearts stopped, the ship became an infinitely thin disc. This state lasted for no time in ship's time, but when it ended several billion years had passed.'

A universal gasp, then pandemonium. Verd had expected it. He waited it out.

'Billion?' 'Kdapt stomp it—' 'Oh my God.' 'Practical joke, Marna. I must say—' 'Shut up and let him finish!'

The shouting died away. A last voice shouted, 'But if our mass was infinite—'

'Only in a region around the ship!'

'Oh,' said a dark stick-figure Verd recognized as Strac Astrophysics. Visibly he shrugged off a vision of suns and galaxies snatched brutally down upon his cringing head by the *Goat's* infinite gravity.

'The zero effect has been used before,' Verd continued in the relative quiet. 'For suspended animation, for very long-range time capsules, et cetera. To my knowledge it has never happened to a spacecraft. Our position is very bad. The Sun has become a greenish-white dwarf. The Earth has lost all its air and has become a one-face world; it turns one side forever to the Sun. Mercury isn't there anymore. Neither is the Moon.

'You can forget the idea of going home, and say goodbye to anyone you knew outside this ship. This is the universe, ourselves and nobody else, and our only duty is to survive. We will keep you informed of developments. Anyone who wishes his passage money refunded is welcome to it.'

In a crackle of weak graveyard laughter, Verd bobbed his head in dismissal.

The passengers weren't taking the hint. Hearing the captain in person was as unique to them as it was to Verd. They sat looking at each other, and a few got up, changed their minds, and sat down again. One called, 'What will you do next?'

'Ask the Brain for suggestions,' said Verd. 'Out now!'

'We'd like to stay and listen,' said the same man. He was short and broad and big footed, probably from one

102

of the heavier planets, and he had the rough-edged compactness of a land tank. 'We've the legal right to consult the Brain at any time. If it takes a translator we should have a translator.'

Verd nodded. 'That's true.' Without further comment he turned to Chanda and said, 'Ask the Brain what actions will maximize our chance of survival for maximal time.'

Chanda tapped her stylus rhythmically against the rim of the Brain speaker.

The dining area was raucous with the sound of breathing and the stealthy shuffling of feet. Everyone seemed to be leaning forward.

The Brain answered in swiftly moving dots of light. Chanda said, 'Immediately replace – Eye of Kdapt!' Chanda looked very startled, then grinned around at Verd. 'Sorry, Captain. "Immediately replace Verd Space-ercaptain with Strac Astrophysics in supreme command over *Hogan's Goat.*" '

In the confusion that followed, Verd's voice was easily the loudest. 'Everybody out! Everybody but Strac Astrophysics.'

Miraculously, he was obeyed.

Strac was a long, tall oldster, old in habits and manners and mode of dress. A streak of black-enamelled steel wool emphasized his chocolate scalp, and his ears spread like wings. Once Verd had wondered why Strac didn't have them fixed. Later he had stopped wondering. Strac obviously made a fetish of keeping what he was born with. His hairline began not between his eyes, but at the very top of his forehead, and it petered out on his neck. His fingernails grew naturally. They must have needed constant trimming.

He sat facing the members of the crew, waiting without impatience.

'I believe you've travelled on my ship before,' said Verd. 'Have you ever said or done anything to give the Brain, or any passenger, the idea that you might want to command the *Hogan's Goat*?'

'Certainly not!' Strac seemed as ruffled by the suggestion as Verd himself. 'The Brain must be insane,' he muttered venomously. Then his own words backlashed him, and in fear he asked, *'Could* the Brain be insane?'

103

'No,' Chanda answered. 'Brains of this type can be damaged, they can be destroyed, but if they come up with an answer it's the right one. There's a built-in doubt factor. Any ambiguity gives you an Insufficient Data.'

'Then why would it try to take my command?'

'I don't know. Captain, there's something I should tell you.'

'What's that?'

'The Brain has stopped answering questions. There seems to be some progressive deterioration going on. It stopped even before the passengers left. If I give it orders in Winsel it obeys, but it won't answer back.'

'Oh, Kdapt take the Brain!' Verd rubbed his temples with his fingertips. 'Parliss, what did the Brain know about Strac?'

'Same as any other passenger. Name, profession, medical state and history, mass, world of origin. That's all.'

'Hmph. Strac, where were you born?'

'The Canyon,' said Strac. 'Is that germane?'

'I don't know. Three hundred thousand is a tiny population for a solar system. but there's no room for more. Above the Canyon rim the air's too thin to breathe. I got out as soon as I could. Haven't been back in nearly a century.'

'I see.'

'Captain, I doubt that. In the Canyon there's no lack of company. It's the culture that's lonely. Everybody thinks just like everybody else. You'd say there's no cultural cross-fertilization. The pressure to conform is brutal.'

'Interesting,' said Verd, but his tone dismissed the subject. 'Strac, do you have any bright ideas that the Brain might have latched on to somehow? Or do you perhaps have a reputation so large in scientific circles that the Brain might know of it?'

'I'm sure that's not the case.'

'Well, do you have any ideas at all? We need them badly.'

'I'm afraid not. Captain, just what is our position? It seems that everyone is dead but us. How do we cope with an emergency like that?'

104

'We don't,' said Verd. 'Not without time travel, and that's impossible. It is, isn't it?'

'Chanda, exactly what did you ask the Brain? How did you phrase it?'

'Maximize the probability of our surviving for maximum time. That's what you asked for. Excuse me, Captain, but the Brain almost certainly assumed that "maximum time" meant forever.'

'All right. Parliss, how long will the ship keep us going?'

Parliss was only thirty years old, and burdened with youth's habitual unsureness; but he knew his profession well enough. 'A long time, Captain. Decades, maybe centuries. There's some boosterspice seeds in our consignment for the Zoo of Earth; if we could grow boosterspice aboard ship we could keep ourselves young. The air plant will work as long as there's sunlight or starlight. But the food converter – well, it can't *make* elements, and eventually they'll get lost somewhere in the circuit, and we'll start getting deficiency diseases, and – hmmm. I could probably keep us alive for a century and a half, and if we institute cannibalism we could—'

'Never mind. Let's call that our limit if we stay in space. We've got other choices, Strac, none of them pleasant.

'We can get to any planet in the solar system using the matter-conversion drive. We've enough solid chemical fuel in the landing rockets to land us on any world smaller than Uranus, or to land and take off from a world the size of Venus or smaller. With the matter-conversion drive we can take off from anywhere, but the photon beam would leave boiling rock behind us. We can do all that, but there's no point to it, because nothing in the solar system is habitable.'

'If I may interrupt,' said Strac. 'Why do we have a matter-conversion drive?'

'Excuse me?'

'The *Hogan's Goat* has the Jumper to move between worlds, and the solids to land and take off. Why does such a ship need another reaction drive? Is the Jumper so imprecise?'

'Oh. No, that's not it. You see, the maths of Jumper

travel postulates a figure for the mass of a very large neighbourhood, a neighbourhood that takes in most of the local group of galaxies. That figure is almost twice the actual rest mass in the neighbourhood. So we have to accelerate until the external universe is heavy enough for us to use the Jumper.'

'I see.'

'Even with total mass conversion we have to carry a tremendous mass of fuel. We use neutronium; anything less massive would take up too much room. Then, without the artificial gravity to protect us it would take over a year to reach the right velocity. The drive gives us a good one hundred gee in uncluttered space.' Verd grinned at Strac's awed expression. 'We don't advertise that. Passengers might start wondering what would happen if the artificial gravity went off.

'Where was I? . . . Third choice : we can go on to other stars. Each trip would take decades, but by refuelling in each system we could reach a few nearby stars in the hundred and fifty years Parliss gives us. But every world we ever used must be dead by now, and the G-type stars we can reach in the time we've got may have no useful worlds. It would be a gamble.'

Strac shifted uneasily. 'It certainly would. We don't necessarily need a G-type sun, we can settle under any star that won't roast us with ultra-violet, but habitable planets are rare enough. Can't you order the Brain to search out a habitable planet and go there?'

'No,' said Lourdi, from across the room. 'The telescope isn't that good, not when it has to peer out of one gravity well into another. The light gets all bent up.'

'And finally,' said Verd, 'if we did land on an Earth-sized planet that looked habitable, and then found out it wasn't, we wouldn't have the fuel to land anywhere else. Well, what do you think?'

Strac appeared to consider. 'I think I'll go have a drink. I think I'll have several. I wish you'd kept our little predicament secret a few centuries longer.' He rose with dignity and turned to the door, then spoiled the exit by turning back. 'By the way, Captain, have you ever been to a one-face world? Or have your travels been confined to the habitable worlds?'

'I've been to the Earth's Moon, but that's all. Why?'

'I'm not sure,' said Strac, and he left looking thoughtful. Verd noticed that he turned right. The bar was aft of the dining-room, to the left.

Gloom settled over the dining area. Verd fumbled in his belt pouch, brought forth a white tube not much bigger than a cigarette. Eyes fixed morosely on a wall, he hung the tube between his lips, sucked through it, inhaled at the side of his mouth. He exhaled cool, thick orange smoke.

The muscles around his eyes lost a little of their tension.

Chanda spoke up. 'Captain, I've been wondering why the Brain didn't answer me directly, why it didn't just give us a set of detailed instructions.'

'Me too. Have you got an answer?'

'It must have computed just how much time it had before its motor aphasia became complete. So instead of trying to give a string of detailed instructions it would never finish, it just named the person most likely to have the right answer. It gave us what it could in the few seconds it had left.'

'But why Strac? Why not me, or one of you?'

'I don't know,' Chanda said wearily. The damage to the Brain had hit her hard. Not surprising; she had always treated the Brain like a beloved but retarded child. She closed her eyes and began to recite, 'Name profession, mass, world of origin, medical history. Strac, astrophysics, the Canyon . . .'

In the next few days, each member of the crew was busy at his own speciality.

Lourdi Coursefinder spent most of her time at the telescope. It was a powerful instrument, and she had the Brain's limited help. But the worlds of even the nearest stars were only circular dots. The sky was thick with black suns, visible only in the infra-red. She did manage to find Earth's Moon – more battered than ever, in a Trojan orbit, trailing sixty degrees behind the parent planet in her path around the Sun.

Parliss Lifesystems spent his waking hours in the ship's library, looking up tomes on the medical aspects of privation. Gradually he was putting together a detailed programme that would keep the passengers healthy for a long time, and alive for a long time after that, with safety factors allowing for breakdown of the more delicate components of his lifesupport system. Later he planned to prepare a similar programme using cannibalism to its best medical advantage. That part would be tricky, involving subtle pyschological effects from moral shock.

Slowly and painfully, with miniature extensible waldos, Chanda searched out the tiny burns in the Brain's cortex and scraped away the charred semiconducting ash. 'Probably won't help much,' she admitted grimly, 'but the ash may be causing short circuits. It can't *hurt* to get it out. I wish I had some fine wire.'

Once he was convinced that the Jumper was stone-cold dead, Verd left it alone. That gave him little to do but worry. He worried about the damage to the Brain, and wondered if Chanda was being over-optimistic. Like a surgeon forced to operate on a sick friend, she refused even to consider that the Brain might get worse instead of better. Verd worried, and he checked the wiring in the manual override systems for the various drives, moving along outside the hull in a vac suit.

He was startled by the sight of the braking spine. Its ultrahard metal was as shiny as ever, but it was two-thirds gone. Sublimation, over several billion years.

He worried about the passengers too. Without the constant entertainment provided by the Brain, they would be facing the shock of their disaster virtually unaided. The log had a list of passengers, and Chanda got the Brain to put it on the screen, but Verd could find few useful professions among them.

Strac Astrophysics.

Jimm Farmer

Avran Zooman

The other professions were all useless here. Taxer, Carmaker, Adman – he was lucky to find anything at all. 'All the same,' he told Lourdi one night, 'I'd give anything to find a Jak FTL-systems aboard.'

'How 'bout a Harlan Alltrades?'

'On this tub? Specializing nonspecialists ride the luxury liners.' He twisted restlessly in the air between the sleeping plates. 'Wanta buy an aircar? It was owned by a snivelling coward—'

Jimm Farmer was a heavy-planet man, with long, smooth muscles and big broad feet. His Jinxian accent implied that he could probably kick holes in hullmetal. 'I've never worked without machinery,' he said. 'Farming takes an awful lot of machinery. Diggers, ploughers, seeders, transplanters, aerators, you name it. Even if you gave me seeds and a world to grow them on, I couldn't do anything by myself.' He scratched his bushy eyebrows. For some reason he'd let them grow outward from the end of his hairline, like the crossbar on an upside-down T. 'But if all the passengers and crew pitched in and followed directions, and if they didn't mind working like robots, I think we could raise something, if we had a planet with good dirt and some seeds.'

'At least we've got the seeds,' said Verd. 'Thanks, Mr Farmer.'

Verd had first seen Avran Zooman walking through the hall at the beginning of the trip. Zooman was a shocking sight. His thin strip of hair was bleached-bone white and started half-way back on his scalp. His skin had faint lines in it, like the preliminary grooves in tooled leather. Verd had avoided him until now. Obviously the man belonged to one of those strange, nearly extinct religious orders which prohibit the taking of boosterspice.

But he didn't behave like a religious nut. Verd found him friendly, alert, helpful, and likeable. His thick We Made It accent was heavy with stressed esses.

'In this one respect we are lucky,' Avran was saying. 'Or you are lucky. I should have been lucky enough to miss my ship. I came to protect your cargo, which is a selection of fertile plant seeds and frozen animal eggs for the Zoo of Earth Authority.'

'Exactly what's in the consignment?'

'Nearly everything you could think of, Captain. The Central Government wished to establish a zoo to show all the life that Earth has lost as a result of her intense population compression. I suspect they wished to encourage emigration. This is the first consignment, and it contains samples of every variety of non-domestic life on We Made It. There were to be other shipments from other worlds, including some expensive mutations from Wunderland designed to imitate the long extinct "big cats". We do not have those, nor the useless decorative plants such as orchids and cactus, but we do have everything we need for farming.'

'Have you got an incubator for the animals?'

'Unfortunately not. Perhaps I could show you how to make one out of other machinery.' Avran smiled humorously. 'But there is a problem. I am fatally allergic to boosterspice extract. Thus I will be dead in less than a century, which unfortunately limits the length of any journey that I can make.'

Verd felt his face go numb. He was no more afraid of death than the next man, but – frantically he tried to sort his climbing emotions before they strangled him. Admiration, wonder, shame, horror, fear. How could Avran live so casually with death? How could he have reached such a state of emotional maturity in what could be no more than fifty years? Shame won out, shame at his own reaction, and Verd felt himself flushing.

Avran looked concerned. 'Perhaps I should come back later,' he suggested.

'No! I'm all right.' Verd had found his tabac stick without thinking. He pulled in a deep, cooling draft of orange smoke, and held it in his lungs for a long moment.

'A few more questions,' he said briskly. 'Does the zoo consignment have grass seed? Are there any bacteria or algae?'

'Grass, yes. Forty-three varieties. No bacteria, I'm afraid.'

'That's not good. It takes bacteria to turn rock dust into fertile soil.'

'Yes.' Avran considered. 'We could start the process with sewage from the ship mixed with intestinal flora. Then add the rock dust. We have earthworms. It might work.'

'Good.'

'Now I have a question, Captain. What is that?'

Verd followed his pointing finger. 'Never seen a tabac stick?'

Avran shook his head.

'There's a funny tranquillizer in tobacco that helps you

110

concentrate, lets you block out distractions. People used to have to inhale tobacco smoke to get it. That caused lung cancer. Now we do it better. Are there tobacco plants in the consignment?'

'I'm afraid not. Can you give up the habit?'

'If I have to. But I'll hate it.'

Verd sat for a moment after Avran had left, then got up and hunted down Parliss. 'Avran claims to be allergic to boosterspice. I want to know if it's true. Can you find out?'

'Sure, Captain. It'll be in the medical record.'

'Good.'

'Why would he lie, Captain?'

'He may have a religious ban on boosterspice. If so, he might think I'd shoot him full of it just because I need him. And he'd be right.'

There was no point in interviewing Strac Astrophysics again. Parliss told him that Strac spent most of his time in his room, and that he had found a pocket computer somewhere.

'He must have something in mind,' said Parliss.

The next day Parliss came to the cabin. 'I've gone through the medical histories,' he said. 'We're all in good shape, except Avran Zooman and Laspia Waitress. Avran told the truth. He's allergic to boosterspice. Laspia has a pair of cultured arms, no telling how she lost the old ones, and both ulnas have machinery in them. One's a dooper, one's a multirange sonic. I wonder what that sweet girl is doing armed to the teeth like that.'

'So do I. Can you sabotage her?'

'I put an extension-recharger in her room. If she tries to shoot anyone she'll find her batteries are drained.'

The sixth day was the day of mutiny.

Verd and Parliss were in the crew common-room, going over Parliss' hundred-and-fifty-year schedule for shipboard living, when the door opened to admit Chanda. The first hint came from Chanda's taut, determined expression. Then Verd saw that someone had followed her in. He stood up to protest, then stood speechless as a line of passengers trooped into the crew common-room, filling it nearly to bursting.

111

'I'm sorry, Captain,' said Chanda. 'We've come to demand your resignation.'

Verd, still standing, let his eyes run over them. The pretty auburn-haired woman in front, the one who held her arms in an inconspicuously strained attitude – she must be Laspia Waitress. Jimm Farmer was also in the front rank. And Strac Astrophysics, looking acutely embarrassed. Many looked embarrassed, and many looked angry; Verd wasn't sure what they were angry at, or who. He gave himself a few seconds to think. Let 'em wait it out . . .

'On what grounds?' he asked mildly.

'On the grounds that it's the best chance we have to stay alive,' said Chanda.

'That's not sufficient grounds. You know that. You need a criminal charge to bring against me: dereliction of duty, sloppiness with the drive beam, murder, violation of religious tenets, drug addiction. Do you wish to make such a charge?'

'Captain, you're talking about impeachment – legal grounds for mutiny. We don't have such grounds. We don't want to impeach you, regardless.'

'Well, just what did you think this was, Chanda? An election?'

'We're inviting you to resign.'

'Thanks, but I think not.'

'We could impeach you, you know.' Jimm Farmer was neither angry nor embarrassed; merely interested. 'We could charge you with addiction to tabac sticks, try you, and convict you.'

'*Tabac sticks?*'

'Sure, everyone knows they're not addictive. The point is that you can't find a higher court to reverse our decision.'

'I guess that's true. Very well, go ahead.'

Parliss broke in, in a harsh whisper. 'Chanda, what are you *doing?*' His face, scalp, and ears burned sunset red.

The tall woman said, 'Quiet, Parl. We're only doing what needs to be done.'

'You're crazy with grief over that damn mechanical moron.'

Chanda flashed him a smoking glare. Parliss returned it. She turned away, aloofly ignoring him.

Strac spoke for the first time. 'Don't make us use force, Captain.'

'Why not? Do you idiots realize what you're asking?' Verd's control was going. He'd been a young man when the *Hogan's Goat* was built. In nearly two centuries he'd flown her farther than the total distance to Andromeda; nursed her and worried about her and lived his life in her lighted, rushing womb. What he felt must have showed in his face, for the girl with the auburn hair raised her left arm and held it innocently bent, pointed right at him. Probably it was the sonic; no doubt he would have been swathed in calming vibrations if her batteries had worked. But all he felt was nausea and a growing rage.

'I do,' Strac said quietly. 'We're asking you to make it possible for us to give you back your ship after this is over.'

Verd jumped at him. A cold corner of his mind was amazed at himself, but most of him only wanted to get his hands around Strac's bony, fragile throat. He glimpsed Laspia Waitress staring in panic at her forearms, and then a steel hand closed around his ankle and *jerked*. Verd stopped in midair.

It was Jimm Farmer. He had jumped across the room like a kangaroo. Verd looked back over his shoulder and carefully kicked him under the jaw. Jimm looked surprised and hurt. He squeezed!

'All right!' Verd yelped. More softly, 'All right. I'll resign.'

The autodoc mended two cracked ankle bones, injected mysterious substances into the badly bruised lower terminal of his Achilles tendon, and ordered a week of bed rest.

Strac's plans were compatible. He had ordered the ship to Earth. Since the *Goat* was still moving at nearly light-speed, and had gone well past the solar system, the trip would take about two weeks.

Verd began to enjoy himself. For the first time since the last disastrous Jump, he was able to stop worrying for more than minutes at a time. The pressure was off. The responsibility was no longer his. He even persuaded Lourdi

113

to co-operate with Strac. At first she would have nothing to do with the mutineers, but Verd convinced her that the passengers depended on her. Professional pride was a powerful argument.

After a week on his back Verd started moving around the ship, trying to get an idea of the state of the ship's morale. He did little else. He was perversely determined not to interfere with the new captain.

Once Laspia Waitress stopped him in the hall. 'Captain, I've decided to take you into my confidence. I am an ARM, a member of the Central Government Police of Earth. There's a badly wanted man aboard this ship.' And before Verd could try to humour her out of it she had produced authentic-looking credentials.

'He's involved in the Free Wunderland conspiracy,' she went on. 'Yes, it still exists. We had reason to believe he was aboard the *Hogan's Goat,* but I wasn't sure of it until he found some way to disarm me. I still haven't identified him yet. He could be anyone, even—'

'Easy, easy,' Verd soothed her. 'I did that. I didn't want anyone wandering around my ship with concealed weapons.'

Her voice cracked. 'You fool! How am I going to arrest him?'

'Why should you? Who would you turn him over to if you did? What harm can he do now?'

'What *harm*? He's a revolutionary, a – a seditionist!'

'Sure. He's fanatically determined to free Wunderland from the tyranny of the Central Government of Earth. But Wunderland and the Central Government have been dead for ages, and we haven't a single Earthman on board. Unless you're one.'

He left her sputtering helplessly.

When he thought about it later it didn't seem so funny. Many of the passengers must be clinging to such an outmoded cause, unwilling to face the present reality. When that defence gave out, he could expect cases of insanity.

Surprisingly, Strac had talked to nobody, except to ask questions of the crew members. If he had plans they were all his own. Perhaps he wanted one last look at Earth, ancient grandmother Earth, dead now of old age. Many passengers felt the same.

114

Verd did not. He and Lourdi had last seen Earth twelve years ago – subjective time – when the *Goat* was getting her life-support systems rejuvenated. They had spent a wonderful two months in Rio de Janeiro, a hive of multi-coloured human beings moving among buildings that reached like frustrated spacecraft towards the sky. Once they had even seen two firemanes, natives of l'Elephant, shouldering their way unconcerned among the bigger humans, but shying like fawns at the sight of a swooping car. Perhaps firemanes still lived somewhere in the smoky arms of this galaxy or another. Perhaps even humans lived, though they must be changed beyond recognition. But Verd did not want to look on the corpse face of Earth. He preferred to keep his memories unspoiled.

He was not asked.

On the tenth day the *Goat* made turnover. Verd thought of the drive beam sweeping its arc across deserted aster-oidal cities. Neutronium converted to a destroying blast of pure light. In civilized space a simple turnover required seconds of calculation on the part of the Brain, just to keep the drive beam pointed safely. Anything that light touched would vanish. But now there was nothing to protect.

On the fifteenth ship's-day morning the Earth was a wide, brilliant crescent, blinding bright where the seas had dried across her sunward face. The Sun shone with eerie greenish-white radiance beyond the polarized windows. Verd and Lourdi were finishing breakfast when Strac appeared outside the one-way transparent door. Lourdi let him in.

'I thought I'd better come personally,' said Strac. 'I've called for a meeting in the crew common-room in an hour. I'd appreciate it if you'd be there, Verd.'

'I'd just as soon not,' said Verd. 'Thanks anyway. Have a roast dove?'

Strac politely declined, and left. He had not repeated his invitation.

'He wasn't just being polite,' Lourdi told him. 'He needs you.'

'Let 'im suffer.'

Lourdi took him gently by the ears and turned him to face her – a trick she had developed to get his undivided attention. 'Friend, this is the wrong time to play prima

115

donna. You talked me into serving the usurper on grounds that the passengers needed my skills. I'm telling you they need yours.'

'Dammit, Lourdi, if they needed me I'd still be captain!'

'They need you as a crewman!'

Verd set his jaw and looked stubborn. Lourdi let go, patted his ears gently, and stepped back. 'That's my say. Think it through, Lord and Master.'

Six people circled the table. Verd was there, and Lourdi and Parliss and Chanda. Strac occupied the captain's chair, beneath the Brain screen. The sixth man was Jimm Farmer.

'I know what we have to do now,' said Strac. His natural dignity had deepened lately, though his shoulders sagged as if ship's gravity were too much for him, and his thin, dark face had lost the ability to smile. 'But I want to consider alternatives first. To that end I want you all to hear the answers to questions I've been asking you individually. Lourdi, will you tell us about the Sun?'

Lourdi stood up. She seemed to know exactly what was wanted.

'It's very old,' she said. 'Terribly old and almost dead. After our Jumper went funny the Sun seems to have followed the main sequence all the way. For a while it got hotter and brighter and bigger, until it blew up into a red giant. That's probably when Mercury disappeared. Absorbed.

'Sol could have left the main sequence then, by going nova for example, but if it had there wouldn't be any inner planets. So it stayed a red giant until there wasn't enough fuel to burn to maintain the pressure, and then the structure collapsed.

'The Sun contracted to a white dwarf. What with unradiated heat working its way out, and heat of contraction, and fusion reactions still going on inside, it continued to give off light, and still does, even though for all practical purposes there's no fuel left. You can't burn iron. So now the Sun's a greenish dwarf, and still cooling. In a few million years it'll be a reddish dwarf, and then a black one.'

116

'Only millions?'

'Yes, Strac. Only millions.'

'How much radiation is being put out now?'

Lourdi considered. 'About the same as in our time, but it's bluer light. The Sun is much hotter than we knew it, but all its light has to radiate through a smaller surface area. Do you want figures?'

'No thanks, Lourdi. Jimm Farmer, could you grow food-stuffs under such a star?'

Peculiar question, thought Verd. He sat up straighter, fighting a horrible suspicion.

Jimm looked puzzled, but answered readily. 'If the air were right and I had enough water, sure I could. Plants like ultraviolet. The animals might need protection from sunburn.'

Strac nodded. 'Lourdi, what's the state of the galaxy?'

'Lousy,' she said promptly. 'Too many dead stars, and most of what's left are blue-white and white giants. Too hot. I'll bet that any planet in this neighbourhood that has the right temperature for life will be a gas giant. The young stars are all in the tips of the galactic arms, and they've been scattered by the spin of the galaxy. We can find *some* young stars in the globular clusters. Do you want to hear about them?'

'We'd never reach them,' said Verd. His suspicion was a certainty. He blew orange smoke and waited, silently daring Strac to put his intention into words.

'Right,' said Strac. 'Chanda, how is the Brain?'

'Very, very sick. It might stop working before the decade's end. It'll never last out the century, crippled as it is.' Chanda wasn't looking so good herself. Her eyes were red, underlined with blue shadows. Verd thought she had lost mass. Her hair hadn't had its usual care. She continued, as if to herself, 'Twice I've given it ordinary commands and got the Insufficient Data sign. That's very bad. It means the Brain is starting to distrust the data in its own memory banks.'

'Just how bad *is* that?'

'It's a one-way street, with a wiped mind at the end. There's no way to stop it.'

'Thanks, Chanda.' Strac was carrying it off, but beneath his battered dignity he looked determined and –

frightened. Verd thought he had reason. 'Now you know everything,' he told them. 'Any comments?'

Parliss said, 'If we're going star hunting we should stop on Pluto and shovel up an air reserve. It'd give us a few decades leeway.'

'Uh huh. Anything else?'

Nobody answered.

'Well, that's that.' Strac drew a deep breath, let it out slowly. 'There's too much risk in searching the nearby stars. We'll have to make do with what we've got. Chanda, please order the Brain to set us down on the highest flat point in Earth's noon-equator region.'

Chanda didn't move. Nobody moved.

'I knew it,' Verd said, very quietly. His voice echoed in the greater quiet. The crew common-room was like a museum exhibit. Everyone seemed afraid to move. Everyone but Jimm Farmer, who in careful silence was getting to his feet.

'Didn't you understand, Strac?' Verd paused and tried to make his voice persuasive. 'The Brain put you in charge because you had more useful knowledge than the rest of us. You were supposed to find a new home for the human race.'

They were all staring at Strac with varying degrees of horror. All but Jimm, who stood patiently waiting for the others to make up their minds.

'You were not supposed to give up and take us home to die!' Verd snapped. But Strac was ignoring him. Strac was glaring at them all in rage and contempt.

Parliss, normally Nordic-pale, was white as moonlight. Strac, it's dead! Leave it! We can find another world—'

'You mewling litter of blind idiots.'

Even Jimm Farmer looked shocked.

'Do you think I'd kill us all for a twinge of homesickness? Verd, you know better than that, even if nobody else does. They were on *your* back, twenty-seven adults and all their potential children, all waiting for you to tell them how to die. Then came the mutiny. Now you're free! They've all shifted to *my* back!'

His eyes left Verd's and ranged over his shocked, silent crew. 'Idiots blindly taking orders from a damaged mech-

118

anical brain. Believing everything you're told. Lourdi!' he snapped. 'What does "one face" mean?'

Lourdi jumped. 'It means the body doesn't rotate with respect to its primary.'

'It doesn't mean the planet has only one face?'

'Wh-at?'

'The Earth has a back side to it.'

'Sure!'

'What does it look like?'

'I don't know.' Lourdi thought a moment. 'The Brain knows. You remember you asked Chanda to make the Brain use the radar to check the back side. Then she couldn't get the Brain to show us the picture. We can't use the telescope because there's no light, not even infrared. It must be terribly cold. Colder than Pluto.'

'You don't know,' said Strac. 'But I do. We're going down. Chanda?'

'Tell us about it,' said Jimm Farmer.

'No,' said Verd.

He had not known that he was going to speak. He had known only that they had given Strac the responsibility without the power to match it. But Strac felt the responsibility; he carried it in his bent shoulders and bleak expression, in his deep, painful breathing, in his previous attempts to pass the buck to someone else. Why would Strac want to land on Earth? Verd didn't know. But Starc must know what he was doing. Otherwise he couldn't have moved at all!

Someone had to back him up.

'No.' Verd spoke with all the authority he could muster. 'Chanda, take her down.'

'Tell us about it,' Jimm repeated. The authority backing his flat, menacing tone was his own titanic physical strength.

Jimm Farmer thought it over, suddenly laughed and sat down. Chanda picked up her stylus and began tapping on the speaker.

The *Hogan's Goat* lay on her side, nearly in the centre of a wide, ancient asteroid crater. There, marring the rounded spine with its long stinger, was the ragged, heat-stained hole that marked a meteor strike. There, along two-thirds of the length of her belly, was the gash a rock had made in the last seconds of the landing. And at the tail, forward of the braking spine, that static explosion of curved metal strips was where the photon drive had been torn free.

A small, fiercely bright Sun burned down from a black sky.

It had been a bad landing. Even at the start the Brain was a fraction of a second slow in adjusting ship's gravity, so that the floor had bucked queasily under them as they dropped. Then, when they were already falling towards the crater, Strac had suddenly added a new order. The photon drive had to be accessible after landing. Chanda had started tapping – and the ship had flipped on its side.

The *Hogan's Goat* had never been built to land on its side. Many of the passengers sported bruises. Avran Zooman had broken an arm. Without boosterspice the bone would be slow to heal.

A week of grinding labour was nearly over.

Only servomachinery now moved on the crater floor. From Verd's viewpoint most of the activity seemed to centre around a gigantic silver tube which was aimed like a cannon at a point ten degrees above the horizon. The drive tube had been towed up against the crater wall, and a mountain of piled, heat-fused earth now buried its lower end. Cables and fuel pipes joined it higher up.

'Hi! Is that you, Captain?'

Verd winced. 'I'm on top of the crater wall,' he said, because Strac couldn't locate him from the sound of his voice. The indeterminate voice had to be Strac. Only Strac would bellow into a suit radio. 'And I'm not the captain.'

Strac floated down beside him. 'I thought I'd see the sights.'

'Good. Have a seat.'

'I find it strange to have to call you Verd,' said the astrophysicist. 'It used to be just "captain".'

'Serves you right for staging a mutiny – Captain.'

'I always knew my thirst for power would get me in trouble.'

They watched as a tractor-mounted robot disconnected a fuel pipe from the drive, then rolled back. A moment later a wash of smoky flame burst from the pipe. The flame changed colour and intensity a dozen times within a few seconds, then died as abruptly as it had begun. The robot waited for the white heat to leave the pipe, then rolled forward to reconnect it.

Verd asked, 'Why are you so calm all of a sudden?'

'My job's over,' Strac said with a shrug in his voice. 'Now it's in the lap of Kdapt.'

'Aren't you taking an awful chance?'

'Oh? You've guessed what I'm trying to do?'

'I hope it wasn't a secret. There's only one thing you could be doing, with the photon drive all laid out and braced like that. You're trying to spin the Earth.'

'Why?' Strac baited him.

'You must be hoping there's air and water frozen on the dark side. But it seems like a thin chance. Why were you afraid to explain?'

'You put it that way, then ask why I didn't put it to a vote? Verd, would you have done what I did?'

'No. It's too risky.'

'Suppose I tell you that I *know* the air and water is there. It has to be there. I can tell you what it looks like. It's a great shallow cap of ice, stratified out according to freezing points, with water ice on the bottom, then carbon dioxide, all the way up through a thick nitrogen layer to a few shifting pools of liquid helium. Surely you don't expect a one-face world to have a gaseous atmosphere? It would all freeze out on the night side. It has to!'

'It's there? There's air there? Your professional word?'

'My word as an astrophysicist. There's frozen gas back there.'

Verd stretched like a great cat. He couldn't help himself. He could actually feel the muscles around his eyes and cheeks rippling as they relaxed, and a great grin crawled towards his ears. 'You comedian!' he laughed. 'Why didn't you say so?'

'Suppose I kept talking?'

Verd turned to look at him.

'You'll have thought of some of these things yourself. Can we breathe that air? Billions of years have passed. Maybe the composition of the air changed before it froze. Maybe too much of it boiled off into space while the Sun was a red giant. Maybe there's too much, generated by outgasing after the Moon was too far away to skim it off. Lourdi said the Sun is putting out about the right amount of heat, but just how close will it be to a livable temperature? Can Jimm Farmer make us topsoil? There'll be live soil on the nightside, possibly containing frozen live bacteria, but can we get there if we have to?

'Worst of all, can we spin the Earth in the first place? I know the drive's strong enough. I don't know about the Earth. There can't be any radioactivity left in the Earth's core, so the planet should be solid rock all the way to the centre. But solid rock flows under pressure. We'll get earthquakes. Kdapt only knows how bad. Well, Captain, would you have taken all those risks?'

'She blows.'

The drive was on.

Traces of hydrogen, too thin to stop a meteor, glowed faintly in the destroying light. A beam like a spotlight beam reached out over the sharp horizon, pointing dead east. Anything that light touched would flame and blow away on the wings of a photon wind. The drive nosed a little deeper into its tomb of lava.

The ground trembled. Verd turned on his flying unit, and Strac rose after him. Together they hovered over the quivering Earth. Other silver specks floated above the plain.

In space the drive would be generating over a hundred savage gravities. Here . . . almost none. Almost.

Little quick ripples came running in from the eastern horizon. They ran across the crater floor in parallel lines of dancing dust, coming closer and closer together. Rocks showered down from the old ringwall.

'Maybe I wouldn't have risked it,' said Verd. 'I don't know.'

'That's why the Brain put me in charge. Did you see the oxygen ice as we went by the night side? Or was it too dark? To you this frozen atmosphere is pure imagination, isn't it?'

'I'll take your professional word.'

'But I don't need to. I *know* it's there.'

Lines of dust danced over the shaking ground. But the ripples were less violent, and were coming less frequently.

'The Brain was damaged,' Verd said softly.

'Yes,' said Strac, frowning down into the old crater. Suddenly he touched his controls and dropped. 'Come on Verd. In a few days there'll be air. We've got to be ready for wind and rain.'

BECALMED IN HELL

I COULD FEEL the heat hovering outside. In the cabin it was bright and dry and cool, almost too cool, like a modern office building in the dead of summer. Beyond the two small windows it was as black as it ever gets in the solar system, and hot enough to melt lead, at a pressure equivalent to three hundred feet beneath the ocean.

'There goes a fish,' I said, just to break the monotony.

'So how's it cooked?'

'Can't tell. It seems to be leaving a trail of breadcrumbs. Fried? Imagine that, Eric. A fried jellyfish.'

Eric sighed noisily. 'Do I have to?'

'You have to. Only way you'll see anything worthwhile in this – this—' Soup? Fog? Boiling maple syrup?

'Searing black calm.'

'Right.'

'Someone dreamed up that phrase when I was a kid, just after the news of the Mariner II probe. An eternal searing black calm, hot as a kiln, under an atmosphere thick enough to keep any light or any breath of wind from reaching the surface.'

I shivered. 'What's the outside temperature now?'

'You'd rather not know. You've always had too much imagination, Howie.'

'I can take it, Doc.'

'Six hundred and twelve degrees.'

'I can't take it, Doc!'

This was Venus, planet of Love, favourite of the science-fiction writers of three decades ago. Our ship hung below the Earth-to-Venus hydrogen fuel tank, twenty miles up and all but motionless in the syrupy air. The tank, nearly empty now, made an excellent blimp. It would keep us aloft as long as the internal pressure matched the external. That was Eric's job, to regulate the tank's pressure by regulating the temperature of the hydrogen gas. We had collected air samples after each ten miles drop from three hundred miles on down, and temperature readings for shorter intervals, and we had dropped the small probe.

124

The data we had got from the surface merely confirmed in detail our previous knowledge of the hottest world in the solar system.

'Temperature just went up to six-thirteen,' said Eric. 'Look, are you through bitching?'

'For the moment.'

'Good. Strap down. We're taking off.'

'Oh, frabjous day!' I started untangling the crash webbing over my couch.

'We've done everything we came to do. Haven't we?'

'Am I arguing? Look, I'm strapped down.'

'Yeah.'

I knew why he was reluctant to leave. I felt a touch of it myself. We'd spent four months getting to Venus in order to spend a week circling her and less than two days in her upper atmosphere, and it seemed a terrible waste of time.

But he was taking too long. 'What's the trouble, Eric?'

'You'd rather not know.'

He meant it. His voice was a mechanical, inhuman monotone; he wasn't making the extra effort to get human expression out of his 'prosthetic' vocal apparatus. Only a severe shock would affect him that way.

'I can take it,' I said.

'Okay. I can't feel anything in the ramjet controls. Feels like I've just had a spinal anaesthetic.'

The cold in the cabin drained into me, all of it. 'See if you can send motor impulses the other way. You could run the rams by guess-and-hope even if you can't feel them.'

'Okay.' One split second later, 'They don't. Nothing happens. Good thinking though.'

I tried to think of something to say while I untied myself from the couch. What came out was, 'It's been a pleasure knowing you, Eric. I've liked being half of this team, and I still do.'

'Get maudlin later. Right now, start checking my attachments. Carefully.'

I swallowed my comments and went to open the access door in the cabin's forward wall. The floor swayed ever so gently beneath my feet.

Beyond the four-foot-square access door was Eric. Eric's

central nervous system, with the brain perched at the top and the spinal cord coiled in a loose spiral to fit more compactly into the transparent glass-and-sponge-plastic housing. Hundreds of wires from all over the ship led to the glass walls, where they were joined to selected nerves which spread like an electrical network from the central coil of nervous tissue and fatty protective membrane.

Space leaves no cripples; and don't call Eric a cripple, because he doesn't like it. In a way he's the ideal space-man. His life support system weighs only half what mine does, and takes up a twelfth as much room. But his other prosthetic aids take up most of the ship. The ramjets were hooked into the last pair of nerve trunks, the nerves which once moved his legs, and dozens of finer nerves in those trunks sensed and regulated fuel feed, ram temperature, differential acceleration, intake aperture dilation, and spark pulse.

These connections were intact. I checked them four different ways without finding the slightest reason why they shouldn't be working.

'Test the others,' said Eric.

It took a good two hours to check every trunk nerve connection. They were all solid. The blood pump was chugging along, and the fluid was rich enough, which killed the idea that the ram nerves might have 'gone to sleep' from lack of nutrients or oxygen. Since the lab is one of his prosthetic aids, I let Eric analyse his own blood sugar, hoping that the 'liver' had goofed and was producing some other compound. The conclusions were appalling. There was nothing wrong with Eric – inside the cabin.

'Eric, you're healthier than I am.'

'I could tell. You look worried, and I don't blame you. Now you'll have to go outside.'

'I know. Let's dig out the suit.'

It was in the emergency tools locker, the Venus suit that was never supposed to be used. NASA had designed it for use at Venusian ground level. Then they had refused to okay the ship below twenty miles until they knew more about the planet. The suit was a segmented armour job. I had watched it being tested in the heat-and-pressure box at Cal Tech, and I knew that the joints stopped moving after five hours, and wouldn't start again until they had been

126

cooled. Now I opened the locker and pulled the suit out by the shoulders and held it in front of me. It seemed to be staring back.

'You still can't feel anything in the ramjets?'

'Not a twinge.'

I started to put on the suit, piece by piece like medieval armour. Then I thought of something else. 'We're twenty miles up. Are you going to ask me to do a balancing act on the hull?'

'No! Wouldn't think of it. We'll just have to go down.'

The lift from the blimp tank was supposed to be constant until takeoff. When the time came Eric could get extra lift by heating the hydrogen to higher pressure, then cracking a valve to let the excess out. Of course he'd have to be very careful that the pressure was higher in the tank, or we'd get Venusian air coming in, and the ship would fall instead of rising. Naturally that would be disastrous.

So Eric lowered the tank temperature and cracked the valve, and down we went.

'Of course there's a catch,' said Eric.

'I know.'

'The ship stood the pressure twenty miles up. At ground level it'll be six times that.'

'I know.'

We fell fast, with the cabin tilted forward by the drag on our tailfins. The temperature rose gradually. The pressure went up fast. I sat at the window and saw nothing, nothing but black, but I sat there anyway and waited for the window to crack. NASA had refused to okay the ship below twenty miles . . .

Eric said, 'The blimp tank's okay, and so's the ship, I think. But will the cabin stand up to it?'

'I wouldn't know.'

'Ten miles.'

Five hundred miles above us, unreachable, was the atomic ion engine that was to take us home. We couldn't get to it on the chemical rocket alone. The rocket was for use after the air became too thin for the ramjets.

'Four miles. Have to crack the valve again.'

The ship dropped.

'I can see ground,' said Eric.

I couldn't. Eric caught me straining my eyes and said, 'Forget it. I'm using deep infra-red, and getting no detail.'

'No vast, misty swamps with weird, terrifying monsters and man-eating plants?'

'All I see is hot, bare dirt.'

But we were almost down, and there were no cracks in the cabin wall. My neck and shoulder muscles loosened. I turned away from the window. Hours had passed while we dropped through the poisoned, thickening air. I already had most of my suit on. Now I screwed on my helmet and three-finger gauntlets.

'Strap down,' said Eric. I did.

We bumped gently. The ship tilted a little, swayed back, bumped again. And again, with my teeth rattling and my armour-plated body rolling against the crash webbing. 'Damn,' Eric muttered. I heard the hiss from above. Eric said, 'I don't know how we'll get back up.'

Neither did I. The ship bumped hard and stayed down, and I got up and went to the airlock.

'Good luck,' said Eric. 'Don't stay out too long.' I waved at his cabin camera. The outside temperature was seven hundred and thirty.

The outer door opened. My suit refrigerating unit set up a complaining whine. With an empty bucket in each hand, and with my headlamp blazing a way through the black murk, I stepped out on to the right wing.

My suit creaked and settled under the pressure, and I stood on the wing and waited for it to stop. It was almost like being under water. My headlamp beam went out thick enough to be solid, penetrating no more than a hundred feet. The air couldn't have been that opaque, no matter how dense. It must have been full of dust, or tiny droplets of some fluid.

The wing ran back like a knife-edged running board, widening toward the tail to where it spread into a tailfin. The two tailfins met back of the fuselage. At each tailfin tip was the ram, a big sculptured cylinder with an atomic engine inside. It wouldn't be hot because it hadn't been used yet, but I had my counter anyway.

I fastened a line to the wing and slid to the ground. As

128

long as we were *here* . . . The ground turned out to be a dry, reddish dirt, crumbly, and so porous that it was almost spongy. Lava etched by chemicals? Almost anything would be corrosive at this pressure and temperature. I scooped one pailful from the surface and another from underneath the first, then climbed up the line and left the buckets on the wing.

The wing was terribly slippery. I had to wear magnetic sandals to stay on. I walked up and back along the two-hundred-foot length of the ship, making a casual inspection. Neither wing nor fuselage showed damage. Why not? If a meteor or something had cut Eric's contact with his sensors in the rams, there should have been evidence of a break in the surface.

Then, almost suddenly, I realized that there was an alternative.

It was too vague a suspicion to put into words yet, and I still had to finish the inspection. Telling Eric would be very difficult if I were right.

Four inspection panels were set into the wing, well protected from the re-entry heat. One was half-way back on the fuselage, below the lower edge of the blimp tank, which was moulded to the fuselage in such a way that from the front the ship looked like a dolphin. Two more were in the trailing edge of the tailfin and the fourth was in the ram itself. All opened, with powered screwdriver on recessed screws, on junctions of the ship's electrical system.

There was nothing out of place under any of the panels. By making and breaking contacts and getting Eric's reactions, I found that his sensation ended somewhere between the second and third inspection panels. It was the same story on the left wing. No external damage, nothing wrong at the junctions. I climbed back to ground and walked slowly beneath the length of each wing, my headlamp tilted up. No damage underneath.

I collected my buckets and went back inside.

'A bone to pick?' Eric was puzzled. 'Isn't this a strange time to start an argument? Save it for space. We'll have four months with nothing else to do.'

'This can't wait. First of all, did you notice anything I

129

didn't?' He'd been watching everything I saw and did through the peeper in my helmet.

'No. I'd have yelled.'

'Okay. Now get this.'

'The break in your circuits isn't inside, because you get sensation up to the second wing inspection panels. It isn't outside because there's no evidence of damage, not even corrosion spots. That leaves only one place for the flaw.'

'Go on.'

'We also have the puzzle of why you're paralysed in both rams. Why should they both go wrong at the same time? There's only one place in the ship where the circuits join.'

'What? Oh, yes, I see. They joined through me.'

'Now let's assume for the moment that you're the piece of equipment with the flaw in it. You're not a piece of machinery, Eric. If something's wrong with you it isn't medical. That was the first thing we covered. But it could be psychological.'

'It's nice to know you think I'm human. So I've slipped a cam, have I?'

'Slightly. I think you've got a case of what used to be called trigger anaesthesia. A soldier who kills too often sometimes finds that his right index finger or even his whole hands has gone numb, as if it were no longer a part of him. Your comment about not being a machine is important, Eric. I think that's the whole problem. You've never really believed that any part of the ship is a part of *you*. That's intelligent, because it's true. Every time the ship is redesigned you get a new set of parts, and it's right to avoid thinking of a change of model as a series of amputations.' I'd been rehearsing this speech, trying to put it so that Eric would have no choice but to believe me. Now I know that it must have sounded phoney. 'But now you've gone too far. Subconsciously you've stopped believing that the rams can *feel* like a part of you, which they were designed to do. So you've persuaded yourself that you don't feel anything.'

With my prepared speech done, and nothing left to say, I stopped talking and waited for the explosion.

'You make good sense,' said Eric.

I was staggered. 'You agree?'

130

'I didn't say that. You spin an elegant theory, but I want time to think about it. What do we do if it's true?'

'Why . . . I don't know. You'll just have to cure yourself.'

'Okay. Now here's *my* idea. I propose that you thought up this theory to relieve yourself of a responsibility for getting us home alive. It puts the whole problem in my lap, metaphorically speaking.'

'Oh, for—'

'Shut up. I haven't said you're wrong. That would be an *ad hominem* argument. We need time to think about this.'

It was lights-out, four hours later, before Eric would return to the subject.

'Howie, do me a favour. Assume, for a while that something mechanical is causing all our trouble. I'll assume it's psychosomatic.'

'Seems reasonable.'

'It is reasonable. What can you do if I've gone psychosomatic? What can I do if it's mechanical? I can't go around inspecting myself. We'd each better stick to what we know.'

'It's a deal.' I turned him off for the night and went to bed.

But not to sleep.

With the lights off it was just like outside. I turned them back on. It wouldn't wake Eric. Eric never sleeps normally, since his blood doesn't accumulate fatigue poisons, and he'd go mad from being awake all the time if he didn't have a Russian sleep inducer plate near his cortex. The ship could implode without waking Eric when his sleep inducer's on. But I felt foolish being afraid of the dark.

While the dark stayed outside it was all right.

But it wouldn't stay there. It had invaded my partner's mind. Because his chemical checks guard him against chemical insanities like schizophrenia, we'd assumed he was permanently sane. But how could any prosthetic device protect him from his own imagination, his own misplaced common sense?

I couldn't keep my bargain. I knew I was right. But what could I do about it?

Hindsight is wonderful. I could see exactly what our mistake had been, Eric's and mine and the hundreds of

131

men who had built his life support after the crash. There was nothing left of Eric then except the intact central nervous system, and no glands except the pituitary. 'We'll regulate his blood composition,' they said, 'and he'll always be cool, calm and collected. No panic reactions from Eric!'

I know a girl whose father had an accident when he was forty-five or so. He was out with his brother, the girl's uncle, on a fishing trip. They were blind drunk when they started home, and the guy was riding on the hood while the brother drove. Then the brother made a sudden stop. Our hero left two important glands on the hood ornament.

The only change in his sex life was that his wife stopped worrying about late pregnancy. His *habits* were developed.

Eric doesn't need adrenal glands to be afraid of death. His emotional patterns were fixed long before the day he tried to land a moonship without radar. He'd grab any excuse to believe that I'd fixed whatever was wrong with the ram connections.

But he was counting on me to do it.

The atmosphere leaned on the windows. Not wanting to, I reached out to touch the quartz with my fingertips. I couldn't feel the pressure. But it was there, inexorable as the tide smashing a rock into sand grains. How long would the cabin hold it back?

If some broken part were holding us here, how could I have missed finding it? Perhaps it had left no break in the surface of either wing. But how?

That was an angle.

Two cigarettes later I got up to get the sample buckets. They were empty, the alien dirt safely stored away. I filled them with water and put them in the cooler, set the cooler for 40° Absolute, then turned off the lights and went to bed.

The morning was blacker than the inside of a smoker's lungs. What Venus really needs, I decided, philosophizing on my back, is to lose ninety-nine per cent of her air. That would give her a bit more than half as much air as Earth, which would lower the greenhouse effect enough to make the temperature livable. Drop Venus' gravity to near zero for a few weeks and the work would do itself.

The whole damn universe is waiting for us to discover antigravity.

132

'Morning,' said Eric. 'Thought of anything?'

'Yes.' I rolled out of bed. 'Now don't bug me with questions. I'll explain everything as I go.'

'No breakfast?'

'Not yet.'

Piece by piece I put my suit on, just like one of King Arthur's gentlemen and went for the buckets only after the gauntlets were on. The ice, in the cold section, was in the chilly neighbourhood of absolute zero. 'This is two buckets of ordinary ice,' I said, holding them up. 'Now let me out.'

'I should keep you here till you talk,' Eric groused. But the doors opened and I went out on to the wing. I started talking while I unscrewed the number two right panel.

'Eric, think a moment about the tests they run on a manned ship before they'll let a man walk into the life-system. They test every part separately and in conjunction with other parts. Yet if something isn't working, either it's damaged or it wasn't tested right. Right?'

'Reasonable.' He wasn't giving away anything.

'Well, nothing caused any damage. Not only is there no break in the ship's skin, but no coincidence could have made both rams go haywire at the same time. Something wasn't tested right.'

I had the panel off. In the buckets the ice boiled gently where it touched the surfaces of the glass buckets. The blue ice cakes had cracked under their own internal pressure. I dumped one bucket into the maze of wiring and contacts and relays, and the ice shattered, giving me room to close the panel.

'So I thought of something last night, something that wasn't tested. Every part of the ship must have been in the heat-and-pressure box, exposed to artifical Venus conditions, but the ship as a whole, a unit, couldn't have been. It's too big.' I'd circled around to the left wing and was opening the number three panel in the trailing edge. My remaining ice was half water and half small chips; I sloshed these in and fastened the panel. 'What cut your circuits must have been the heat or the pressure or both. I can't help the pressure, but I'm cooling these relays with ice. Let me know which ram gets its sensation back first, and we'll know which inspection panel is the right one.'

133

'Howie. Has it occurred to you what the cold water might do to those hot metals?'

'It could crack them. Then you'd lose all control over the ramjets, which is what's wrong right now.'

'Uh. Your point, partner. But I still can't feel anything.'

I went back to the airlock with my empty buckets swinging, wondering if they'd get hot enough to melt. They might have, but I wasn't out that long. I had my suit off and was refilling the buckets when Eric said, 'I can feel the right ram.'

'How extensive? Full control?'

'No, I can't feel the temperature. Oh, here it comes. We're all set, Howie.'

My sigh of relief was sincere.

I put the buckets in the freezer again. We'd certainly want to take off with the relays cold. The water had been chilling for perhaps twenty minutes when Eric reported, 'Sensation's going.'

'What?'

'Sensation's going. No temperature, and I'm losing fuel feed control. It doesn't stay cold long enough.'

'Ouch! Now what?'

'I hate to tell you. I'd almost rather let you figure it out for yourself.'

I had. 'We go as high as we can on the blimp tank, then I go out on the wing with a bucket of ice in each hand—'

We had to raise the blimp tank temperature to almost eight hundred degrees to get pressure, but from then on we went up in good shape. To sixteen miles. It took three hours.

'That's as high as we go,' said Eric. 'You ready?'

I went to get the ice. Eric could see me, he didn't need an answer. He opened the airlock for me.

Fear I might have felt, or panic, or determination or self sacrifice – but there was nothing. I went out feeling like a used zombie.

My magnets were on full. It felt like I was walking through shallow tar. The air was thick, though not as heavy as it had been down there. I followed my headlamp to the number two panel, opened it, poured ice in and threw the bucket high and far. The ice was in one cake. I couldn't close the panel. I left it open and hurried around to the other wing. The second bucket was filled with exploded chips; I sloshed them in and locked the number two left panel and came back with both hands free. It still looked like limbo in all directions, except where the headlamp cut a tunnel through the darkness, and – my feet were getting hot. I closed the right panel on boiling water and sidled back along the hull into the airlock.

'Come in and strap down,' said Eric. 'Hurry!'

'Gotta get my suit off.' My hands had started to shake from reaction. I couldn't work the clamps.

'No you don't. If you start right now we may get home. Leave the suit on and come in.'

I did. As I pulled my webbing shut, the rams roared. The ship shuddered a little, then pushed forward as we dropped from under the blimp tank. Pressure mounted as the rams reached operating speed. Eric was giving it all he had. It would have been uncomfortable even without the metal suit around me. With the suit on it was torture. My couch was afire from the suit, but I couldn't get breath to say so. We were going almost straight up.

We had gone twenty minutes when the ship jerked like a galvanized frog. 'Ram's out,' Eric said calmly. 'I'll use the other.' Another lurch as we dropped the dead one. The ship flew on like a wounded penguin, but still accelerating.

One minute . . . two . . .

The other ram quit. It was as if we'd run into molasses. Eric blew off the ram and the pressure eased. I could talk.

'Eric.'

'What?'

'Got any marshmallows?'

'*What*? Oh, I see. Is your suit tight?'

'Sure.'

'Live with it. We'll flush the smoke out later. I'm going to coast above some of this stuff, but when I use the rocket it'll be savage. No mercy.'

'Will we make it?'

'I think so. It'll be close.'

The relief came first, icy cold. The the anger. 'No more inexplicable numbnesses?' I asked.

'No. Why?'

'If any come up you'll be sure and tell me, won't you?'

'Are you getting at something?'

'Skip it.' I wasn't angry any more.

'I'll be damned if I do. You know perfectly well it was mechanical trouble. You fixed it yourself!'

'No. I convinced you I must have fixed it. You needed to believe the rams *should* be working again. I gave you a miracle cure, Eric. I just hope I don't have to keep dreaming up new placebos for you all the way home.'

'You thought that, but you went out on the wing sixteen miles up?' Eric's machinery snorted. 'You've got guts where you need brains, Shorty.'

I didn't answer.

'Five thousand says the trouble was mechanical. We let the mechanics decide after we land.'

'You're on.'

'Here comes the rocket. Two, one—'

It came, pushing me down into my metal suit. Sooty flames licked past my ears, writing black on the green metal ceiling, but the rosy mist before my eyes was not fire.

The man with the thick glasses spread a diagram of the Venus ship and jabbed a stubby finger at the trailing edge of the wing. 'Right around here,' he said. 'The pressure from outside compressed the wiring channel a little, just enough so there was no room for the wire to bend. It had to act as if it were rigid, see? Then when the heat expanded the metal these contacts pushed past each other.'

'I suppose it's the same design on both wings?'

He gave me a queer look. 'Well, naturally.'

I left my check for $5000 in a pile of Eric's mail and hopped a plane for Brasilia. How he found me I'll never know, but the telegram arrived this morning.

HOWIE COME HOME ALL IS FORGIVEN
DONOVANS BRAIN

I guess I'll have to.

DEATH BY ECSTASY

FIRST CAME THE routine request for a Breach of Privacy permit. A police officer took down the details and forwarded the request to a clerk, who saw that the tape reached the appropriate civic judge. The judge was reluctant, for privacy is a precious thing in a world of eighteen billion; but in the end he could find no reason to refuse. On November 2, 2123, he granted the permit.

The tenant's rent was two weeks in arrears. If the manager of Monica Apartments had asked for eviction he would have been refused. But Owen Jennison did not answer his doorbell or his room phone. Nobody could recall seeing him in many weeks. Apparently the manager only wanted to know that he was all right.

And so they found the tenant of 1809.

And when they had looked in his wallet, they called me.

I was at my desk at ARMs Headquarters, making useless notes and wishing it were lunchtime.

At this stage the Loren case was all correlate-and-wait. It involved an organlegging gang, apparently run by a single man, yet big enough to cover half the North American west coast. We had considererable data on the gang — methods of operation, centres of activity, a few former customers, even a tentative handful of names — but nothing that would give us an excuse to act. So it was a matter of shoving what we had into the computer, watching the few suspected associates of the ganglord Loren, and waiting for a break.

The months of waiting were ruining my sense of involvement.

My phone buzzed.

I put the pen down and said, 'Gil Hamilton.'

A small dark face regarded me with soft black eyes. 'I am Detective-Inspector Julio Ordaz of the Los Angeles Police Department. Are you related to an Owen Jennison?'

'Owen? No, we're not related. Is he in trouble?'

'You do know him, then.'

'Sure I know him. Is he here, on Earth?'

'It would seem so.' Ordaz had no accent, but the lack of colloquialisms in his speech made him sound vaguely foreign. 'We will need positive identification, Mr Hamilton, Mr Jennison's ident lists you as next of kin.'

'That's funny. I – back up a minute. Is Owen dead?'

'Somebody is dead, Mr Hamilton. He carried Mr Jennison's ident in his wallet.'

'Okay. Now, Owen Jennison was a citizen of the Belt. This may have interworld complications. That makes it ARMs business. Where's the body?'

'We found him in an apartment rented under his own name. Monica Apartments, Lower Los Angeles, room 1809.'

'Good. Don't move anything you haven't moved already. I'll be right over.'

Monica Apartments was a nearly featureless concrete block, eighty storeys tall, a thousand feet across the edges of its square base. Lines of small balconies gave the sides a sculptured look, above a forty-foot inset ledge that would keep tenants from dropping objects on pedestrians. A hundred buildings just like it made Lower Los Angeles look lumpy from the air.

Inside, a lobby done in anonymous modern. Lots of metal and plastic showing; lightweight, comfortable chairs without arms; big ashtrays; plenty of indirect lighting; a low ceiling; no wasted space. The whole room might have been stamped out with a die. It wasn't supposed to look small, but it did, and that warned you what the rooms would be like. You'd pay your rent by the cubic centimetre.

I found the manager's office, and the manager, a soft-looking man with watery blue eyes. His conservative paper suit, dark red, seemed chosen to render him invisible, as did the style of his brown hair, worn long and combed straight back without a part. 'Nothing like this has ever happened here,' he confided as he led me to the elevator banks. 'Nothing. It would have been bad enough without his being a Belter, but *now*—' He cringed at the thought. 'Newsmen. They'll *smother* us.'

The elevator was coffin-sized, but with the handrails

on the inside. It went up fast and smooth. I stepped out into a long, narrow hallway.

What would Owen have been doing in a place like this? Machinery lived here, not people.

Maybe it wasn't Owen. Ordaz had been reluctant to commit himself. Besides, there's no law against picking pockets. You couldn't enforce such a law on this crowded planet. Everyone on Earth was a pickpocket.

Sure. Someone had died carrying Owen's wallet.

I walked down the hallway to 1809.

It was Owen who sat grinning in the armchair. I took one good look at him, enough to be sure, and then I looked away and didn't look back. But the rest of it was even more unbelievable.

No Belter could have taken that apartment. I was born in Kansas; but even I felt the awful anonymous chill. It would have driven Owen bats.

'I don't believe it,' I said.

'Did you know him well, Mr Hamilton?'

'About as well as two men can know each other. He and I spent three years mining rocks in the main asteroid belt. You don't keep secrets under those conditions.'

'Yet you didn't know he was on Earth.'

'That's what I can't understand. Why the blazes didn't he phone me if he was in trouble?'

'You're an ARM,' said Ordaz. 'An operative in the United Nations Police.'

He had a point. Owen was as honourable as any man I knew; but honour isn't the same in the Belt. Belters think flatlanders are all crooks. They don't understand that to a flatlander, picking pockets is a game of skill. Yet a Belter sees smuggling as the same kind of game, with no dishonesty involved. He balances the thirty per cent tariff against possible confiscation of his cargo, and if the odds are right he gambles.

Owen could have been doing something that would look honest to him but not to me.

'He could have been in something sticky,' I admitted. 'But I can't see him killing himself over it. And . . . not here. He wouldn't have come here.'

1809 was a living-room and a bathroom and a closet.

139

I'd glanced into the bathroom, knowing what I would find. It was the size of a comfortable shower stall. An adjustment panel outside the door would cause it to extrude various appurtenances in memory plastic, to become a washroom, a shower stall, a toilet, a dressing-room, a steam cabinet. Luxurious in everything but size, as long as you pushed the right buttons.

The living-room was more of the same. A King bed was invisible behind a wall. The kitchen alcove, with basin and oven and grill and toaster, would fold into another wall; the sofa, chairs, and tables would vanish into the floor. One tenant and three guests would make a crowded cocktail party, a cosy dinner gathering, a closed poker game. Card table, dinner table, coffee table were all there, surrounded by the appropriate chairs; but only one set at a time would emerge from the floor. There was no refrigerator, no freezer, no bar. If a tenant needed food or drink he phoned down, and the super-market on the third floor would send it up.

The tenant of such an apartment had his comfort. But he owned nothing. There was room for him; there was none for his possessions. This was one of the inner apartments. An age ago there would have been an air shaft; but air shafts took up expensive room. The tenant didn't even have a window. He lived in a comfortable box.

Just now the items extruded were the overstuffed reading armchair, two small side tables, a footstool, and the kitchen alcove. Owen Jennison sat grinning in the armchair. Naturally he grinned. Little more than dried skin covered the natural grin of his skull.

'It's a small room,' said Ordaz, 'but not too small. Millions of people live this way. In any case a Belter would hardly be a claustrophobe.'

'No. Owen flew a singleship before he joined us. Three months at a stretch, in a cabin so small you couldn't stand up with the airlock closed. Not claustrophobia, but—' I swept my arm about the room. 'What do you see that's his?'

Small as it was, the closet was nearly empty. A set of street clothes, a paper shirt, a pair of shoes, a small brown overnight case. All new. The few items in the bathroom medicine chest had been equally new and equally anonymous.

Ordaz said, 'Well?'

'Belters are transients. They don't own much, but what they do own, they guard. Small possessions, relics, souvenirs. I can't believe he wouldn't have had *something*.'

Ordaz lifted an eyebrow. 'His space suit?'

'You think that's unlikely? It's not. The inside of his pressure suit is a Belter's home. Sometimes it's the only home he's got. He spends a fortune decorating it. If he loses his suit, he's not a Belter anymore.

'No, I don't insist he'd have brought his suit. But he'd have had *something*. His phial of Marsdust. The bit of nickel-iron they took out of his chest. Or, if he left all his souvenirs home, he'd have picked up things on Earth. But in this room – there's *nothing*.'

'Perhaps,' Ordaz suggested delicately, 'he didn't notice his surroundings.'

And somehow that brought it all home.

Owen Jennison sat grinning in a water-stained silk dressing gown. His space-darkened face lightened abruptly beneath his chin, giving way to normal suntan. His blond hair, too long, had been cut Earth style; no trace remained of the Belter strip cut he'd worn all his life. A month's growth of untended beard covered half his face. A small black cylinder protruded from the top of his head. An electric cord trailed from the top of the cylinder and ran to a wall socket.

The cylinder was a droud, a current addict's transformer.

I stepped closer to the corpse and bent to look. The droud was a standard make, but it had been altered. Your standard current addict's droud will pass only a trickle of current into the brain. Owen must have been getting ten times the usual charge, easily enough to damage his brain in a month's time.

I reached out and touched the droud with my imaginary hand.

Ordaz was standing quietly beside me, letting me make my examination without interruption. Naturally he had no way of knowing about my restricted psi powers.

Restricted was the operative word. I had two psychic

powers: telekinesis and esper. With the esper sense I could sense the shapes of objects at a distance; but the distance was the reach of an extra right arm. I could lift small objects, if they were no farther away than the fingertips of an imaginary right hand. The restriction was a flaw in my own imagination. Since I could not believe my imaginary hand would reach farther than that . . . it wouldn't.

Even so limited a psi power can be useful. With my imaginary fingertips I touched the droud in Owen's head, then ran them down to a tiny hole in his scalp, and farther.

It was a standard surgical job. Owen could have had it done anywhere. A hole in his scalp, invisible under the hair, nearly impossible to find even if you knew what you were looking for. Even your best friends wouldn't know, unless they caught you with the droud plugged in. But the tiny hole marked a bigger plug set in the bone of the skull. I touched the ecstasy plug with my imaginary fingertips, then ran them down the hair-fine wire going deep into Owen's brain, down into the pleasure centre.

No, the extra current hadn't killed him. What had killed Owen was his lack of will power. He had been unwilling to get up.

He had starved to death sitting in that chair. There were plastic squeezebottles all around his feet, and a couple still on the end tables. All empty. They must have been full a month ago. Owen hadn't died of thirst. He had died of starvation, and his death had been planned.

Owen my crewmate. Why hadn't he come to me? I'm half a Belter myself. Whatever his trouble, I'd have got him out somehow. A little smuggling – what of it? Why had he arranged to tell me only after it was over?

The apartment was so clean, so clean. You had to bend close to smell the death; the air conditioning whisked it all away.

He'd been very methodical. The kitchen was open so that a catheter could lead from Owen to the sink. He'd given himself enough water to last out the month; he'd paid his rent a month in advance. He'd cut the droud cord by hand, and he'd cut it short, deliberately tethering himself to a wall socket beyond reach of the kitchen.

A complex way to die, but rewarding in its way. A month of ecstasy, a month of the highest physical pleasure man can attain. I could imagine him giggling every time he remembered he was starving to death. With food only a few footsteps away . . . but he'd have to pull out the droud to reach it. Perhaps he postponed the decision, and postponed it again . . .

Owen and I and Homer Chandrasekhar, we had lived for three years in a cramped shell surrounded by vacuum. What was there to know about Owen Jennison that I hadn't known? Where was the weakness we didn't share? If Owen had done this, so could I. And I was afraid.

'Very neat,' I whispered. 'Belter neat.'

'Typically Belter, would you say?'

'I would not. Belters don't commit suicide. Certainly not this way. If a Belter had to go, he'd blow his ship's drive and die like a star. The neatness is typical. The result isn't.'

'Well,' said Ordaz. 'Well.' He was uncomfortable. The facts spoke for themselves, yet he was reluctant to call me a liar. He fell back on formality.

'Mr Hamilton, do you identify this man as Owen Jennison?'

'It's him.' He'd always been a touch overweight, yet I'd recognized him the moment I saw him. 'But let's be sure.' I pulled the dirty dressing gown back from Owen's shoulder. A near-perfect circle of scar tissue, eight inches across, spread over the left side of his chest. 'See that?'

'We noticed it, yes. An old burn?'

'Owen's the only man I know who could show you a meteor scar on his skin. It blasted him in the shoulder one day while he was outside the ship. Sprayed vaporized pressure-suit steel all over his skin. The doc pulled a tiny grain of nickle-iron from the centre of the scar, just below the skin. Owen always carried that grain of nickel-iron. Always,' I said, looking at Ordaz.

'We didn't find it.'

'Okay.'

'I'm sorry to put you through this, Mr Hamilton. It was you who insisted we leave the body in situ.'

'Yes. Thank you.'

Owen grinned at me from the reading chair. I felt the

143

pain, in my throat and in the pit of my stomach. Once I had lost my right arm. Losing Owen felt the same way.

'I'd like to know more about this,' I said. 'Will you let me know the details as soon as you get them?'

'Of course. Through the ARMs office?'

'Yes.' This wasn't ARMs business, despite what I'd told Ordaz; but ARMs prestige would help. 'I want to know why Owen died. Maybe he just cracked up . . . culture shock or something. But if someone hounded him to death, I'll have his blood.'

'Surely the administration of justice is better left to—' Ordaz stopped, confused. Did I speak as an ARM or as a citizen?

I left wondering.

The lobby held a scattering of tenants, entering and leaving elevators or just sitting around. I stood outside the elevator for a moment, searching passing faces for the erosion of personality that must be there.

Mass-produced comfort. Room to sleep and eat and watch tridee, but no room to *be* anyone. Living here, one would own nothing. What kind of people would live like that? They should have looked all alike, moved in unison, like the string of images in a barber's mirrors.

Then I spotted wavy brown hair and a dark red paper suit. The manager? I had to get close before I was sure. His face was the face of a permanent stranger.

He saw me coming and smiled without enthusiasm. 'Oh, hello, Mr . . . uh . . . Did you find . . .' He couldn't think of the right question.

'Yes,' I said, answering it anyway. 'But I'd like to know some things. Owen Jennison lived here for six weeks, right?'

'Six weeks and two days, before we opened his room.'

'Did he ever have visitors?'

The man's eyebrows went up. We drifted in the direction of his office, and I was close enough to read the name on the door: JASPER MILLER, *Manager*. 'Of course not,' he said. 'Anyone would have noticed that something was wrong.'

'You mean he took the room for the express purpose of dying? You saw him once, and never again?'

'I suppose he might . . . no, wait.' The manager thought

144

deeply. 'No. He registered on a Thursday. I noticed the Belter tan, of course. Then on Friday he went out. I happened to see him pass.'

'Was that the day he got the droud? No. skip it, you wouldn't know that. Was it the last time you saw him go out?'

'Yes, it was.'

'Then he could have had visitors late Thursday or early Friday.'

The manager shook his head, very positively.

'Why not?'

'You see, Mr, uh ...'

'Hamilton.'

'We have a holo camera on every floor, Mr Hamilton. It takes a picture of each tenant the first time he goes to his room, and then never again. Privacy is one of the services a tenant buys with his room.' The manager drew himself up a little as he said this. 'For the same reason, the holo camera takes a picture of anyone who is *not* a tenant. The tenants are thus protected from unwarranted intrusions.'

'And there were no visitors to any of the rooms on Owen's floor?'

'No, sir, there were not.'

'Your tenants are a solitary bunch.'

'Perhaps they are.'

'I suppose a computer in the basement decides who is and is not a tenant.'

'Of course.'

'So for six weeks Owen Jennison sat alone in his room. In all that time he was totally ignored.'

Miller tried to turn his voice cold, but he was too nervous. 'We try to give our guests privacy. If Mr Jennison had wanted help of any kind he had only to pick up the house phone. He could have called me, or the pharmacy, or the supermarket downstairs.'

'Well, thank you, Mr Miller. That's all I wanted to know. I wanted to know how Owen Jennison could wait six weeks to die while nobody noticed.'

Miller swallowed. 'He was dying all that time?'

'Yah.'

'We had no way of knowing. How could we? I don't see how you can blame us.'

'I don't either,' I said, and brushed by. Miller had been close enough, so I had lashed out at him. Now I was ashamed. The man was perfectly right. Owen could have had help if he'd wanted it.

I stood outside, looking up at the jagged blue line of sky that showed between the tops of the buildings. A taxi floated into view, and I beeped my clicker at it, and it dropped.

I went back to ARM Headquarters. Not to work – I couldn't have done any work, not under the circumstances – but to talk to Julie.

Julie. A tall girl, pushing thirty, with green eyes and long hair streaked red and gold. And two wide brown forceps marks above her right knee; but they weren't showing now. I looked into her office, through the one-way glass, and watched her at work.

She sat in a contour couch, smoking. Her eyes were closed. Sometimes her brow would furrow as she concentrated. Sometimes she would snatch a glance at the clock, then close her eyes again.

I didn't interrupt her. I knew the importance of what she was doing.

Julie. She wasn't beautiful. Her eyes were a little too far apart, her chin too square, her mouth too wide. It didn't matter. Because Julie could read minds.

She was the ideal date. She was everything a man needed. A year ago, the day after the night I killed my first man, I had been in a terribly destructive mood. Somehow Julie had turned it into a mood of manic exhilaration. We'd run wild through a supervised anarchy park, running up an enormous bill. We'd hiked five miles without going anywhere, facing backwards on a downtown slidewalk. At the end we'd been utterly fatigued, too tired to think . . . But two weeks ago it had been a warm, cuddly, comfortable night. Two people happy with each other; no more than that. Julie was what you needed, anytime, anywhere.

Her male harem must have been the largest in history. To pick up on the thoughts of a male ARM, Julie had

146

to be in love with him. Luckily there was no room in her for a lot of love. She didn't demand that we be faithful. A good half of us were married. But there had to be love for each of Julie's men, or Julie couldn't protect him.

She was protecting us now. Each fifteen minutes, Julie was making contact with a specific ARM agent. Psi powers are notoriously undependable, but Julie was an exception. If we got in a hole, Julie was always there to get us out . . . provided some idiot didn't interrupt her at work.

So I stood outside, waiting, with a cigarette in my imaginary hand.

The cigarette was for practice, to stretch the mental muscles. In its way my 'hand' was as dependable as Julie's mind-touch, possibly because of its very limitations. Doubt your psi powers and they're gone. A rigidly defined third arm was more reasonable than some warlock ability to make objects move by wishing at them. I knew how an arm felt, and what it would do.

Why do I spend so much time lifting cigarettes? Well, it's the biggest weight I can lift without strain. And there's another reason . . . something taught me by Owen.

At ten minutes to fifteen Julie opened her eyes, rolled out of the contour couch, and came to the door. 'Hi, Gil,' she said sleepily. 'Trouble?'

'Yah. A friend of mine just died. I thought you'd better know.' I handed her a cup of coffee.

She nodded. We had a date tonight, and this would change its character. Knowing that, she probed lightly.

'Jesus!' she said, recoiling. 'How . . . how horrible. I'm terribly sorry, Gil. Date's off, right?'

'Unless you want to join the ceremonial drunk.'

She shook her head vigorously. 'I didn't know him. It wouldn't be proper. Besides, you'll be wallowing in your own memories, Gil. A lot of them will be private. I'd cramp your style if you knew I was there to probe. Now if Homer Chandrasekhar were here, it'd be different.'

'I wish he were. He'll have to throw his own drunk. Maybe with some of Owen's girls, if they're around.'

'You know what I feel,' she said.

'Just what I do.'

147

'I wish I could help.'

'You always help.' I glanced at the clock. 'Your coffee break's about over.'

'Slave driver.' Julie took my earlobe between thumb and forefinger. 'Do him proud,' she said, and went back to her soundproof room.

She always helps. She doesn't even have to speak, Just knowing that Julie has read my thoughts, that someone understands ... that's enough.

All alone at three in the afternoon, I started my ceremonial drunk.

The ceremonial drunk is a young custom, not yet tied down by formality. There is no set duration. No specific toasts must be given. Those who participate must be close friends of the deceased, but there is no set number of participants.

I started at the Luau, a place of cool blue light and running water. Outside it was fifteen-thirty in the afternoon, but inside it was evening in the Hawaiian Islands of centuries ago. Already the place was half-full. I picked a corner table with considerable elbow room and dialled for a Luau grog. It came, cool, brown, and alcoholic, its straw tucked into a cone of ice.

There had been three of us at Cubes Forsythe's ceremonial drunk, one black Ceres night four years ago. A jolly group we were too; Owen and me and the widow of our third crewman. Gwen Forsythe blamed us for her husband's death. I was just out of the hospital with a right arm that ended at the shoulder and I blamed Cubes and Owen and myself, all at once. Even Owen had turned dour and introspective. We couldn't have picked a worse trio, or a worse night for it.

But custom called, and we were there. Then as now, I found myself probing my own personality for the wound that was a missing crewman, a missing friend. Introspecting.

Gilbert Hamilton. Born of flatlander parents, in April, 2093, in Topeka, Kansas. Born with two arms and no sign of wild talents.

Flatlander: a Belter term referring to earthmen, and particularly to earthmen who had never seen space. I'm not sure my parents ever looked at the stars. They managed the third largest farm in Kansas, ten square miles of arable land between two wide strips of city paralleling two strips of turnpike. We were city people, like all flatlanders, but when the crowds got to be too much for my brothers and me, we had vast stretches of land to be alone in. Ten square miles of playground, with nothing to hamper us but the crops and automachinery.

We looked at the stars, my brothers and I. You can't see stars from the city; the lights hide them. Even in the fields you couldn't see them around the lighted horizon. But straight overhead, they were there: black sky scattered with bright dots, and sometimes a flat white moon.

At twenty I gave up my UN citizenship to become a Belter. I wanted stars, and the Belt government holds title to most of the solar system. There are fabulous riches in the rocks, riches belonging to a scattered civilization of a few hundred thousand Belters; and I wanted my share of that, too.

It wasn't easy. I wouldn't be eligible for a single-ship licence for ten years. Meanwhile I would be working for others, and learning to avoid mistakes before they killed me. Half the flatlanders who join the Belt die in space before they can earn their licences.

I mined tin on Mercury and exotic chemicals from Jupiter's atmosphere. I hauled ice from Saturn's rings and quicksilver from Europa. One year our pilot made a mistake pulling up to a new rock, and we damn near had to walk home. Cubes Forsythe was with us then. He managed to fix the com laser and aim it at Icarus to bring help. Another time the mechanic who did the maintenance job on our ship forgot to replace an absorber, and we all got roaring drunk on the alcohol that built up in our breathing-air. The three of us caught the mechanic six months later. I hear he lived.

Most of the time I was part of a three-man crew. The members changed constantly. When Owen Jennison joined us he replaced a man who had finally earned his single-ship licence, and couldn't wait to start hunting rocks on his own. He was too eager. I learned that he'd made one round trip and half of another.

Owen was my age, but more experienced, a Belter

born and bred. His blue eyes and blond cockatoo's crest were startling against the dark of his Belter tan, the tan that ended so abruptly where his neck ring cut off the space-intense sunlight his helmet let through. He was permanently chubby, but in free fall it was as if he'd been born with wings. I took to copying his way of moving, much to Cubes' amusement.

I didn't make my own mistake until I was twenty-six.

We were using bombs to put a rock in a new orbit. A contract job. The technique is older than fusion drives, as old as early Belt colonization, and it's still cheaper and faster than using a ship's drive to tow the rock. You use industrial fusion bombs, small and clean, and you set them so that each explosion deepens the crater to channel the force of later blasts.

We'd set four blasts already, four white fireballs that swelled and faded as they rose. When the fifth blast went off we were hovering nearby on the other side of the rock.

The fifth blast shattered the rock.

Cubes had set the bomb. My own mistake was a shared one, because any of the three of us should have had the sense to take off right then. Instead, we watched, cursing, as valuable oxygen-bearing rock became near-valueless shards. We watched the shards spread slowly into a cloud . . . and while we watched one fast-moving shard reached us. Moving too slowly to vaporize when it hit, it nonetheless sheared through a triple crystal-iron hull, slashed through my upper arm, and pinned Cubes Forsythe to a wall by his heart.

A couple of nudists came in. They stood blinking among the booths while their eyes adjusted to the blue twilight, then converged with glad cries on the group two tables over. I watched and listened with an eye and an ear, thinking how different flatlander nudists were from Belter nudists. These all looked alike. They all had muscles, they had no interesting scars, they carried their credit cards in identical shoulder pouches, and they all shaved the same areas.

. . . We always went nudist in the big bases. Most people did. It was a natural reaction to the pressure suits we wore day and night while out in the rocks. Get him into a shirtsleeve environment, and your normal Belter sneers at a shirt. But it's only for comfort. Give him a good reason and your Belter will don shirt and pants as quickly as the next guy.

But not Owen. After he got that meteor scar, I never saw him wear a shirt. Not just in the Ceres domes, but anywhere there was air to breathe. He just had to show that scar.

A cool blue mood settled on me and I remembered . . .

. . . Owen Jennison lounging on a corner of my hospital bed, telling me of the trip back. I couldn't remember anything after that rock had sheared through my arm.

I should have bled to death in seconds. Owen hadn't given me the chance. The wound was ragged; Owen had sliced it clean to the shoulder with one swipe of a com laser. Then he'd tied a length of fibreglass curtain over the flat surface and knotted it tight under my remaining arm-pit. He told me about putting me under two atmospheres of pure oxygen as a substitute for replacing the blood I'd lost. He told me how he'd reset the fusion drive for four gees to get me back in time. By rights we should have gone up in a cloud of starfire and glory.

'So there goes my reputation. The whole Belt knows how I rewired our drive. A lot of 'em figure if I'm stupid enough to risk my own life like that I'd risk theirs too.'

'So you're not safe to travel with.'

'Just so. They're starting to call me Four Gee Jennison.'

'You think you've got problems? I can just see how it'll be when I get out of this bed. "You do something stupid, Gil?" The hell of it is, it *was* stupid.'

'So lie a little.'

'Uh huh. Can we sell the ship?'

'Nope. Gwen inherited a third interest in it from Cubes. She won't sell.'

'Then we're effectively broke.'

'Except for the ship. We need another crewman.'

'Correction. *You* need *two* crewmen. Unless you want to fly with a one-armed man. I can't afford a transplant.'

Owen hadn't tried to offer me a loan. That would have been insulting, even if he'd had the money. 'What's wrong with a prosthetic?'

'An iron arm? Sorry, no. I'm squeamish.'

151

Owen had looked at me strangely, but all he'd said was, 'Well, we'll wait a bit. Maybe you'll change your mind.'

He hadn't pressured me. Not then, and not later, after I'd left the hospital and taken an apartment while I waited to get used to a missing arm. If he thought I would eventually settle for a prosthetic, he was mistaken.

Why? It's not a question I can answer. Others obviously feel differently; there are millions of people walking around with metal and plastic and silicone parts. Part man, part machine, and how do they themselves know which is the real person?

I'd rather be dead than part metal. Call it a quirk. Call it, even, the same quirk that makes my skin crawl when I find a place like Monica Apartments. A human being should be all human. He should have habits and possessions peculiarly his own, he should not try to look like or to behave like anyone but himself, and he should not be half robot.

So there I was, Gil the Arm, learning to eat with my left hand.

An amputee never entirely loses what he's lost. My missing fingers itched. I moved to keep from barking my missing elbow on sharp corners. I reached for things, then swore when they didn't come.

Owen had hung around, though his own emergency funds must have been running low. I hadn't offered to sell my third of the ship, and he hadn't asked.

There had been a girl. Now I'd forgotten her name. One night I was at her place waiting for her to get dressed – a dinner date – and I'd happened to see a nail file she'd left on a table. I'd picked it up. I'd almost tried to file my nails, but remembered in time. Irritated, I had tossed the file back on the table – and missed.

Like an idiot I'd tried to catch it with my right hand. And I'd caught it.

I'd never suspected myself of having psychic powers. You have to be in the right frame of mind to use a psi power. But who had ever had a better opportunity than I did that night, with a whole section of brain tuned to the nerves and muscles of my right arm, and no right arm?

I'd held the nail file in my imaginary hand. I'd felt it, just as I'd felt my missing fingernails getting too long. I had run my thumb along the rough steel surface; I had turned the file in my fingers. Telekinesis for lift, esper for touch.

'That's it,' Owen had said the next day. 'That's all we need. One crewman, and you with your eldritch powers. You practise, see how strong you can get that lift. I'll go find a sucker.'

'He'll have to settle for a sixth of net. Cubes' widow will want her share.'

'Don't worry. I'll swing it.'

'Don't worry!' I'd waved a pencil stub at him. Even in Ceres' gentle gravity, it was as much as I could lift – then. 'You don't think TK and esper can make do for a real arm, do you?'

'It's better than a real arm. You'll see. You'll be able to reach through your suit with it without losing pressure. What Belter can do that?'

'Sure.'

'What the hell do you want, Gil? Someone should give you your arm back? You can't have that. You lost it fair and square, through stupidity. Now it's your choice. Do you fly with an imaginary arm, or do you go back to Earth?'

'I can't go back. I don't have the fare.'

'Well?'

'Okay, okay. Go find us a crewman. Someone I can impress with my imaginary arm.'

I sucked meditatively on a second Luau grog. By now all the booths were full, and a second layer was forming around the bar. The voices made a continuous hypnotic roar. Cocktail hour had arrived.

. . . He'd swung it, all right. On the strength of my imaginary arm, Owen had talked a kid named Homer Chandrasekhar into joining our crew.

He'd been right about my arm, too.

Others with similar senses can reach farther, up to halfway around the world. My unfortunately literal imagination had restricted me to a psychic hand. But my esper fingertips were more sensitive, more dependable. I could lift more weight. Today, in Earth's gravity, I can lift a full shot glass.

I found I could reach through a cabin wall to feel for breaks in the circuits behind it. In vacuum I could brush dust from the outside of my faceplate. In port I did magic tricks.

I'd almost ceased to feel like a cripple. It was all due to Owen. In six months of mining I had paid off my hospital bills and earned my fare back to Earth, with a comfortable stake left over.

'Finagle's Black Humour!' Owen had exploded when I told him. 'Of all places, why Earth?'

'Because if I can get my UN citizenship back, Earth will replace my arm. Free.'

'Oh. That's true,' he said dubiously.

The Belt had organ banks too, but they were always under-supplied. Belters didn't give things away. Neither did the Belt government. They kept the prices on transplants as high as they would go. Thus they dropped the demand to meet the supply, and kept taxes down to boot.

In the Belt I'd have had to buy my own arm. And I didn't have the money. On Earth there was social security, and a vast supply of transplant material.

What Owen had said couldn't be done, I'd done. I'd found someone to hand me my arm back.

Sometimes I'd wondered if Owen held the choice against me. He'd never said anything, but Homer Chandrasekhar had spoken at length. A Belter would have earned his arm or done without. Never would he have accepted charity.

Was that why Owen hadn't tried to call me?

I shook my head. I didn't believe it.

The room continued to lurch after my head stopped shaking. I'd had enough for the moment. I finished my third grog and ordered dinner.

Dinner sobered me for the next lap. It was something of a shock to realize that I'd run through the entire lifespan of my friendship with Owen Jennison. I'd known him for three years, though it had seemed like half a lifetime. And it was. Half my six-year lifespan as a Belter.

I ordered coffee grog and watched the man pour it: hot, milky coffee laced with cinnamon and other spices, and high-proof rum poured in a stream of blue fire. This was one of the special drinks served by a human headwaiter,

154

and it was the reason they kept him around. Phase two of the ceremonial drunk : blow half your fortune, in the grand manner.

But I called Ordaz before I touched the drink.

'Yes, Mr. Hamilton? I was just going home for dinner.'

'I won't keep you long. Have you found out anything new?'

Ordaz took a closer look at my phone image. His disapproval was plain. 'I see that you have been drinking. Perhaps you should go home now, and call me tomorrow.'

I was shocked. 'Don't you know *anything* about Belt customs?'

'I do not understand.'

I explained the ceremonial drunk. 'Look, Ordaz, if you know that little about the way a Belter thinks, then we'd better have a talk. Soon. Otherwise you're likely to miss something.'

'You may be right. I can see you at noon, over lunch.'

'Good. What have you got?'

'Considerable, but none of it is very helpful. Your friend landed on Earth two months ago, arriving on the *Pillar of Fire*, operating out of Outback Field, Australia. He was wearing a haircut in the style of Earth. From there—'

'That's funny. He'd have had to wait two months for his hair to grow out.'

'That occurred even to me. I understand that a Belter commonly shaves his entire scalp, except for a strip two inches wide running from the nape of his neck forward.'

'The strip cut, yah. It probably started when someone decided he'd live longer if his hair couldn't fall in his eyes during a tricky landing. But Owen could have let his hair grow out during a singleship mining trip. There'd be nobody to see.'

'Still, it seems odd. Did you know that Mr. Jennison has a cousin on Earth? One Harvey Peele, who manages a chain of supermarkets.'

'So I wasn't his next of kin, even on Earth.'

Mr. Jennison made no attempt to contact him.'

'Anything else?'

'I've spoken to the man who sold Mr. Jennison his droud and plug. Kenneth Graham owns an office and operating room on Gayley in Near West Los Angeles. Graham claims that the droud was a standard type, that your friend must have altered it himself.'

'Do you believe him?'

'For the present. His permits and his records are all in order. The droud was altered with a soldering iron, an amateur's tool.'

'Uh huh.'

'As far as the police are concerned, the case will probably be closed when we locate the tools Mr. Jennison used.'

'Tell you what. I'll wire Homer Chandrasekhar tomorrow. Maybe he can find out things – why Owen landed without a strip haircut, why he came to Earth at all.'

Ordaz shrugged witht his eyebrows. He thanked me for my trouble and hung up.

The coffee grog was still hot. I gulped at it, savouring the sugary, bittery sting of it, trying to forget Owen dead and remember him in life. He was always slightly chubby, I remembered, but he never gained a pound and he never lost a pound. He could move like a whippet when he had to.

And now he was terribly thin, and his death-grin was ripe with obscene joy.

I ordered another coffee grog. The waiter, a showman, made sure he had my attention before he lit the heated rum, then poured it from a foot above the glass. You can't drink that drink slowly. It slides down too easily, and there's the added spur that if you wait too long it might get cold. Rum and strong coffee. Two of these and I'd be drunkenly alert for hours.

Midnight found me in the Mars Bar, running on Scotch and soda. In between I'd been bar hopping. Irish coffee at Bergin's, cold and smoking concoctions at the Moon Pool, Scotch and wild music at Beyond. I couldn't get drunk, and I couldn't find the right mood. There was a barrier to the picture I was trying to rebuild.

It was the memory of the last Owen, grinning in an armchair with a wire leading down into his brain.

I didn't know that Owen. I had never met the man, and never would have wanted to. From bar to nightclub to restaurant I had run from the image, waiting for the alcohol to break the barrier between present and past.

So I sat at a corner table, surrounded by 3D panoramic views of an impossible Mars. Crystal towers and long, straight blue canali, six-legged beasts and beautiful, impossibly slender men and women, looked out at me across never-never land. Would Owen have found it sad or funny? He'd seen the real Mars, and had not been impressed.

I had reached that stage where time becomes discontinuous, where gaps of seconds or minutes appear between the events you can remember. Somewhere in that period I found myself staring at a cigarette. I must have just lighted it, because it was near its original two-hundred-millimetre length. Maybe a waiter had snuck up behind me. There it was, at any rate, burning between my middle and index fingers.

I stared at the coal as the mood settled on me. I was calm, I was drifting, I was lost in time . . .

. . . We'd been two months in the rocks, our first trip out since the accident. Back we came to Ceres with a hold full of gold, fifty per cent pure, guaranteed suitable for rustproof wiring and conductor plates. At nightfall we were ready to celebrate.

We walked along the city limits, with neon blinking and beckoning on the right, a melted rock cliff to the left, and stars blazing through the dome overhead. Homer Chandrasekhar was practically snorting. On this night his first trip out culminated in his first homecoming: and homecoming is the best part.

'We'll want to split up about midnight,' he said. He didn't need to enlarge on that. Three men in company might conceivably be three singleship pilots, but chances are they're a ship's crew. They don't have their singleship licences yet; they're too stupid or too inexperienced. If we wanted companions for the night—

'You haven't thought this through,' Owen answered. I saw Homer's double-take, then his quick look at where my shoulder ended, and I was ashamed. I didn't need my crewmates to hold my hand, and in this state I'd only slow them down.

Before I could open my mouth to protest, Owen went on. 'Think it through. We've got a draw here that we'd be idiots to throw away. Gil, pick up a cigarette. No, not with your left hand—'

I was drunk, gloriously drunk and feeling immortal. The attenuated martians seemed to move in the walls, the walls that seemed to be picture windows on a Mars that never was. For the first time that night, I raised my glass in toast.

'To Owen, from Gil the Arm. Thanks.'

I transferred the cigarette to my imaginary hand.

By now you've got the idea I was holding it in my imaginary fingers. Most people have the same impression, but it isn't so. I held it clutched ignominiously in my fist. The coal couldn't burn me, of course, but it still felt like a lead ingot.

I rested my imaginary elbow on the table, and that seemed to make it easier – which is ridiculous, but it works. Truly, I'd expected my imaginary arm to disappear after I got the transplant. But I'd found I could dissociate from the new arm to hold small objects in my invisible hand, to feel tactile sensations in my invisible fingertips.

I'd earned the title Gil the Arm, that night in Ceres. It had started with a floating cigarette. Owen had been right. Everyone in the place eventually wound up staring at the floating cigarette smoked by the one-armed man. All I had to do was find the prettiest girl in the room with my peripheral vision, then catch her eye.

That night we had been the centre of the biggest impromptu party ever thrown in Ceres Base. It wasn't planned that way at all. I'd used the cigarette trick three times, so that each of us would have a date. But the third girl already had an escort, and he was celebrating something; he'd sold some kind of patent to an Earth-based industrial firm. He was throwing money around like confetti. So we let him stay. I did tricks, reaching esper fingers into a closed box to tell what was inside, and by the time I finished all the tables had been pushed together and I was in the centre, with Homer and Owen and three girls. Then we got to singing old songs, and the bartenders joined us, and suddenly everything was on the house.

Eventually about twenty of us wound up in the orbiting mansion of the First Speaker for the Belt Government. The goldskin cops had tried to bust us up earlier, and the First Speaker had behaved very rudely indeed, then compensated by inviting them to join us ...

And that was why I used TK on so many cigarettes.

Across the width of the Mars Bar, a girl in a peach coloured dress sat studying me with her chin on her fist. I got up and went over.

My head felt fine. It was the first thing I checked when I woke up. Apparently I'd remembered to take a hangover pill.

A leg was hooked over my knee. It felt good, though the pressure had put my foot to sleep. Fragrant dark hair spilled beneath my nose. I didn't move. I didn't want her to know I was awake.

It's damned embarrassing when you wake up with a girl and can't remember her name.

Well, let's see. A peach dress neatly hung from a doorknob ... I remembered a whole lot of travelling last night. The girl at the Mars Bar. A puppet show. Music of all kinds. I'd talked about Owen, and she'd steered me away from that because it depressed her. Then—

Hah! Taffy. Last name forgotten.

'Morning,' I said.

'Morning,' she said. 'Don't try to move, we're hooked together ...' In the sober morning light she was lovely. Long black hair, brown eyes, creamy untanned skin. To be lovely this early was a neat trick, and I told her so, and she smiled.

My lower leg was dead meat until it started to buzz with renewed circulation, and then I made faces until it calmed down. Taffy kept up a running chatter as we dressed. 'That third hand is strange. I remember you holding me with two strong arms and stroking the back of my neck with the third. *Very* nice. It reminded me of a Fritz Leiber story.'

' "The Wanderer". The panther girl.'

'Mm hmm. How many girls have you caught with that cigarette trick?'

'None as pretty as you.'

159

'And how many girls have you told that to?'

'Can't remember. It always worked before. Maybe this time it's for real.'

We exchanged grins.

A minute later I caught her frowning thoughtfully at the back of my neck. 'Something wrong?'

'I was just thinking. You really crashed and burned last night. I hope you don't drink that much all the time.'

'Why? You worried about me?'

She blushed, then nodded.

'I should have told you. In fact, I think I did, last night. I was on a ceremonial drunk. When a good friend dies it's obligatory to get smashed.'

Taffy looked relieved. 'I didn't mean to get—'

'Personal? Why not. You've the right. Anyway, I like –' *maternal types,* but I couldn't say that. 'People who worry about me.'

Taffy touched her hair with some kind of complex comb. A few strokes snapped her hair instantly into place. Static electricity?

'It was a good drunk,' I said. 'Owen would have been proud. And that's all the mourning I'll do. One drunk and—' I spread my hands. 'Out.'

'It's not a bad way to go,' Taff mused reflectively. 'Current stimulus, I mean. I mean, if you've got to bow out—'

'Now drop that!' I don't know how I got so angry so fast. Ghoul-thin and grinning in a reading chair, Owen's corpse was suddenly vivid before me. I'd fought that image for too many hours. 'Walking off a bridge is enough of a cop-out.' I snarled. 'Dying for a month while current burns out your brain is nothing less than sickening.'

Taffy was hurt and bewildered. 'But your friend did it, didn't he? You didn't make him sound like a weakling.'

'Nuts.' I heard myself say. 'He didn't do it. He was—'

Just like that, I was sure. I must have realized it while I was drunk or sleeping. Of *course* he hadn't killed himself. *That* wasn't Owen. And current addiction wasn't Owen either.

'He was murdered,' I said. 'Sure he was. Why didn't I see it?' And I made a dive for the phone.

'Good morning, Mr. Hamilton.' Detective-Inspector Ordaz looked very fresh and neat this morning. I was sud-

160

denly aware that I hadn't shaved. 'I see you remembered to take your hangover pills.'

'Right. Ordaz, has it occurred to you that Owen might have been murdered?'

'Naturally. But it isn't possible.'

'I think it might be. Suppose he—'

'Mr. Hamilton.'

'Yah?'

'We have an appointment for lunch. Shall we discuss it then? Meet me at Headquarters at twelve hundred.'

'Okay. One thing you might take care of this morning. See if Owen registered for a nudist's licence.'

'Do you think he might have?'

'Yah. I'll tell you why at lunch.'

'Very well.'

'Don't hang up. You said you'd found the man who sold Owen his droud-and-plug. What was his name again?'

'Kenneth Graham.'

'That's what I thought.' I hung up.

Taffy touched my shoulder. 'Do – do you really think he might have been – killed?'

'Yah. The whole set-up depended on him not being able to—'

'No. Wait. I don't want to know about it.'

I turned to look at her. She really didn't. The very subject of a stranger's death was making her sick to her stomach.

'Okay. Look, I'm a jerk not to at least offer you breakfast, but I've got to get on this right away. Can I call you a cab?'

When the cab came I dropped a ten-mark coin in the slot and helped her in. I got her address before it took off.

ARM Headquarters hummed with early morning activity. Hellos came my way, and I answered them without stopping to talk. Anything important would filter down to me eventually.

As I passed Julie's cubicle I glanced in. She was hard at work, limply settled in her contour couch, jotting notes with her eyes closed.

Kenneth Graham.

A hook-up to the basement computer formed the greater

part of my desk. Learning how to use it had taken me several months. I typed an order for coffee and doughnuts, then: INFORMATION RETRIEVAL. KENNETH GRAHAM. LIMITED LICENCE: SURGERY. GENERAL LICENCE: DIRECT CURRENT STIMU-LUS EQUIPMENT SALES. ADDRESS: NEAR WEST LOS ANGELES.

Tape chattered out of the slot, an instant response, loop after loop of it curling on my desk. I didn't need to read it to know I was right.

New technologies create new customs, new laws, new ethics, new crimes. About half the activity of the United Nations Police, the ARMs, dealt with control of a crime that hadn't existed a century ago. The crime of organleg-ging was the result of thousands of years of medical pro-gress, of millions of lives selflessly dedicated to the ideal of healing the sick. Progress had brought these ideals to reality, and, as usual, had created new problems.

1900 A.D. was the year Karl Landsteiner classified hu-man blood into four types, giving patients their first real chance to survive a transfusion. The technology of trans-plants had grown with the growing of the twentieth cen-tury. Whole blood, dry bone, skin, live kidneys, live hearts could all be transferred from one body to another. Donors had saved tens of thousands of lives in that hundred years, by willing their bodies to medicine.

But the number of donors was limited, and not many died in such a way that anything of value could be saved.

The deluge had come something less than a hundred years ago. One healthy donor (but of course there was no such animal) could save a dozen lives. Why, then, should a con-demned murderer die to no purpose? First a few states, then most of the nations of the world had passed new laws. Criminals condemned to death must be executed in a hos-pital, with surgeons to save as much as could be saved for the organ banks.

The world's billions wanted to live, and the organ banks were life itself. A man could live forever as long as the doctors could shove spare parts into him faster than his own parts wore out. But they could do that only as long as the world's organ banks were stocked.

162

A hundred scattered movements to abolish the death penalty died silent, unpublicized deaths. Everybody gets sick sometime.

And still there were shortages in the organ banks. Still patients died for the lack of parts to save them. The world's legislators had responded to steady pressure from the world's people. Death penalties were established for first, second, and third degree murder. For assault with a deadly weapon. Then for a multitude of crimes: rape, fraud, embezzlement, having children without a licence, four or more counts of false advertising. For nearly a century the trend had been growing, as the world's voting citizens acted to protect their right to live forever.

Even now there weren't enough transplants. A woman with kidney trouble might wait a year for a transplant: one healthy kidney to last the rest of her life. A thirty-five-year-old heart patient must live with a sound but forty-year-old heart. One lung, part of a liver, prosthetics that wore out too fast or weighed too much or did too little . . . there weren't enough criminals. Not surprisingly, the death penalty *was* a deterrent. People stopped committing crimes rather than face the donor room of a hospital.

For instant replacement of your ruined digestive system, for a *young* healthy heart, for a whole liver when you'd ruined yours with alcohol . . . you had to go to an organ-legger.

There are three aspects to the business of organlegging. One is the business of kidnap-murder. It's risky. You can't fill an organ bank by waiting for volunteers. Executing condemned criminals is a government monopoly. So you go out and *get* your donors: on a crowded city sidewalk, in an air terminal, stranded on a freeway by a car with a busted capacitor . . . anywhere.

The selling end of the business is just as dangerous, because even a desperately sick man sometimes has a conscience. He'll buy his transplant, then go straight to the ARMs, curing his sickness and his conscience by turning in the whole gang. Thus the sales end is somewhat anonymous, but as there are few repeat sales, that hardly matters.

Third is the technical, medical aspect. Probably this is the

163

safest part of the business. Your hospital is big, but you can put it anywhere. You wait for the donors, who arrive still alive; you ship out livers and glands and square feet of live skin, correctly labelled for rejection reactions.

It's not as easy as it sounds. You need doctors. Good ones.

That was where Loren came in. He had a monopoly.

Where did he get them? We were still trying to find out. Somehow, one man had discovered a foolproof way to recruit talented but dishonest doctors practically en masse. Was it really one man? All our sources said it was. And he had half the North American west coast in the palm of his hand.

Loren. No holographs, no fingerprints or retina prints, not even a description. All we had was that one name, a few possible contacts.

One of these was Kenneth Graham.

The holograph was a good one. Probably it had been posed in a portrait shop. Kenneth Graham had a long Scottish face with a lantern jaw and a small, dour mouth. In the holo he was trying to smile and look dignified simultaneously. He only looked uncomfortable. His hair was sandy and close cut. Above his light grey eyes his eyebrows were so light as to be nearly invisible.

My breakfast arrived. I dunked a doughnut and bit it, and found out I was hungrier than I'd throught.

A string of holos had been reproduced on the computer tape. I ran through the others fairly quickly, eating with one hand and flipping the key with the other. Some were fuzzy; they had been taken by spy beams through the windows of Graham's shop. None of the prints were in any way incriminating. Not one showed Graham smiling.

He had been selling electrical joy for twelve years now.

A current addict has an advantage over his supplier. Electricity is cheap. With a drug, your supplier can always raise the price on you; but not with electricity. You see the ecstasy merchant once, when he sells you your operation and your droud, and never again. Nobody gets hooked by accident. There's an honesty to current addiction. The customer always knows just what he's getting into, and what it will do for him – and to him.

Still, you'd need a certain lack of empathy to make a living the way Kenneth Graham did. Else he'd have had to turn away his customers. Nobody becomes a current addict gradually. He decides all at once, and he buys the operation before he has ever tasted its joy. Each of Kenneth Graham's customers had reached his shop after deciding to drop out of the human race.

What a stream of the hopeless and the desperate must have passed through Graham's shop! How could they help but haunt his dreams? And if Kenneth Graham slept well at night, then—

Then, small wonder if he had turned organlegger.

He was in a good position for it. Despair is characteristic of the would-be current addict. The unknown, the unloved, the people nobody knew and nobody needed and nobody missed, these passed in a steady stream through Kenneth Graham's shop.

So a few didn't come out. Who'd notice?

I flipped quickly through the tape to find out who was in charge of watching Graham. Jackson Bera. I called down through the desk phone.

'Sure,' said Bera, 'we've had a spy beam on him about three weeks now. It's a waste of good salaried ARM agents. Maybe he's clean. Maybe he's been tipped somehow.'

'Then why not stop watching him?'

Bera looked disgusted. 'Because we've only been watching for three weeks. How many donors do you think he needs a year? Two. Read the reports. Gross profit on a single donor is over a million UN marks. Graham can afford to be careful who he picks.'

'Yah.'

'At that, he wasn't careful enough. At least two of his customers disappeared last year. Customers with families. That's what put us on to him.'

'So you could watch him for the next six months without a guarantee. He could be just waiting for the right guy to walk in.'

'Sure. He has to write up a report on every customer. That gives him the right to ask personal questions. If the guy has relatives, you know. Then again,' Bera said dis-

165

consolately, 'he could be clean. Sometimes a current addict disappears without help.'

'How come I didn't see any holos of Graham at home? You can't be watching just his shop.'

Jackson Bera scratched at his hair. Hair like black steel wool worn long like a bushman's mop. 'Sure we're watching his place, but we can't get a spy beam in there. It's an inside apartment. No windows. You know anything about spy beams?'

'Not much. I know they've been around awhile.'

'They're as old as lasers. Oldest trick in the book is to put a mirror in the room you want to bug. Then you run a laser beam through a window, or even through heavy drapes, and bounce it off the mirror. When you pick it up it's been distorted by the vibrations in the glass. That gives you a perfect recording of anything that's been said in that room. But for pictures you need something a little more sophisticated.'

'How sophisticated can we get?'

'We can put a spy beam in any room with a window. We can send one through some kind of wall. Give us an optically flat surface and we can send one around corners.'

'But you need an outside wall.'

'Yup.'

'What's Graham doing now?'

'Just a sec.' Bera disappeared from view. 'Someone just came in. Graham's talking to him. Want the picture?'

'Sure. Leave it on. I'll turn it off from here when I'm through with it.'

The picture of Bera went dark. A moment later I was looking into a doctor's office. If I'd seen it cold I'd have thought it was run by a podiatrist. There was the comfortable tilt-back chair with the headrest and the footrest; the cabinet next to it with instruments lying on top, on a clean white cloth; the desk over in one corner. Kenneth Graham was talking to a homely, washed-out-looking girl.

I listened to Graham's would-be-fatherly reassurances and his glowing description of the magic of current addiction. When I couldn't take it any longer I turned the sound down. The girl took her place in the chair, and Graham placed something over her head.

The girl's homely face turned suddenly beautiful.

Happiness is beautiful, all by itself. A happy person is beautiful, per se. Suddenly and totally, the girl was full of joy and I realized that I hadn't known everything about droud sales. Apparently Graham had an inductor to put the current where he wanted it, without wires. He *could* show a customer what current addiction felt like, without first implanting the wires.

What a powerful argument that was!

Graham turned off the machine. It was as if he'd turned off the girl. She sat stunned for a moment, then reached frantically for her purse and started scrabbling inside.

I couldn't take anymore. I turned it off.

Small wonder if Graham had turned organlegger. He had to be totally without empathy just to sell his merchandise.

Even there, I thought, he'd had a head start.

So he was a little more callous than the rest of the world's billions. But not much. Every voter had a bit of the organlegger in him. In voting the death penalty for so many crimes, the law makers had only bent to pressure from the voters. There was a spreading lack of respect for life, the evil side of transplant technology. The good side was a longer life for everyone. One condemned criminal could save a dozen deserving lives. Who could complain about that?

We hadn't thought that way in the Belt. In the Belt survival was a virtue in itself, and life was a precious thing, spread so thin among the sterile rocks, hurtling in single units through all that killing emptiness between the worlds.

So I'd had to come to Earth for my transplant.

My request had been accepted two months after I landed. So quickly? Later I'd learned that the banks always have a surplus of certain items. Few people lose their arms these days. I had also learned, a year after the transplant had taken, that I was using an arm taken from a captured organlegger's storage bank.

That had been a shock. I'd hoped my arm had come from a depraved murderer, someone who'd shot fourteen nurses from a rooftop. Not at all. Some faceless, nameless victim had had the bad luck to encounter a ghoul, and I had benefited thereby.

Did I turn in my new arm in a fit of revulsion? No,

surprising to say, I did not. But I had joined the ARMs, once the Amalgamation of Regional Militia, now the United Nations Police. Though I had stolen a dead man's arm, I would hunt the kin of those who had killed him.

The noble urgency of that resolve had been drowned in paperwork these past few years. Perhaps I was becoming callous, like the flatlanders – the *other* flatlanders around me, voting new death penalties year after year. *Income-tax evasion. Operating a flying vehicle on manual controls, over a city.*

Was Kenneth Graham so much worse than they?

Sure he was. The bastard had put a wire in Owen Jennison's head.

I waited twenty minutes for Julie to come out. I could have sent her a memorandum, but there was plenty of time before noon, and too little time to get anything accomplished, and . . . I wanted to talk to her.

'Hi,' she said. 'Thanks,' taking the coffee. 'How went the ceremonial drunk? Oh, I *see*. Mmmmm. Very good. Almost poetic.' Conversation with Julie has a way to taking shortcuts.

Poetic, right. I remembered how inspiration had struck like lightning through a mild high glow. Owen's floating cigarette lure. What better way to honour his memory than to use it to pick up a girl?

'Right,' Julie agreed. 'But there's something you may have missed. What's Taffy's last name?'

'I can't remember. She wrote it down on—'

'What does she do for a living?'

'How should I know?'

'What religion is she? Is she a pro or an anti? Where did she grow up?'

'Dammit—'

'Half an hour ago you were very complacently musing on how depersonalized all us flatlanders are except you. What's Taffy, a person or a foldout?' Julie stood with her hands on her hips, looking up at me like a short school-teacher.

How many people is Julie? Some of us have never seen this Guardian aspect. She's frightening, the Guardian. If it

168

ever appeared on a date, the man she was with would be struck impotent forever.

It never does. When a reprimand is deserved, Julie delivers it in broad daylight. This serves to separate her functions, but it doesn't make it easier to take.

No use pretending it wasn't her business, either.

I'd come here to ask for Julie's protection. Let me turn unlovable to Julie, even a little bit unlovable, and as far as Julie was concerned I would have an unreadable mind. How, then, would she know when I was in trouble? How could she send help to rescue me from whatever? My private life *was* her business, her single vastly important job.

'I *like* Taffy,' I protested. 'I didn't care who she was when we met. Now I like her, and I think she likes me. What do you want from a first date?'

'You know better. You can remember other dates when two of you talked all night on a couch, just from the joy of learning about each other' She mentioned three names, and I flushed. Julie knows the words that will turn you inside out in an instant. 'Taffy is a person, not an episode, not a symbol of anything, not just a pleasant night. What's your judgment of her?'

I thought about it, standing there in the corridor. Funny: I've faced the Guardian Julie on other occasions, and it has never occurred to me to just walk out of the unpleasant situation. Later I think of that. At the time I just stand there, facing the Guardian/Judge/Teacher. I thought about Taffy . . .

'She's nice,' I said. '*Not* depersonalized. Squeamish, even. She wouldn't make a good nurse. She'd want to help too much, and it would tear her apart when she couldn't. I'd say she was one of the vulnerable ones.'

'Go on.'

'I want to see her again, but I won't dare talk shop with her. In fact . . . I'd better not see her till this business of Owen is over. Loren might take an interest in her. Or . . . she might take an interest in me, and I might get hurt . . . have I missed anything?'

'I think so. You owe her a phone call. If you won't be dating her for a few days, call her and tell her so.'

169

'Check.' I spun on my heel, spun back. 'Finagle's Jest! I almost forgot. The reason I came here—'

'I know, you want a time slot. Suppose I check on you at oh nine forty-five every morning?'

'That's a little early. When I get in deadly danger it's usually at night.'

'I'm off at night. Oh nine-forty-five is all I've got. I'm sorry, Gil, but it is. Shall I monitor you or not?'

'Sold. Nine forty-five.'

'Good. Let me know if you get real proof Owen was murdered. I'll give you two slots. You'll be in a little more concrete danger then.'

'Good.'

'I love you. Yeep, I'm late.' And she dodged back into her office, while I went to call Taffy.

Taffy wasn't home, of course, and I didn't know where she worked, or even what she did. Her phone offered to take a message. I gave my name and said I'd call back.

And then I sat there sweating for five minutes.

It was half an hour to noon. Here I was at my desk phone. I couldn't decently see any way to argue myself out of sending a message to Homer Chandrasekhar.

I didn't want to talk to him, then or ever. He'd chewed me out but good, last time I'd seen him. My free arm had cost me my Belter life, and it had cost me Homer's respect. I didn't want to talk to him, even on a one-way message, and I most particularly didn't want to have to tell him Owen was dead.

But someone had to tell him.

And maybe he could find out something.

And I'd put it off nearly a full day.

For five minutes I sweated, and then I called long distance and recorded a message and sent it off to Ceres. More accurately, I recorded six messages before I was satisfied. I don't want to talk about it.

I tried Taffy again; she might come home for lunch. Wrong.

I hung up wondering if Julie had been fair. What had we bargained for, Taffy and I, beyond a pleasant night? And we'd had that, and would have others, with luck.

But Julie would find it hard not to be fair. If she

170

thought Taffy was the vulnerable type, she'd take her information from my own mind.

Mixed feelings. You're a kid, and your mother has just laid down the law. But it *is* a law, something you can count on . . . and she *is* paying attention to you . . . and she *does* care . . . when, for so many of those outside, nobody cares at all.

'Naturally I thought of murder,' said Ordaz. 'I always consider murder. When my sainted mother passed away after three years of the most tender care by my sister Maria Angela, I actually considered searching for evidence of needle holes about the head.'

'Find any?'

Ordaz' face froze. He put down his beef and started to get up.

'Cool it,' I said hurriedly. 'No offence intended.' He glared a moment, then sat down half mollified.

We'd picked an outdoor restaurant on the pedestrian level. On the other side of a hedge (a real live hedge, green and growing and everything) the shoppers were carried past in a steady oneway stream. Beyond them, a slidewalk carried a similar stream in the opposite direction. I had the dizzy feeling that it was we who were moving.

A waiter like a bell-bottomed chess pawn produced steaming dishes of chili size from its torso, put them precisely in front of us, and slid away on a cushion of air.

'Naturally I considered murder. Believe me, Mr Hamilton, it does not hold up.'

'I think I could make a pretty good case.'

'You may try, of course. Better, I will start you on your way. First, we must assume that Kenneth Graham the happiness pedlar did not sell a droud-and-plug to Owen Jennison. Rather, Owen Jennison was forced to undergo the operation. Graham's records, including the written permission to operate, were forged. All this we must assume, is it not so?'

'Right. And before you tell me Graham's escutcheon is unblemished, let me tell you that it isn't.'

'Oh?'

'He's connected with an organlegging gang. That's classified information. We're watching him, and we don't want him tipped.'

171

'That is news.' Ordaz rubbed his jaw. 'Organlegging. Well. What would Owen Jennison have to do with organlegging?'

'Owen's a Belter. The Belt's always drastically short of transplant materials.'

'Yes, they import quantities of medical supplies from Earth. Not only organs in storage, but also drugs and prosthetics. So?'

'Owen ran a good many cargoes past the goldskins in his day. He got caught a few times, but he's still way ahead of the government. He's on the records as a successful smuggler. If a big organlegger wanted to expand his market, he might very well send a feeler out to a Belter with a successful smuggling record.'

'You never mentioned that Mr Jennison was a smuggler.'

'What for? All Belters are smugglers, if they think they can get away with it. To a Belter, smuggling isn't immoral. But an organlegger wouldn't know that. He'd think Owen was already a criminal.'

'Do you think your friend—' Ordaz hesitated delicately.

'No, Owen wouldn't turn organlegger. But he might, he just *might* try to turn one in. The rewards for information leading to the capture and conviction of, et cetera, are substantial. If someone contacted Owen, Owen might very well have tried to trace the contact by himself.

'Now, the gang we're after covers half the west coast of this continent. That's big. It's the Loren gang, the one Graham may be working for. Suppose Owen had a chance to meet Loren himself?'

'You think he might take it, do you?'

'I think he did. I think he let him hair grow out so he'd look like an Earthman, to convince Loren he wanted to look inconspicuous. I think he collected as much information as he could, then tried to get out with a whole skin. But he didn't make it.

'Did you find his application for a nudist licence?'

'No. I saw your point there,' said Ordaz. He leaned back, ignoring the food in front of him. 'Mr Jennison's tan was uniform except for the characteristic darkening of the face. I presume he was a practising nudist in the Belt.'

'Yah. We don't need licences there. He'd have been one here, too, unless he was hiding something. Remember that scar. He never missed a chance to show it off.'

'Could he really have thought to pass for a—' Ordaz hesitated – 'flatlander?'

'With that Belter tan? No! He was overdoing it a little with the haircut. Maybe he thought Loren would underestimate him. But he wasn't advertising his presence, or he wouldn't have left his most personal possessions home.'

'So he was dealing with organleggers, and they found him out before he could reach you. Yes, Mr Hamilton, this is well thought out. But it won't work.'

'Why not? I'm not trying to prove it's murder. Not yet. I'm just trying to show you that murder is at least as likely as suicide.'

'But it's not, Mr. Hamilton.'

I looked the question.

'Consider the details of the hypothetical murder. Owen Jennison is drugged no doubt, and taken to the office of Kenneth Graham. There, an ecstasy plug is attached. A standard droud is fitted, and is then amateurishly altered with soldering tools. Already we see, on the part of the killer, minute attention to details. We see it again in Kenneth Graham's forged papers of permission to operate. They were impeccable.

'Owen Jennison is then taken back to his apartment. It would be his own, would it not? There would be little point in moving him to another. The cord from his droud is shortened, again in amateurish fashion. Mr Jennison is tied up—'

'I wondered if you'd see that.'

'But why should he not be tied up? He is tied up, and allowed to waken. Perhaps the arrangement is explained to him, perhaps not. That would be up to the killer. The killer then plugs Mr Jennison into a wall. A current trickles through his brain and Owen Jennison knows pure pleasure for the first time in his life.

'He is left tied up for, let us say, three hours. In the first few minutes he would be a hopeless addict, I think—'

'You must have known more current addicts than I have.'

'Even I would not want to be pinned down. Your

173

normal current addict is an addict after a few minutes. But then, your normal current addict asked to be made an addict, knowing what it would do to his life. Current addiction is symptomatic of despair. Your friend might have been able to fight free of a few minutes' exposure.'

'So they kept him tied up for three hours. Then they cut the ropes.' I felt sickened. Ordaz' ugly, ugly pictures matched mine in every detail.

'No more than three hours, by our hypothesis. They would not dare stay longer than a few hours. They would cut the ropes and leave Owen Jennison to starve to death. In the space of a month the evidence of his drugging would vanish, as would any abrasions left by ropes, lumps on his head, mercy needle punctures, and the like. A carefully detailed, well-thought-out plan, don't you agree?'

I told myself that Ordaz was not being ghoulish. He was just doing his job. Still, it was difficult to answer objectively.

'It fits our picture of Loren. He's been very careful with us. He'd love carefully detailed, well-thought-out plans.'

Ordaz leaned forward. 'But don't you see? A carefully detailed plan is all wrong. There is a crucial flaw in it. Suppose Mr Jennison pulls out the droud?'

'Could he do that? Would he?'

'Could he? Certainly. A simple tug of the fingers. The current wouldn't interfere with motor co-ordination. Would he?' Ordaz pulled meditatively at his beer. 'I know a good deal about current addictions, but I don't know what it *feels* like, Mr Hamilton. Your normal addict pulls his droud out as often as he inserts it, but your friend was getting ten times normal current. He might have pulled the droud out a dozen times, and instantly plugged it back each time. Yet Belters are supposed to be strong-willed men, very individualistic. Who knows whether, even after a week of addiction, your friend might not have pulled the droud loose, coiled the cord, slipped it in his pocket, and walked away scot free?

'There is the additional risk that someone might walk in on him – an automachinery serviceman, for instance. Or someone might notice that he had not bought any food in a month. A suicide would take that risk. Suicides routinely leave themselves a chance to change their minds. But a murderer?

'No. Even if the chance were one in a thousand, the man who created such a detailed plan would never have taken such a chance.'

The sun burned down hotly on our shoulders. Ordaz suddenly remembered his lunch and began to eat.

I watched the world ride by beyond the hedge. Pedestrians stood in little conversational bunches; others peered into shop windows on the pedestrian strip, or glanced over the hedge to watch us eat. There were the few who pushed through the crowd with set expressions, impatient with the ten-mile-per-hour speed of the slidewalk.

'Maybe they *were* watching him. Maybe the room was bugged.'

'We searched the room thoroughly,' said Ordaz. 'If there had been observational equipment, we would have found it.'

'It could have been removed.'

Ordaz shrugged.

I remembered the spy-eyes in Monica Apartments. Someone would have had to physically enter the room to carry a bug out. He could ruin it with the right signal, maybe, but it would surely leave traces.

And Owen had had an inside room. No spy-eyes.

'There's one thing you've left out,' I said presently.

'And what would that be?'

'My name in Owen's wallet, listed as next of kin. He was directing my attention to the thing I was working on. The Loren gang.'

'That is possible.'

'You can't have it both ways.'

Ordaz lowered his fork. 'I *can* have it both ways, Mr Hamilton. But you won't like it.'

'I'm sure I won't.'

'Let us incorporate your assumption. Mr Jennison was contacted by an agent of Loren, the organlegger, who intended to sell transplant material to Belters. He accepted. The promise of riches was too much for him.

'A month later, something made him realize what a terrible thing he had done. He decided to die. He went

175

to an ecstasy pedlar and he had a wire put in his head. Later, before he plugged in the droud, he made one attempt to atone for his crime. He listed you as his next of kin, so that you might guess why he had died, and perhaps so that you could use that knowledge against Loren.'

Ordaz looked at me across the table. 'I see that you will never agree. I cannot help that. I can only read the evidence.'

'Me too. But I knew Owen. He'd never have worked for an organlegger, he'd never have killed himself, and if he had, he'd never have done it that way.'

Ordaz didn't answer.

'What about fingerprints?'

'In the apartment? None.'

'None but Owen's?'

'Even his were found only on the chairs and end tables. I curse the man who invented the cleaning robot. Every smooth surface in that apartment was cleaned exactly forty-four times during Mr Jennison's tenancy.' Ordaz went back to his chili size.

'Then try this. Assume for the moment that I'm right. Assume Owen was after Loren, and Loren got him. Owen knew he was doing something dangerous. He wouldn't have wanted me to get on to Loren before he was ready. He wanted the reward for himself. But he might have left me something, just in case.

'Something in a locker somewhere, an airport or spaceport locker. Evidence. Not under his own name, or mine either, because I'm a known ARM. But—'

'Some name you both know.'

'Right. Like Homer Chandrasekhar. Or – got it. Cubes Forsythe. Owen would have thought that was apt. Cubes is dead.'

'We will look. You must understand that it will not prove your case.'

'Sure. Anything you find, Owen could have arranged in a fit of conscience. Screw that. Let me know what you get,' I said, and stood up and left.

I rode the slidewalk, not caring where it was taking me. It would give me a chance to cool off.

Could Ordaz be right? Could he?

But the more I dug into Owen's death, the worse it made Owen look.

Therefore Ordaz was wrong.

Owen work for an organlegger? He'd rather have been a donor.

Owen getting his kicks from a wall socket? He never even watched tridee!

Owen kill himself? No. If so, not that way.

But even if I could have swallowed all that . . .

Owen Jennison, letting me know he'd worked with organleggers? Me, Gil the Arm Hamilton? Let *me* know *that*?

The slidewalk rolled along, past restaurants and shopping centres and churches and banks. Ten storeys below, the hum of cars and scooters drifted up faintly from the vehicular level. The sky was a narrow, vivid slash of blue between black shadows of skycrapers.

Let *me* know *that*? Never.

But Ordaz' strangely inconsistent murderer was no better.

I thought of something even Ordaz had missed. Why would Loren dispose of Owen so elaborately? Owen need only disappear into the organ banks, never to bother Loren again.

The shops were thinning out now, and so were the crowds. The slidewalk narrowed, entered a residential area, and not a very good one. I'd let it carry me a long way. I looked around trying to decide where I was.

And I was four blocks from Graham's place.

My subconscious had done me a dirty. I wanted to look at Kenneth Graham, face to face. The temptation to go on was nearly irresistible, but I fought it off and changed direction at the next disc.

A slidewalk intersection is a rotating disc, its rim tangent to four slidewalks and moving with the same speed. From the centre you ride up an escalator and over the slidewalks to reach stationary walks along the buildings. I could have caught a cab at the centre of the disc, but I still wanted to think, so I just rode halfway around the rim.

I could have walked into Graham's shop and got away

177

with it. Maybe. I'd have looked hopeless and bored and hesitant, told Graham I wanted an ecstasy plug, worried loudly about what my wife and friends would say, then changed my mind at the last moment. He'd have let me walk out, knowing I'd be missed. Maybe.

But Loren had to know more about the ARMs than we know about him. Some time or other, had Graham been shown a holo of yours truly? Let a known ARM walk into his shop, and Graham would panic. It wasn't worth the risk.

Then, dammit, what *could* I do?

Ordaz' inconsistent killer. If we assumed Owen was murdered, we couldn't get away from the other assumptions. The care, the nitpicking detail – and then Owen left alone to pull out the plug and walk away, or to be discovered by a persistent salesman or a burglar, or—

No. Ordaz' hypothetical killer, and mine, would have watched Owen like a hawk. For a month.

That did it. I stepped off at the next disc and got a taxi.

The taxi dropped me on the roof of Monica Apartments. I took an elevator to the lobby.

If the manager was surprised to see me, he didn't show it as he gestured me into his office. The office seemed much more roomier than the lobby had, possibly because there were things to break the anonymous-modern decor: paintings on the wall, a small black worm track in the rug that must have been caused by a visitor's cigarette, a holo of Miller and his wife on the wide, nearly empty desk. He waited until I was settled, then leaned forward expectantly.

'I'm here on ARMs business,' I said, and passed him my ident.

He passed it back without checking it. 'I presume it's the same business,' he said without cordiality.

'Yah. I'm convinced Owen Jennison must have had visitors while he was here.'

The manager smiled. 'That's ridic – impossible.'

'Nope, it's not. Your holo cameras take pictures of visitors, but they don't snap the tenants, do they?'

'Of course not.'

'Then Owen could have been visited by any tenant in the building.'

178

The manager looked shocked. 'No, certainly not. Really, I don't see why you pursue this, Mr Hamilton. If Mr Jennison had been found in such a condition, it would have been reported!'

'I don't think so. Could he have been visited by any tenant in the building?'

'No. No. The cameras would have taken a picture of anyone from another floor.'

'How about someone from the same floor?'

Reluctantly the manager bobbed his head. 'Ye-es. As far as the holo cameras are concerned, that's possible. But—'

'Then I'd like to ask for pictures of any tenant who lived on the eighteenth floor during the past six weeks. Send them to the ARMs Building, Central LA. Can do?'

'Of course. You'll have them within an hour.'

'Good. Now, something else occurred to me. Suppose a man got out on the nineteenth floor and walked down to the eighteenth. He'd be holoed on the nineteenth, but not on the eighteenth, right?'

The manager smiled indulgently. 'Mr. Hamilton, there are no stairs in this building.'

'Just the elevators? Isn't that dangerous?'

'Not at all. There is a separate self-contained emergency power source for each of the elevators. It's common practice. After all, who would want to walk up eighty storeys if the elevator failed?'

'Okay, fine. One last point. Could someone tamper with the computer? Could someone make it decide not to take a certain picture, for instance?'

'I . . . am not an expert on how to tamper with computers, Mr. Hamilton. Why don't you go straight to the company? Caulfield Brains, Inc.'

'Okay. What's your model?'

'Just a moment.' He got up and leafed through a drawer in a filing cabinet. 'EQ 144.'

'Okay.'

That was all I could do here, and I knew it . . . and still I didn't have the will to get up. There ought to be *something* . . .

Finally Miller cleared his throat. 'Will that be all, sir?'

'Yes,' I said. 'No. Can I get into 1809?'

'I'll see if we've rented it yet.'

'The police are through with it?'

'Certainly.' He went back to the filing cabinet. 'No, it's still available. I'll take you up. How long will you be?'

'I don't know. No more than half an hour. No need to come up.'

'Very well.' He handed me the key and waited for me to leave. I did.

The merest flicker of blue light caught my eye as I left the elevator. I would have thought it was in my optic nerve, not in the real world, if I hadn't known about the holo cameras. Maybe it was. You don't need laser light to make a holograph, but it does get you clearer pictures.

Owen's room was a box. Everything was retracted. There was nothing but the bare walls. I had never seen anything so desolate, unless it was some asteroidal rock, too poor to mine, too badly placed to be worth a base.

The control panel was just beside the door. I turned on the lights, then touched the master button. Lines appeared, outlined in red and green and blue. A great square on one wall for the bed, most of another wall for the kitchen, various outlines across the floor. Very handy. You wouldn't want a guest to be standing on the table when you expanded it.

I'd come here to get the feel of the place, to encourage a hunch, to see if I'd missed anything. Translation: I was playing. Playing, I reached through the control panel to find the circuits. The printed circuitry was too small and too detailed to tell me anything, but I ran imaginary fingertips along a few wires and found that they looped straight to their action points, no detours. No sensors to the outside. You'd have to be in the room to know what was expanded, what retracted.

So a supposedly occupied room had had its bed retracted for six weeks. But you'd have to be in the room to know it.

I pushed buttons to expand the kitchen nook and the reading chair. The wall slid out eight feet; the floor humped itself and took form. I sat down in the chair, and the kitchen nook blocked my view of the door.

Nobody could have seen Owen from the hall.

If only someone had noticed that Owen wasn't ordering food. That might have saved him.

I thought of something else, and it made me look around for the air conditioner. There was a grill at floor level. I felt behind it with my imaginary hand. Some of these apartment air-conditioning units go on when the CO_2 level hits half a per cent. This one was geared to temperature and manual control.

With the other kind, our careful killer could have tapped the air-conditioner current to find out if Owen was still alive and present. As it was, 1809 had behaved like an empty room for six weeks.

I flopped back in the reading chair.

If my hypothetical killer had watched Owen, he'd done it with a bug. Unless he'd actually lived on this floor for the four or five weeks it took Owen to die, there was no other way.

Okay, think about a bug. Make it small enough and nobody would find it except the cleaning robot, who would send it straight to the incinerator. You'd have to make it big, so the robot wouldn't get it. No worry about Owen finding it! And then, when you knew Owen was dead, you'd use the self-destruct.

But if you burned it to slag, you'd leave a burn hole somewhere. Ordaz would have found it. So. An asbestos pad? You'd want the self-destruct to leave something that the cleaning robot would sweep up.

And if you'll believe that you'll believe anything. It was too chancy. *Nobody* knows what a cleaning robot will decide is garbage. They're made stupid because it's cheaper. So they're programmed to leave large objects alone.

There had to be someone on this floor, either to watch Owen himself or to pick up the bug that did the watching. I was betting everything I had on a human watcher.

I'd come here mainly to give my intuition a chance. It wasn't working. Owen had spent six weeks in this chair, and for at least the last week he'd been dead. Yet I couldn't feel it with him. It was just a chair with two end tables. He had left nothing in the room, not even a restless ghost.

The call caught me half-way back to Headquarters.

'You were right,' Ordaz told me over the wristphone.

'We have found a locker at Death Valley Port registered to Cubes Forsythe. I am on my way there now. Will you join me?'

'I'll meet you there.'

'Good. I am as eager as you to see what Owen Jennison left us.'

I doubted that.

The Port was something more than 230 miles away, an hour at taxi speeds. It would be a big fare. I typed out a new address on the destination board, then called in at Headquarters. An ARM agent is fairly free; he doesn't have to justify every little move. There was no question of getting permission to go. At worst they might disallow the fare on my expense account.

'Oh, and there'll be a set of holos coming in from Monica Apartments,' I told the man. 'Have the computer check them against known organleggers and associates of Loren.'

The taxi rose smoothly into the sky and headed east. I watched tridee and drank coffee until I ran out of coins for the dispenser.

If you go between November and May, when the climate is ideal, Death Valley can be a tourist's paradise. There is the Devil's Golf Course, with its fantastic ridges and pinnacles of salt; Zabriskie Point and its weird badlands topography; the old borax mining sites; and all kinds of strange, rare plants, adapted to the heat and the death-dry climate. Yes, Death Valley has many points of interest, and someday I was going to go see them. So far all I'd seen was the spaceport. But the Port was impressive in its own way.

The landing field used to be part of a sizeable inland sea. It is now a sea of salt. Alternating red and blue concentric circles mark the field for ships dropping from space, and a century's developments in chemical, fission, and fusion reaction motors have left blast pits striped like rainbows by esoteric, often radio-active salts. But mostly the field retains its ancient glare white.

And out across the salt are ships of many sizes and many shapes. Vehicles and machinery dance attendance, and, if you're willing to wait, you may see a ship land. It's worth the wait.

The Port building, at the edge of the major salt flat, is a pastel green tower set in a wide patch of fluorescent orange concrete. No ship has ever landed on it – yet. The taxi dropped me at the entrance and moved away to join others of its kind. And I stood inhaling the dry, balmy air.

Four months of the year, Death Valley's climate is ideal. One August the Furnace Creek Ranch recorded 134° Fahrenheit shade temperature.

A man behind a desk told me that Ordaz had arrived before me. I found him and another officer in a labyrinth of pay lockers, each big enough to hold two or three suitcases. The locker Ordaz had opened held only a lightweight plastic briefcase.

'He may have taken other lockers,' he said.

'Probably not. Belters travel light. Have you tried to open it?'

'Not yet. It is a combination lock. I thought perhaps . . .'

'Maybe.' I squatted to look at it.

Funny: I felt no surprise at all. It was as if I'd known all along that Owen's suitcase would be there. And why not? He was bound to try to protect himself somehow. Through me, because I was already involved in the UN side of organlegging. By leaving something in a spaceport locker, because Loren couldn't find the right locker or get into it if he did, and because I would naturally connect Owen with spaceports. Under Cubes' name, because I'd be looking for that, and Loren wouldn't.

Hindsight is wonderful.

The lock had five digits. 'He must have meant me to open it. Let's see . . .' and I moved the tumblers to 42217. April 22, 2117, the day Cubes died, stapled suddenly to a plastic partition.

The lock clicked open.

Ordaz went instantly for the manila folder. More slowly, I picked up two glass phials. One was tightly sealed against Earth's air, and half full of an incredibly fine dust. So fine was it that it slid about like oil inside the glass. The other phial held a blackened grain of nickel-iron, barely big enough to see.

Other things were in that case, but the prize was that

folder. The story was in there . . . at least up to a point. Owen must have planned to add to it.

A message had been waiting for him in the Ceres mail dump when he returned from his last trip out. Owen must have laughed over parts of that message. Loren had taken the trouble to assemble a complete dossier of Owen's smuggling activities over the past eight years. Did he think he could ensure Owen's silence by threatening to turn the dossier over to the goldskins?

Maybe the dossier had given Owen the wrong idea. In any case, he'd decided to contact Loren and see what developed. Ordinarily he'd have sent me the entire message and let me try to track it down. I was the expert, after all. But Owen's last trip out had been a disaster.

His fusion drive had blown somewhere beyond Jupiter's orbit. No explanation. The safeties had blown his life-system capsule free of the explosion, barely. A rescue ship had returned him to Ceres. The fee had nearly broken him. He needed money. Loren may have known that, and counted on it.

The reward for information leading to Loren's capture would have bought him a new ship.

He'd landed at Outback Field, following Loren's instructions. From there, Loren's men had moved him about a good deal : to London, to Bombay, to Amberg, Germany. Owen's personal, written story ended in Amberg. How had he reached California? He had not had a chance to say.

But in between, he had learned a good deal. There were snatches of detail on Loren's organization. There was Loren's full plan for shipping illicit transplant materials to the Belt, and for finding and contacting customers. Owen had made suggestions there. Most of them sounded reasonable and would be unworkable in practice. Typically Owen. I could find no sign that he'd overplayed his hand.

But of course he hadn't known it when he did.

And there were holos, twenty-three of them, each a member of Loren's gang. Some of the pictures had markings on the back; others were blank. Owen had been unable to find out where each of them stood in the organization.

I leafed through them twice, wondering if one of them could be Loren himself. Owen had never known.

'It would seem you were right,' said Ordaz. 'He could not have collected such detail by accident. He must have planned from the beginning to betray the Loren gang.'

'Just as I told you. And he was murdered for it.'

'It seems he must have been. What motive could he have had for suicide?' Ordaz' round, calm face was doing its best to show anger. 'I find I cannot believe in our inconsistent murderer either. You have ruined my digestion, Mr. Hamilton.'

I told him my idea about other tenants on Owen's floor. He smiled and nodded. 'Possibly, possibly. This is your department now. Organlegging is the business of the ARMs.'

'Right.' I closed the briefcase and hefted it. 'Let's see what the computer can do with these. I'll send you photocopies of everything in here.'

'You'll let me know about the other tenants?'

'Of course.'

I walked into ARM Headquarters swinging that precious briefcase, feeling on top of the world. Owen had been murdered. He had died with honour, if not – oh, definitely not – with dignity. Even Ordaz knew it now.

Then Jackson Bera, snarling and panting, went by at a dead run.

'What's up?' I called after him. Maybe I wanted a chance to brag. I had twenty-three faces, twenty-three organleggers, in my briefcase.

Bera slid to a stop beside me. 'Where *you* been?'

'Working. Honest. What's the hurry?'

'Remember that pleasure pedlar we were watching?'

'Graham? Kenneth Graham?'

'That's the one. He's dead. We blew it.' And Bera took off.

He'd reached the lab by the time I caught up with him.

Kenneth Graham's corpse was face up on the operating table. His long, lantern-jawed face was pale and slack without expression; empty. Machinery was in place above and below his head.

'How you doing?' Bera demanded.

'Not good,' the doctor answered. 'Not your fault. You

185

got him into the deepfreeze fast enough. It's just that the current—' he shrugged.

I shook Bera's shoulder. 'What happened?'

Bera was panting a little from his run. 'Something must have leaked. Graham tried to make a run for it. We got him at the airport.'

'You could have waited. Put someone on the plane with him. Flooded the plane with TY-4.'

'Remember the stink the last time we used TY-4 on civilians? Damn newscasters.' Bera was shivering. I didn't blame him.

ARMs and organleggers play a funny kind of game. The organleggers have to turn their donors in alive, so they're always armed with hypo guns, firing slivers of crystalline anaesthetic that melt instantly in the blood. We use the same weapon, for somewhat the same reason: a criminal has to be saved for trial, and then for the government hospitals. So no ARM ever expects to kill a man.

There was a day I learned the truth. A small-time organlegger named Raphael Haine was trying to reach a call button in his own home. If he'd reached it all kinds of hell would have broken loose, Haine's men would have hypoed me, and I would have regained consciousness a piece at a time, in Haine's organ-storage tanks. So I strangled him.

The report was in the computer, but only three human beings knew about it. One was my immediate superior, Lucas Carner. The other was Julie. So far, he was the only man I'd ever killed.

And Graham was Bera's first killing.

'We got him at the airport,' said Bera. 'He was wearing a hat. I wish I'd noticed that, we might have moved faster. We started to close in on him with hypo guns. He turned and saw us. He reached under his hat, and then he fell.'

'Killed himself?'

'Uh huh.'

'How?'

'Look at his head.'

I edged closer to the table, trying to stay out of the doctor's way. The doctor was going through the routine of trying to pull information from a dead brain by induction. It wasn't going well.

There was a flat oblong box on top of Graham's head. Black plastic, about half the size of a pack of cards, I touched it and knew at once that it was attached to Graham's skull.

'A droud. Not a standard type. Too big.'

'Uh huh.'

Liquid helium ran up my nerves. 'There's a battery in it.'

'Right.'

'I often wonder what the vintners buy, et cetera. A cordless droud. Man, that's what *I* want for Christmas.'

Bera twitched all over. 'Don't *say* that.'

'Did you know he was a current addict?'

'No. We were afraid to bug his home. He might have found it and be tipped. Take another look at that thing.'

The shape was wrong, I thought. The black plastic case had been half melted.

'Heat,' I mused. 'Oh!'

'Uh huh. He blew the whole battery at once. Sent the whole killing charge right through his brain, right through the pleasure centre of his brain. And, Jesus, Gil, the thing I keep wondering is, what did it feel like? Gil, what could it possibly have *felt* like?'

I thumped him across the shoulders in lieu of giving him an intelligent answer. He'd be a long time wondering. And so would I.

Here was the man who had put the wire in Owen's head. Had his death been momentary Hell, or all the delights of paradise in one singing jolt? Hell, I hoped, but I didn't believe it.

At least Kenneth Graham wasn't somewhere else in the world, getting a new face and new retinas and new fingertips from Loren's illicit organ banks.

'Nothing,' said the doctor. 'His brain's too badly burned. There's just nothing there that isn't too scrambled to make sense.'

'Keep trying,' said Bera.

I left quietly. Maybe later I'd buy Bera a drink. He seemed to need it. Bera was one of those with empathy. I knew that he could almost feel that awful surge of ecstasy and defeat as Kenneth Graham left the world behind.

187

The holos from Monica Apartments had arrived hours ago. Miller had picked not only the tenants who had occupied the eighteenth floor during the past six weeks, but tenants from the nineteenth and seventeenth floors too. It seemed an embarrassment of riches. I toyed with the idea of someone from the nineteenth floor dropping over his balcony to the eighteenth, every day for five weeks. But 1809 hadn't had an outside wall, let alone a window, not to mention a balcony.

Had Miller played with the same idea? Nonsense. He didn't even know the problem. He'd just overkilled with the holos to show how co-operative he was.

None of the tenants during the period in question matched known or suspected Loren men.

I said a few appropriate words and went for coffee. Then I remembered the twenty-three possible Loren men in Owen's briefcase. I'd left them with a programmer, since I wasn't quite sure how to get them into the computer myself. He ought to be finished by now.

I called down. He was.

I persuaded the computer to compare them with the holos from Monica Apartments.

Nothing. Nobody matched anybody.

I spent the next two hours writing up the Owen Jennison case. A programmer would have to translate it for the machine. I wasn't that good yet.

We were back with Ordaz' inconsistent killer.

That, and a tangle of dead ends. Owen's death had bought us a handful of new pictures, pictures which might even be obsolete by now. Organleggers changed their faces at the drop of a hat. I finished the case outline, sent it down to a programmer, and called Julie. I wouldn't need her protection now.

Julie had left for home.

I started to call Taffy, stopped with her number half dialled. There are times not to make a phone call. I needed to sulk; I needed a cave to be alone in. My expression would probably have broken a phone screen. Why inflict it on an innocent girl?

I left for home.

It was dark when I reached the street. I rode the pedestrian bridge across the slidewalks, waited for a taxi at the intersection disc. Presently one dropped, the white FREE sign blinking on its belly. I stepped in and deposited my credit card.

Owen had collected his holos from all over the Eurasian continent. Most of them, if not all, had been Loren's foreign agents. Why had I expected to find them in Los Angeles?

The taxi rose into the white night sky. City lights turned the cloud cover into a flat white dome. We penetrated the clouds, and stayed there. The taxi autopilot didn't care if I had a view or not.

. . . So what did I have now? Someone among dozens of tenants was a Loren man. That, or Ordaz' inconsistent killer, the careful one, had left Owen to die for five weeks, alone and unsupervised.

. . . Was the inconsistent killer so unbelievable?

He was, after all, my own hypothetical Loren. And Loren had committed murder, the ultimate crime. He'd murdered routinely, over and over, with fabulous profits. The ARMs hadn't been able to touch him. Wasn't it about time he started getting careless?

Like Graham. How long had Graham been selecting donors among his customers, choosing a few nonentities a year? And then, twice within a few months, he took clients who were missed. Careless.

Most criminals are not too bright. Loren had brains enough; but the men on his payroll would be about average. Loren would deal with the stupid ones, the ones who turned to crime because they didn't have enough sense to make it in real life.

If a man like Loren got careless, this was how it would happen. Unconsciously he would judge ARM intelligence by his own men. Seduced by an ingenious plan for murder, he might ignore the single loophole and go through with it. With Graham to advise him, he knew more about current addiction than we did; perhaps enough to trust the effects of current addiction on Owen.

Then Owen's killers had delivered him to his apartment and never seen him again. It was a small gamble Loren had taken, and it had paid off, this time.

189

Next time he'd grow more careless. One day we'd get him.

But not today.

The taxi settled out of the traffic pattern, touched down on the roof of my apartment building in the Hollywood Hills. I got out and moved towards the elevators.

An elevator opened. Someone stepped out.

Something warned me, something about the way he moved. I turned, quick-drawing from the shoulder. The taxi might have made good cover – if it hadn't been already rising. Other figures had stepped from the shadows.

I think I got a couple before something stung my cheek. Mercybullets, slivers of crystalline anaesthetic melting in my bloodstream. My head spun, and the roof spun, and the centrifugal force dropped me limply to the roof. Shadows loomed above me, then receded to infinity.

Fingers on my scalp shocked me awake.

I woke standing upright, bound like a mummy in soft, swaddling bandages. I couldn't so much as twitch a muscle below my neck. By the time I knew that much it was too late. The man behind me had finished removing electrodes from my head and stepped into view, out of reach of my imaginary arm.

There was something of the bird about him. He was tall and slender, small-boned, and his triangular face reached a point at the chin. His wild, silken blond hair had withdrawn from his temples, leaving a sharp widow's peak. He wore impeccably tailored wool street shorts in orange and brown stripes. Smiling brightly, with his arms folded and his head cocked to one side, he stood waiting for me to speak.

And I recognized him. Owen had taken a holo of him, somewhere.

'Where am I?' I groaned, trying to sound groggy. 'What time is it?'

'Time? It's already morning,' said my captor. 'As for where you are, I'll let you wonder.'

Something about his manner . . . I took a guess and said, 'Loren?'

Loren bowed, not overdoing it. 'And you are Gilbert Hamilton of the United Nations Police. Gil the Arm.'

Had he said Arm or ARM? I let it pass. 'I seem to have slipped.'

'You underestimated the reach of my own arm. You also underestimated my interest.'

I had. It isn't much harder to capture an ARM than any other citizen, if you catch him off guard, and if you're willing to risk the men. In this case his risk had cost him nothing. Cops use hypo guns for the same reason organ-leggers do. The men I'd shot, if I'd hit anyone in those few seconds of battle, would have come around long ago. Loren must have set me up in these bandages, then left me under 'russian sleep' until he was ready to talk to me.

The electrodes were the 'russian sleep'. One goes on each eyelid, one on the nape of the neck. A small current goes through the brain, putting you right to sleep. You get a full night's sleep in an hour. If it's not turned off you can sleep forever.

So this was Loren.

He stood watching me with his head cocked to one side, bird-like, with his arms folded. One hand held a hypo gun, rather negligently. I thought.

What time was it? I didn't dare ask again, because Loren might guess something. But if I could stall him until 0945, Julie could send help . . .

She could send help where?

Finagle in hysterics! Where was I? If I didn't know that, Julie wouldn't know either!

And Loren intended me for the organ banks. One crystalline sliver would knock me out without harming any of the delicate, infinitely various parts that made me Gil Hamilton. Then Loren's doctors would take me apart.

In government operating rooms they flash-burn the criminal's brain for later urn burial. God knows what Loren would do with my own brain. But the rest of me was young and healthy. Even considering Loren's over-head, I was worth more than a million UN marks on the hoof.

'Why me?' I asked. 'It was me you wanted, not just any ARM. Why the interest in me?'

'It was you who were investigating the case of Owen Jennison. *Much* too thoroughly.'

'Not thoroughly enough, dammit!'

191

Loren looked puzzled. 'You really don't understand?'

'I really don't.'

'I find that highly interesting,' Loren mused. 'Highly.'

'All right, why am I still alive?'

'I was curious, Mr. Hamilton. I hoped you'd tell me about your imaginary arm.'

So he'd said Arm, not ARM. I bluffed anyway. 'My *what?*'

'No need for games, Mr. Hamilton. If I think I'm losing I'll use this.' He wiggled the hypo gun. 'You'll never wake up.'

Damn! He knew. The only things I could move were my ears and my imaginary arm, and Loren knew all about it! I'd never be able to lure him into reach.

Provided he knew *all* about it.

I had to draw him out.

'Okay,' I said, 'but I'd like to know how you found out about it. A plant in the ARMs?'

Loren chuckled. 'I wish it were so. No. We captured one of your men some months ago, quite by accident. When I realized what he was, I induced him to talk shop with me. He was able to tell me something about your remarkable arm. I hope you'll tell me more.

'Who was it?'

'Really, Mr. Hamil—'

'Who was it?'

'Do you really expect me to remember the name of every donor?'

Who had gone into Loren's organ banks? Stranger, acquaintance, friend? Does the manager of a slaughter-house remember every slaughtered steer?

'So-called psychic powers interest me,' said Loren. 'I remembered you. And then, when I was on the verge of concluding an agreement with your Belter friend Jennison, I remembered something unusual about a crewman he had shipped with. They called you Gil the Arm, didn't they? Prophetic. In port your drinks came free if you could use your imaginary arm to drink them.'

'Then damn you. You thought Owen was a plant, did you? Because of me! Me!'

'Breast beating will earn you nothing, Mr. Hamilton,' Loren put steel in his voice. 'Entertain me, Mr. Hamilton.'

I'd been feeling around for anything that might release me from my upright prison. No such luck. I was wrapped like a mummy in bandages too strong to break. All I could feel with my imaginary hand were cloth bandages up to my neck, and a bracing rod along my back to hold me upright. Beneath the swathing I was naked.

'I'll show you my eldritch powers,' I told Loren, 'if you'll loan me a cigarette.' Maybe that would draw him close enough . . .

He knew something about my arm. He knew its reach. He put one single cigarette on the edge of a small table-on-wheels and slid it up to me. I picked it up and stuck it in my mouth and waited hopefully for him to come to light it. 'My mistake,' he murmured; and he pulled the table back and repeated the whole thing with a lighted cigarette.

No luck. At least I'd got my smoke. I pitched the dead one as far as it would go : about two feet. I have to move slowly with my imaginary hand. Otherwise what I'm holding simply slips through my fingers.

Loren watched in fascination. A floating, disembodied cigarette, obeying my will! His eyes held traces of awe and horror. That was bad. Maybe the cigarette had been a mistake.

Some people see psi powers as akin to witchcraft, and psychic people as servants of Satan. If Loren feared me, then I was dead.

'Interesting,' said Loren. 'How far will it reach?'

He knew that. 'As far as my real arm, of course.'

'But why? Others can reach much farther. Why not you?'

He was clear across the room, a good ten yards away, sprawled in an armchair. One hand held a drink, the other held the hypo gun. He was superbly relaxed. I wondered if I'd ever see him move from that comfortable chair, much less come within reach.

The room was small and bare, with the look of a basement. Loren's chair and a small portable bar were the only furnishings, unless there were others behind me.

A basement could be anywhere. Anywhere in Los Angeles, or out of it. If it was really morning, I could be anywhere on Earth by now.

'Sure,' I said, 'others can reach farther than I can. But they don't have my strength. It's an imaginary arm, sure enough, and my imagination won't make it ten feet long. Maybe someone could convince me it was, if he tried hard enough. But maybe he'd ruin what belief I have. Then I'd have two arms, just like everyone else. I'm better off . . .' I let it trail away, because Loren was going to take all my damn arms anyway.

My cigarette was finished. I pitched it away.

'Want a drink?'

'Sure, if you've got a jigger glass. Otherwise I can't lift it.'

He found me a shot glass and sent it to me on the edge of the rolling table. I was barely strong enough to pick it up. Loren's eyes never left me as I sipped and put it down.

The old cigarette lure. Last night I'd used it to pick up a girl. Now it was keeping me alive.

Did I really want to leave the world with something gripped tightly in my imaginary fist? Entertaining Loren. Holding his interest until—

Where was I? Where?

And suddenly I knew. 'We're at Monica Apartments,' I said. 'Nowhere else.'

'I knew you'd guess that eventually.' Loren smiled. 'But it's too late. I got to you in time.'

'Don't be so damn complacent. It was my stupidity, not your luck. I should have *smelled* it. Owen would never have come here of his own choice. You ordered him here.'

'And so I did. By then I already knew he was a traitor.'

'So you sent him here to die. Who was it that checked on him every day to see he'd stayed put? Was it Miller, the manager? He has to be working for you. He's the one who took the holographs of you and your men out of the computer.'

'He was the one,' said Loren. 'But it wasn't every day. I had a man watching Jennison every second, through a portable camera. We took it out after he was dead.'

'And then waited a week. Nice touch.' The wonder was that it had taken me so long. The atmosphere of the place . . . what kind of people would live in Monica Apartments? The faceless ones, the ones with no identity, the ones who would surely be missed by nobody. They would stay put in their apartments while Loren checked on them, to see that they really did have nobody to miss them. Those who qualified would disappear, and their papers and possessions with them, and their holos would vanish from the computer.

Loren said, 'I tried to sell organs to the Belters, through your friend Jennison. I know he betrayed me, Hamilton. I want to know how badly.'

'Badly enough.' He'd guess that. 'We've got detailed plans for setting up an organ-bank dispensary in the Belt. It wouldn't have worked anyway, Loren. Belters don't think that way.'

'No pictures.'

'No.' I didn't want him changing his face.

'I was sure he'd left something,' said Loren. 'Otherwise we'd have made him a donor. Much simpler. More profitable, too. I needed the money, Hamilton. Do you know what it costs the organization to let a donor go?'

'A million or so. Why'd you do it?'

'He'd left something. There was no way to get at it. All we could do was try to keep the ARMs from looking for it.'

'Ah.' I had it then. 'When anyone disappears without a trace, the first thing any idiot thinks of is organleggers.'

'Naturally. So he couldn't just disappear, could he? The police would go to the ARMs, the file would go to you, and you'd start looking.'

'For a spaceport locker.'

'Oh?'

'Under the name of Cubes Forsythe.'

'I knew that name.' Loren said between his teeth. 'I should have tried that. You know, after we had him hooked on current, we tried pulling the plug on him to get him to talk. It didn't work. He couldn't concentrate on anything but getting the droud back in his head. We looked high and low—'

'I'm going to kill you,' I said, and meant every word.

Loren cocked his head, frowning. 'On the contrary, Mr. Hamilton. Another cigarette?'

'Yah.'

He sent it to me, lighted, on the rolling table. I picked it up, holding it a trifle ostentatiously. Maybe I could focus

195

his attention on it – on his only way to find my imaginary hand.

Because if he kept his eyes on the cigarette, and I put it in my mouth at a crucial moment – I'd leave my hand free without his noticing.

What crucial moment? He was still in the armchair. I had to fight the urge to coax him closer. Any move in that direction would make him suspicious.

What time was it? And what was Julie doing? I thought of a night two weeks past. Remembered dinner on the balcony of the highest restaurant in Los Angeles, just a fraction less than a mile up. A carpet of neon that spread below us to touch the horizon in all directions. Maybe she'd pick it up . . .

She'd be checking on me at 0945.

'You must have made a remarkable spacemen,' said Loren. 'Think of being the only man in the solar system who can adjust a hull antenna without leaving the cabin.'

'Antennas take a little more muscle than I've got.' So he knew I could reach through things. If he'd seen that far— 'I should have stayed,' I told Loren. 'I wish I were on a mining ship, right this minute. All I wanted at the time was two good arms.'

'Pity. Now you have three. Did it occur to you that using psi powers against men was a form of cheating?'

'What?'

'Remember Raphael Haine?' Loren's voice had become uneven. He was angry, and holding it down with difficulty.

'Sure. Small-time organlegger in Australia.'

'Raphael Haine was a friend of mine. I know he had you tied up at one point. Tell me, Mr. Hamilton : if your imaginary hand is as weak as you say, how did you untie the ropes?'

'I didn't. I couldn't have. Haine used handcuffs. I picked his pocket for the key . . . with my imaginary hand, of course.'

'You used psi powers against him. You had no right !'

Magic. Anyone who's not psychic himself feels the same way, just a little. A touch of dread, a touch of envy. Loren thought he could handle ARMs; he'd killed at least one of us. But to send warlocks against him was grossly unfair.

196

That was why he'd let me wake up. Loren wanted to gloat. How many men have captured a warlock?

'Don't be an idiot,' I said. 'I didn't volunteer to play your silly game, or Haine's either. *My* rules make you a wholesale murder.'

Loren got to his feet (what time was it?) and I suddenly realized my time was up. He was in a white rage. His silky blond hair seemed to stand on end.

I looked into the tiny needle hole in the hypo gun. There was nothing I could do. The reach of my TK was the reach of my fingers. I felt all the things I would never feel: the quart of Trastine in my blood to keep the water from freezing in my cells, the cold bath of half-frozen alcohol, the scalpels and the tiny, accurate surgical lasers. Most of all, the scalpels.

And my knowledge would die when they threw away my brain. I knew what Loren looked like. I knew about Monica Apartments, and who knew how many others of the same kind? I knew where to go to find all the loveliness in Death Valley, and someday I was going to go. What time was it? What time?

Loren had raised the hypo gun and was sighting down the stiff length of his arm. Obviously he thought he was at target practice. 'It really is a pity,' he said, and there was only the slightest tremor in his voice. 'You should have stayed a spaceman.'

What was he waiting for? 'I can't cringe unless you loosen these bandages,' I snapped, and I jabbed what was left of my cigarette at him for emphasis. It jerked out of my grip, and I reached and caught it and—

And stuck it in my left eye.

At another time I'd have examined the idea a little more closely. But I'd still have done it. Loren already thought of me as his property. As live skin and healthy kidneys and lengths of artery, as parts in Loren's organ banks, I was property worth a million UN marks. And I was destroying my eye! Organleggers are always hunting for eyes; anyone who wears glasses could use a new pair, and the organleggers themselves are constantly wanting to change retina prints.

What I hadn't anticipated was the pain. I'd read somewhere that there are no sensory nerves in the eyeball. Then it was my lids that hurt. Terribly!

But I only had to hold on for a moment.

Loren swore and came for me at a dead run. He knew how terribly weak was my imaginary arm. What could I do with it? He didn't know; he'd never know, though it stared him in the face. He ran at me and slapped at the cigarette, a full swing that half knocked my head off my neck and sent the now dead butt ricocheting off a wall. Panting, snarling, speechless with rage, he stood – within reach.

My eye closed like a small tormented fist.

I reached past Loren's gun, through his chest wall, and found his heart. And squeezed.

His eyes became very round, his mouth gaped wide, his larynx bobbed convulsively. There was time to fire the gun. Instead he clawed at his chest with a half-paralysed arm. Twice he raked his fingernails across his chest, gaping upward for air that wouldn't come. He thought he was having a heart attack. Then his rolling eyes found my face.

My face. I was a one-eyed carnivore, snarling with the will to murder. I would have his life if I had to tear the heart out of his chest! How could he help but know?

He knew!

He fired at the floor, and fell.

I was swearing and shaking with reaction and disgust. The scars! He was all scars; I'd felt them going in. His heart was a transplant. And the rest of him – he'd looked about thirty from a distance, but this close it was impossible to tell. Parts were younger, parts older. How much of Loren was Loren? What parts had he taken from others? And none of the parts quite matched.

He must have been chronically ill, I thought. And the Board wouldn't give him the transplants he needed. And one day he'd seen the answer to all his problems . . .

Loren wasn't moving. He wasn't breathing. I remembered the way his heart had jumped and wriggled in my imaginary hand, and then suddenly given up.

He was lying on his left arm, hiding his watch. I was all alone in an empty room, and I still didn't know what time it was.

I never found out. It was hours before Miller finally

198

dared to interrupt his boss. He stuck his round, blank face around the door jamb, saw Loren sprawled at my feet, and darted back with a squeak. A minute later a hypo gun came around the jamb, followed by a watery blue eye. I felt the sting in my cheek.

'I checked you early,' said Julie. She settled herself uncomfortably at the foot of the hospital bed. 'Rather, you called me. When I came to work you weren't there, and I wondered why, and *wham*. It was bad, wasn't it?'

'Pretty bad,' I said.

'I've never sensed anyone so scared.'

'Well, don't tell anyone about it.' I hit the switch to raise the bed to sitting position. 'I've got an image to maintain.'

My eye and the socket around it were bandaged and numb. There was no pain, but the numbness was obtrusive, a reminder of two dead men who had become part of me. One arm, one eye.

If Julie was feeling that with me, then small wonder if she was nervous. She was. She kept shifting and twisting on the bed.

'I kept wondering what time it was. What time was it?'

'About nine-ten.' Julie shivered. 'I thought I'd faint when that — that vague little man pointed his hypo gun around the corner. Oh, don't! Don't, Gil. It's *over*.'

That close? Was it *that* close? 'Look,' I said, 'you go back to work. I appreciate the sick call, but this isn't doing either of us any good. If we keep it up we'll both wind up in a state of permanent terror.'

She nodded jerkily and got up.

'Thanks for coming. Thanks for saving my life too.'

Julie smiled from the doorway. 'Thanks for the orchids.'

I hadn't ordered them yet. I flagged down a nurse and got her to tell me that I could leave tonight, after dinner, provided I went straight home to bed. She brought me a phone, and I used it to order the orchids.

Afterwards I dropped the bed back and lay there awhile. It was nice being alive. I began to remember promises I had made, promises I might never have kept. Perhaps it was time to keep a few.

I called down to Surveillance and got Jackson Bera.

After letting him drag from me the story of my heroism, I invited him up to the infirmary for a drink. His bottle, but I'd pay. He didn't like that part, but I bullied him into it.

I had dialled half of Taffy's number before, as I had last night, I changed my mind. My wristphone was on the bedside table. No pictures.

' 'Lo.'

'Taffy? This is Gil. Can you get a weekend free?'

'Sure. Starting Friday?'

'Good.'

'Come for me at ten. Did you ever find out about your friend?'

'Yah. I was right. Organleggers killed him. It's over now, we got the guy in charge.' I didn't mention the eye. By Friday the bandages would be off. 'About that weekend. How would you like to see Death Valley?'

'You're kidding, right?'

'I'm kidding, wrong. Listen—'

'But it's hot! It's dry! It's as dead as the Moon! You did say Death Valley, didn't you?'

'It's not hot this month. Listen . . .' And she did listen. She listened long enough to be convinced.

'I've been thinking,' she said then. 'If we're going to see a lot of each other, we'd better make a – a bargain. No shop talk. All right?'

'A good idea.'

'The point is, I work in a hospital,' said Taffy. 'Surgery. To me organic transplant material is just the tools of my trade, tools to use in healing. It took me a long time to get that way. I don't want to know where the stuff comes from and I don't want to know anything about organleggers.'

'Okay, we've got a covenant. See you at ten hundred Friday.'

A doctor, I thought afterwards. Well. The weekend was going to be a good one. Surprising people are always the ones most worth knowing.

Bera came in with a pint of J&B. 'My treat,' he said. 'No use arguing, 'cause you can't reach your wallet anyway.' And the fight was on.